THE TRUTH, AT LAST

Dr. Baskerville was serious. "It's imperative that we do the surgery immediately. I can't stress that strongly enough. Consider the episode you experienced in the judge's chambers a big red flag. I hate to sound like a walking cliché, but time is of the essence."

"Too bad," Aunt Jay said. "There's something I have to clear up first."

An alarm went off somewhere deep behind my eyes. I sensed another Mack truck on my horizon.

Baskerville rubbed his forehead, as if fighting fatigue. "I can't see what could possibly be more important than your life."

"Nothing is," Jay said. "But your definition of life is different from mine, because you've got a lot more in front of you than behind you. Me, I'm flirting with eighty and life to me is my past, whether the way I've lived and the things I've done were done for the right reason. When I know that, you can cut away."

A muscle in his jaw moved rhythmically, as if he was clenching his teeth. "If that's the case, I would advise you to find out as soon as you can. You're running out of time."

———

Books by Chassie West

Sunrise
Loss of Innocence

Published by HarperPaperbacks

LOSS OF INNOCENCE

Chassie West

HarperPaperbacks
A Division of HarperCollins Publishers

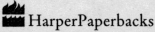

HarperPaperbacks
A Division of HarperCollinsPublishers
10 East 53rd Street, New York, N.Y. 10022-5299

This is a work of fiction. The characters, incidents, and
dialogues are products of the author's imagination and are not to
be construed as real. Any resemblance to actual events or
persons, living or dead, is entirely coincidental.

ISBN 0-06-108111-6

HarperCollins®, ®, and HarperPaperbacks™
are trademarks of HarperCollinsPublishers, Inc.

Cover illustration by Merritt Dekle
Author photo by Christopher Happel

First printing: March 1997

Printed in the United States of America

Visit HarperPaperbacks on the World Wide Web at
http://www.harpercollins.com/paperbacks

❖ 10 9 8 7 6 5 4 3 2 1

This one's for my editor, Carolyn Marino, with my eternal gratitude for her patience. Thank you, Carolyn.
CLW

Acknowledgment

Sincere appreciation is due Dr. Jean Wheeler Smith Young, M.D., who made certain I avoided making a complete idiot of myself when it came to things medical in *Loss of Innocence*. Her assistance was invaluable. Any blunders in this area are solely mine, not hers.

LOSS OF INNOCENCE

1

I'd just lapsed into the kind of bowels-of-the-earth-deep sleep you go into five minutes before your alarm goes off, when the phone rang. Even without waking up, I knew it meant trouble. It had to. Face it, things had been going too smoothly. I'd managed to get my parents onto the train to Miami, Dad grousing about the expense, even though it wasn't costing him a cent. Unless he figured some way to stop an Amtrak train en route, they would board the cruise ship tomorrow and spend their fortieth anniversary in the Bahamas, paid for by me and my brothers.

On the work front, commencement ceremonies at the Adult Ed Center had gone off without a hitch. Thirteen women, most of them from a nearby shelter, had earned GEDs. Seven more were now computer literate, about to start new jobs, and could give the finger to all the statisticians who had written them off as permanent residents on the welfare rolls. I was damned proud of that.

As for me, I was finally celebrating a commencement of

my own. After three years of working twelve- and thirteen-hour days at the Center, I was over the hump and could let myself relax. No more trying to fill every waking moment to keep from drowning in memories and feeling sorry for myself. This was the first day of my first vacation since I'd started at the Center and I intended to wallow in bed all day. A call this early had to mean somebody wanted me for something and I wasn't going for it. No way. I picked up the phone ready to lie my ass off, whatever it took.

"This the residence of Mr. Troy Burdette?"

The "Mr." didn't bother me. It's a common mistake when you've got a boy's name. What did wake me up and fast was the voice, which was soft, slow in cadence, the vowels elastic, the accent definitely Carolinian. North or South, I wasn't sure. And Caucasian. Of that I was.

"*Ms.* Burdette. The residence of, I mean. Speaking." I stopped, embarrassed by my garbled syntax. Teachers of computer word processing programs—and anything else for that matter—aren't supposed to talk like that. I focused on the clock. Seven-ten. This had to be an early rising telemarketer. "Whatever you're selling, I'm not buying. Please take my name and phone number off your list."

"I'm not selling anything, ma'am," he said quickly. "This is Officer Haskins calling from Incense, South Carolina."

I'd been suckered. I groaned and turned over, dislodging The Deacon—he's a cat, not a person, worse luck—off my feet. "Who is this? Jimmy? No, it's Graham, isn't it?" With a love of practical jokes embedded in the family chromosomes, I had any number of relatives to choose from. And my brother Graham was good at accents.

"No, ma'am, the name's Haskins, like I said. Do you know a Miz Julia Wingate?"

Julia Wingate. It was a moment before all the synapses fired in the correct sequence. Aunt Jay, my ex-husband's only remaining blood relative. Apprehension sent my pulse into overdrive. Auntie Jay was somewhere between seventy-five and ninety, depending on the day of the week you asked her, and lived in North Carolina on several acres she kept up with little or no help because that's the way she wanted it.

"Julia Wingate's a great-aunt," I said, neglecting to specify whose. "What's happened?"

I steeled myself for the response. Aunt Jay still drove, her vehicle of choice a big, black 1938 Buick in mint condition. It hugged the road like a layer of asphalt. Turn Jay loose in it on a highway and she could run Mario Andretti into the ground. If the police were calling, she must have had an accident. "Is she all right?"

"Well, that's what I was hopin' you could tell me, Miz Burdette. Miz Wingate showed up here 'bout an hour ago insistin' that we arrest her for murder."

"What?" My stomach plummeted. "Ohmigod, she hit someone with the Buick?"

"With the . . . ? Uh, no, ma'am. She says she killed a man back in Nineteen and forty-three and—"

"What?"

"Yes, ma'am. The thing is—"

I relaxed a little. This was obviously a mistake. Aunt Jay wouldn't even kill spiders, not intentionally, anyway. She might help a black widow relocate from a corner of her garden shed to a corner of her garden, but it would never occur to her to take the sole of her shoe to one. "Whoever you have there," I said, "it isn't Julia Wingate. What's she look like?"

"She's a black lady, upwards of seventy—way upwards, I suspect—five feet tall, maybe ninety pounds. Dark complexion, light brown eyes, white hair in a sort of topknot. Oh, and rings on every finger."

The twinge of apprehension returned. That was Julia Wingate, all right.

"Says she's lived with this thing on her conscience long enough," the officer continued, "and is turning herself in to pay her debt to society. The problem is—"

"Wait a minute," I interrupted, scenting a rat. Aunt Jay's sense of humor bordered on the bizarre. "I'm sorry, Officer," I said, wondering how to soften the blow for him. "She's pulling your leg."

"I wish I could agree with you, ma'am, but I can't. This lady's as serious as a snake bite. Says she's not gonna let us put her off this time. She's—"

"What do you mean, this time? She's done this before?"

"So she says. I don't know who she talked to before. All I know is, wasn't me."

This was crazy. "Just a minute, please." I hit the Hold button, got up, and trotted into the bedroom I use as an office to get my reading glasses. They help me think more clearly. As nothing he'd said made sense, I needed all the help I could get. The Deacon followed, gliding up onto the windowsill, no mean feat for a sixteen-pound pussycat. "Still there, Officer?" I asked, using the speakerphone on my desk.

"Still here. I have to ask you, ma'am," he said, lowering his voice, "does Miz Wingate have all her faculties?"

I felt a sudden liking for this man and how delicately he'd broached the subject. "She sounded okay the last time I talked to her." How long had it been? Guilt whacked me across the backside. It had been understood: divorce or no, Wade's great-aunt was still family until death did us part. How could I have let so much time pass without calling her? "That's been a while ago," I admitted. "Six months or so."

"Well, I've checked the records and made a call or

two," the officer said. "Far as I can determine, there weren't no homicides or unexplained deaths here that year or the one before or after. Looks to me as if your auntie's slipping a bit. No surprise at her age. We're willin' to see that she gets back to where she belongs, even though she's not one of ours, but she won't leave. I've never seen nobody as bound and determined to get locked up as she is. We'd sure 'preciate some help on this."

"Let me speak to her," I suggested. "Maybe I can persuade her to go home."

"She doesn't know I'm talking to you. Claimed she didn't have any family and that this is home. I found your business card case under the front seat of her car and thought I'd take a chance you knew her."

God almighty. I'd lost half the contents of my purse, including that card case, during a panic stop she'd made the last time I'd ridden with her. That had to have been four years before, when she'd driven up from Greensboro to see us. We hadn't been able to talk her into taking the train then, and chances were, nothing I said over the phone would convince her to go home now.

Only Wade could get through to her, but the last thing I wanted to do was call him. Just because I was finally over him—well, practically, anyway—didn't mean I wanted to test the sensitivity of the scar tissue. But he loved that old lady. He'd want to do something.

"Look, Officer, there is one person she might listen to. Let me give you his numbers."

"Er . . ." He cleared his throat and lowered his voice even further. "We've got a touchous situation here, the place not being all that big. Only reason I was able to call you without her hearing is because she's giving my partner what-for about the condition of our facilities. I'd 'preciate it if you could contact this person for me and ask him to come get her. Short of that, maybe him talking to her would be enough."

Damn. This was payback for not getting the blasted answering machine fixed last month when I should have. Why couldn't I have simply let the phone ring just now? Now I was stuck. I couldn't say no. I agreed to play messenger, took his number, and asked him to keep Aunt Jay occupied as long as he could. "The person I'll try to contact is a great-nephew. His name is Wade Prentiss. I'll have him call as soon as I find him."

He thanked me and hung up. I sat there listening to the dial tone burr like a mad hornet while I worked up the backbone to phone California. Wade's wife would be none too pleased to have me calling at four-twenty in the morning their time, but waiting for a more decent hour was out of the question. Reluctantly, I dialed his house. And got his answering machine.

There was only one activity during which Wade could resist the ringing of a telephone, but at four in the morning, for God sakes? Trying to blank out the picture in my head of what he was probably doing, I made myself listen to the voice of the new Mrs. Prentiss explain that neither she nor her husband was available, etc., etc. I'm quoting her here. "Neither I nor my husband . . ."

I can't tell you how much that "neither-nor" business made my teeth itch. Why the hell couldn't she have said, "Wade and I aren't available." Better still, go my dad's route. "We're busy. Leave your name and number. We'll get back to you—maybe." And there wasn't the slightest trace of the South in her voice. She'd been born and raised on the West Coast by parents born and raised on the West Coast and by God, she sounded like it.

I left a message, hoping Wade might hear my voice and

pick up, but no luck. So I hung up, bugged at being bugged at my replacement and her chirpy little voice. Latrice had to be an okay person or Wade wouldn't have married her. He had good taste; he'd married me, hadn't he? If Big Mama Nature hadn't double-crossed us, we'd have still been married. And I had to hope that, making love or not, he'd have answered the first time I'd mentioned his great-aunt's name. Okay, he probably wasn't there. I had to find the boy.

I dialed his beeper, then checked the time. I'd give him fifteen minutes to call back before trying his numbers at work. Unless he'd changed, he just might still be at the plant, his nose glued to a monitor screen. I used the quarter-hour wait to feed The Deacon, brush my teeth, and make faces in the mirror as I checked for wrinkles. My first gray hair had popped out on my thirtieth birthday, sending me into a depression so deep it had made the Grand Canyon look like a gully alongside an unpaved road. Now at thirty-one I had four more wiry gray hairs, but otherwise, few signs that the Grim Reaper was waiting outside the bathroom door.

All things considered, I decided, I looked pretty good. My weight was okay for somebody five-feet-five. My mom swore I was too skinny, but that's what moms do; it's in their job description. In fact, I could have used another pound or two. Skin, a cinnamon-toast brown, still smooth and unlined. Dark topaz irises still clear, no pale rings around them. My 34-C's hadn't lost the fight with gravity yet. I was twisting around to see if the same could be said of my tush when the phone rang. I sprinted out of the john and caught it before it had chirped the second time.

"Troy? Hi, baby. Is something wrong?"

All right, I admit it. His voice could still get me. "Hi, Wade. Thanks for calling back so soon," I said, keeping it light but heading straight to the point. "There's a problem or I wouldn't have bothered you, especially at this hour. It's your Aunt Jay."

His quick intake of breath was audible. "What's happened?"

I ran it down to him, agreeing that, yes, it sounded as if she must have deteriorated mentally since we'd last been in touch with her. "The officer I talked to is hoping you'll come get her or at least call and talk to her to convince her to go home."

"Oh, God. Oh, man, what the hell am I gonna do?"

There was no mistaking the anguish in his voice. For the first time I began to wonder what was happening on his side of the world. "What's wrong, Wade?"

"Shit, Troy! I can call, but you know how much good that'll do. No one's ever changed Aunt Jay's mind about anything. And I can't leave now. I just can't."

"What's going on, honey?" So I slipped, sue me.

The responding silence spun itself out for so long, I was afraid he thought I'd crossed the line now that he was someone else's honey. "I'm calling from Mercy Hospital," he said finally. "Latrice just had twins but they're almost seven weeks premature and hanging on by threads. I can't leave them, Troy. You understand that, don't you?"

I'd thought I was past the pain, but it sliced across my belly with such intensity that my knees went wobbly and I lowered myself to the floor. The Deacon, sensing something amiss, hopped down and plopped his fat behind on my lap. I grabbed him and buried my nose in his coat, needing something alive and warm to hang on to.

"Troy?" Wade said.

I evicted the frogs from my throat. "Yeah. Congratulations, Wade. I'm very happy for you, I really mean that."

And for the most part, I did. "The twins will be all right, I'm sure of it. What are they?"

"One of each. God, they're so little, Troy. The boy is two pounds, nine ounces, and the girl is two pounds, four." His voice was hoarse with emotion. "They're having respiratory problems, and they've got to be at least five pounds before they can go home, so they'll be in incubators for I don't know how long. The problem is, the doctors say it's important that we're here as much as possible to hold them, help feed them, things like that, so they'll thrive. And Latrice isn't in that great a shape. It was a Caesarean birth, so—"

"I understand," I interrupted, unable to take much more. "This craziness with Aunt Jay couldn't have happened at a worse time for you."

"Understatement." He paused, and I knew what was coming. It's kind of hard not to see a Mack truck barreling down on you. "I'd call her, baby, but we both know from experience she's not going to budge. Will you handle it for me—I mean, go get her and take her home? It's a lot to ask, but I don't know what else to do."

"Sure, Wade," I said, as the tires rolled over my back. "You stay there and look after your twins—and Latrice. I'll do what I can."

I could feel his relief from three thousand miles away. "Thanks, baby. I'll—we'll owe you for this. In fact, let me know how much the airfare or gas is and any other expenses you run up and I'll reimburse you. You know I'm good for it. And keep me posted, okay? Use the beeper number."

I agreed, disconnected, and didn't move, cat in lap, my back against the desk drawers, as I waited for a return of the numbness it had taken me three years to achieve. Eventually something told me Jay Wingate might be pushing up daisies before I reached that point again, so I dislodged The

Deacon, got up and logged onto the computer to check airline schedules. Then it occurred to me, I didn't have the slightest notion where Incense, South Carolina, was. After a return call to a much relieved Officer Haskins, I made reservations for the first flight into Savannah, Georgia. That necessitated a second call to the policeman, who was beginning to feel like an old family friend, to let him know about what time I'd be there. I was told, to my delight, that he would have a driver pick me up at the airport. That left me with an hour and forty minutes to pack, dress, and figure out what the hell to do with The Deacon.

The problem was, I couldn't be sure how long I'd be gone. A day or two would be no problem. If for some reason I had to stay longer, he wouldn't starve to death, not with the fat he carried around his middle, but my apartment would be in shreds. And damned smelly. Leaving him at a kennel or with the vet was out of the question. I had parked him there before while away on business trips and had been told, upon picking him up, that in the future I should make other arrangements.

The thing is, The Deacon liked me, but as far as I could determine, I was the only human he liked. My family and friends and the vet had learned to keep their distance and if called upon to handle him, to wear heavy-duty gloves. The one time I'd engaged a service to come in to feed him was a disaster. As far as The Deacon was concerned, his territory was being invaded and he acted accordingly. Fortunately the lady really liked animals and was willing to let bygones be bygones if I paid her medical bill. I paid. The only thing I could do now was take the hellion with me. I wasn't sure how much it would cost, but since Wade would be paying for it, I wasn't going to worry about it, either. Resigned to the kind of subterfuge involved in getting his furry ass into his carrier, I headed for the shower, still not completely convinced that this business in South Carolina was anything other than a big misunderstanding. Aunt Jay a murderer? Uh-uh. No way.

I guess I assumed that the car and driver waiting for me at the Savannah airport would be whatever served as metropolitan Incense police issue. My first clue that I had sized up the situation as far off the mark as I could get was when I spotted the elderly white gentleman in a chauffeur's cap and uniform standing inside the airport at my gate with a sign that read "Innocence." I missed a step, causing a minor rear-end collision with a lady pushing rather than pulling one of those suitcases on wheels. Innocence? No wonder I hadn't been able to find the place on the map. I'd been looking for Incense.

For some reason, he seemed to know I was his quarry. Smiling, his face creasing with an extraordinary collection of wrinkles, he stepped forward to meet me, cap in hand. "Miz Burdette," he said. It was not a question. "How do. I'm here to take you up to Innocence. The name's Henry. Any more luggage?" he asked, relieving me of my under-the-seater. I hesitated before giving it up. The man had to be seventy if he was a day.

"Just a pet carrier," I responded, extending a hand to shake, which caused a bit of burden-shuffling since he had his cap in one hand and my bag in the other. "It was nice of Mr. Haskins to do this. I could have rented a car."

"No trouble at all," he said, leading me toward the luggage retrieval area. "It's my job. I pick up visitors alla time. Bring your dog, did you?"

"My cat," I corrected him. "He's so mean, no one will take care of him for me. He travels okay in a car, but this is his first flight. I hope he's all right."

I needn't have worried. The Deacon peered at me from the carrier, and after a low growl to let me know what he thought of keeping company with suitcases, yawned and settled down.

Henry eyed him with respect. "Big feller, ain't he?" He'd gotten the point. I was the one who'd carry The Deacon. Henry had the better deal. I'm a light packer. Even with clothes, shoes, and toiletries, my suitcase probably weighed less than the cat and his carrier. I was puffing a bit by the time we got out to the car.

About that. It wasn't a car, it was a station wagon, older than I was by several years, a 1950-something Ford, the kind with wood paneling on the sides. My grandfather had owned one. Henry's was in excellent condition, as clean and shiny as if it had just come off the dealer's parking lot. It sported a sign painted on its front doors: Innocence Island Courtesy Car. I hadn't realized the place was an island.

"A beauty, ain't it?" Henry said, as he helped me and The Deacon get settled to his satisfaction. It was as immaculate inside as out, no splits in the seat covers, no scratches on the dash. "Runs like a top, too. They don't make 'em like this anymore. Everybody ready?" He turned the ignition and the engine roared to life. I hadn't heard a thrum like it in years.

There wasn't all that much to see on the way to Innocence. The ride through the countryside, and an assortment of small towns, recognizable only because the speed limit would drop for a hundred yards or so, began to remind me of jaunts made during the summers my brothers and I spent with our grandparents. Granddad would hop under the wheel of his Country Squire given the flimsiest excuse. He loved that station wagon. And Henry drove the same way Granddad did, as if the numbers on the speed limit signs had been handed down on tablets etched by the finger of God. The sign said thirty-five. Henry, humming tunelessly under his breath, drove thirty-five, not a mile faster or slower, over the state line into South Carolina. Cars zipped by us with a rush of wind, drivers glaring at us, a single long blast of their horns supplying exclamation points. The needle on the Ford's speedometer never wavered.

Whereas it had been fun riding anywhere with Granddad back then, I wasn't a kid anymore. I knew the risks of someone barreling down on us from behind and realizing at the last minute how much slower we were going. The prospect of an inattentive driver winding up with his car parked in the back seat with The Deacon made the ride to our destination seem twice as long. By the time we approached a causeway with a sign promising that Innocence was a mile away, I was so on edge that if you'd touched me, I'd have twanged like a guitar string.

We crossed an expanse of water and I relaxed a little as Henry reached the island and slowed at a tiny gatehouse. All I saw of the gatekeeper, or whatever he was, was an arm stuck out of the window, waving Henry on. A sign posted just beyond bore a warning that all visitors were required to register and a visitor pass had to be visible in their cars at all times. Just below it was a second sign: "Visiting Minors' Curfew: Midnight Unless Accompanied by an Adult. Strictly Enforced." Visitors' passes? A curfew? I began to wonder exactly what kind of place Innocence was.

2

Other than signs warning "Dozen Pines–10 Days to Go," there certainly wasn't anything remarkable about the first mile or so—marshes punctuated by reeds on one side of the road and buff-colored sand littered with sea oats on the other. By my reckoning, the ocean was somewhere off to my right. I could hear it and smell it, but it wasn't visible. Perhaps this island was larger than I'd thought.

When we passed the fourth warning about ten days to go, I had to ask. "What's Dozen Pines?"

Henry snorted. "A big deal golf tournament the Chamber of Commerce's pushing. Expecting folks from all over. Never seen so much to-do over knocking a little white ball into a hole. Seems a right silly thing for a grown man to do, you ask me."

I had been married to a man whose passion for the afore-mentioned was on a par with his passion for lovemaking. Wade was dynamite in bed. He was also a helluva good golfer. I'd never been sure what connection there was between the two, but since I'd enjoyed the benefits so much, I decided that the most expedient thing to do now would be to keep my mouth shut.

We entered a grove of trees, live oaks, I thought, Spanish moss sagging from their boughs like dirty rags, but I had yet to see a building of any kind. Once past the trees and a sharp left, however, a sign announced a speed limit of twenty-five miles an hour and Henry slowed from the rip-snorting thirty-five he'd maintained since the gatehouse. We'd hit civilization. "Main Street," Henry said.

His explanation was unnecessary. It couldn't have been called anything else. It was wide, and cleaner than a doctor's examining room, with bike racks lining sparkling white curbs, an occasional palmetto tree jutting skyward along the sidewalk, and more than the occasional sign proclaiming the number of days until the Dozen Pines tournament.

The first place we passed was a clear indication of what was to come if I'd been perceptive enough to home in on it: a movie theater called the Roxy, its gaudy Art Deco marquee announcing a Bogart festival this week and a Gable marathon to come. Next door to it was a diner, the kind modeled after a railroad car, chrome galore glistening in the afternoon sun. Every third store seemed to be trilling a siren song to antiques hounds and collectors of one sort or another—comic books, radios, clocks. A music store advertised sheet music, Guy Lombardo and Perry Como albums. The drugstore had a soda fountain clearly visible through its broad front window, and on the corner was an honest-to-God glass-enclosed telephone booth with folding doors. I hadn't seen one like it in years. There was a certain look about the stores but it still escaped me. Each establishment had a canvas awning and a few, like the barbershop—cigar store Indian to the right of the door, barber pole to the left—had benches outside in front of their windows.

The gas station did it for me. No self-serve pumps here; every one of them looked nearly as old as I was. And not only were the attendants in crisp, snappy uniforms, they wore caps and smiles and were cleaning their customers' front and rear windows, while others had their heads stuck under the hoods checking oil. I swiveled around to look back at the stores we'd passed, wondering why it had taken me so long to catch on. No McDonald's, Kentucky Fried, or 7-Eleven; in fact nothing of recent vintage. We had driven into a time warp. The whole scene was straight out of the Truman and Eisenhower eras. My only frame of reference was old movies, Andy Griffith's Mayberry and *Leave It to Beaver* reruns, fortified by photos of my grandparents' hometown, High Point, North Carolina, before the super-duper grocery stores and shopping malls sprang up. Regardless, there was no doubt why this place was called Innocence. They'd simply dumped the last forty years. Nostalgia was king.

Henry peered around, brow furrowed. "Wonder where everybody is. Never seen the streets this empty. Guess the heat drove 'em indoors. Whatcha think so far? I seen you looking."

"It's very . . . quaint. Is this a resort or a theme park or something?"

He chuckled. "Don't let Hizzoner the mayor hear you say that. This here's a retirement community. Have to be fifty-five to buy or rent. And if you own, there's no using your property for time-sharing and such. You can let family or friends camp in it when you aren't here, but if you do, they have to register and abide by the Allenby rules, or zip, they're gone. Makes for a right peaceful place to live."

That explained the signs at the gatehouse. "What are the Allenby rules?" I asked.

"The Reverend Allenby's Commandments, some folks call them. Sort of a code of conduct, ya might call them."

"So the island is church property?"

"No'm," Henry said, a wry grin playing around his mouth, "although there's some who say it might as well be. The Reverend was on the board that decided the direction Innocence should go years back. He helped plan things, had a lot of say. Still does, come to that, mostly because he's outlived everybody else. But he was right. This ain't paradise, but it ain't far short of it, either."

"Why is it I've never heard of it?" I asked.

"Don't reckon you would unless you used to read *Modern Maturity* and the like. Hizzoner stopped advertisin' a couple of years ago, 'cause we're full up. Folks clammerin' to move here 'cause the weather's easy on old folks' joints. Don't have tourists like over Hilton Head way—nothing much to see, for one thing—and don't have any crime. Not many places like that anymore. Now, I'm 'sposed to take you to the courthouse. That's just around the corner here." He turned right at a stately pace and frowned, squinting ahead intently. "What the Sam Hill . . . ?"

The reason for his question escaped me. Whereas Main was the buy-and-sell district, this appeared to be strictly business business. No high-rises—the tallest was five floors—but most were clearly banks, savings and loans, professional office buildings for lawyers and accountants, and from the signs in the windows, a bumper crop of investment counselors.

The street dead-ended at a T intersection a couple of long blocks ahead where an island of green forced traffic to circle around it. Its backdrop was an official-looking building, two stories of sparkling white marble, the gold weathervane on its spire almost blinding in the sun. A crowd, a good many spilling over into the intersection, milled about in front of the building. If these were Henry's retirees, they sure looked a heck of a lot younger than I'd have expected. And healthy. Several wore tennis outfits and carried rackets. There were a few with canes and three in wheelchairs, but even they looked anything but infirm.

For some reason, barricades blocked entry onto the circle. Barely visible because of the crowd, a police car was parked in front of the building, chase lights whirling. From somewhere in the distance, a siren wailed.

"Sounds like Aaron's car a-comin'. Maybe an accident up here somewhere," Henry muttered, pulling over to the curb. "Yonder's Junior Haskins." He pointed at a florid face towering above the crowd nearest a ground-level door to the left of the front steps.

"My goodness. How tall is he?" I asked.

"Middlin' height. Must be standing on the bench. Why's he peekin' in his own window? And where's Ficker? If he's supposed to be directing traffic, he's doing a piss-poor job, 'scuse m' French. Don't see no accident, though. Wonder what's going on."

A little worm of uneasiness slithered down my spine. "Where's the jail, Mr. Henry?"

"The name's actually Henry E. Henry, ma'am, so just Henry will do. Jail's on the ground floor right where Junior's standin'. Ain't much of a jail, really. Don't need what they got. Like I said, no crime. Why don't you stay put while I go tell Junior you're here. He—" The remainder of the sentence was lost in the explosive blast of a gunshot. "God a'mighty!" Henry yelled and scrunched down in his seat.

The crowd scattered, some ducking behind parked cars, others hightailing to parts unknown. Considering their ages, they were moving at a pretty good clip. Officer Haskins remained frozen on the bench for a second, his expression one of disbelief. Then as if to make up for lost time, he hopped down and pounded toward the street.

I have no memory of my reasoning, I simply reacted, throwing open the door and practically falling out of the station wagon. Regaining my balance, I ran toward Mr. Haskins, who had reached the one tree decorating the traffic island, a sizable oak, but nowhere nearly thick enough to hide his paunch, which protruded from behind the trunk. He heard me coming and looked back over his shoulder.

"Lady, you hard of hearing or something? Go back before you get yourself shot!"

Ignoring his warning, I kept running until I'd reached his side. Behind me on the far side of the circle, a second police car screeched to a halt, knocking over one of the sawhorse barricades, and an officer who could have been Mr. Haskins's twin hurried toward us, crouched low. "That was a shot!" he announced, eyes wide. "What the hell's goin' on, Junior? Where'd it come from?"

"The jail. Crazy ol' bat's holding Ficker hostage in there. Ficker!" he yelled. "You all right?"

A voice, to my surprise, a young one, responded. "I have to tell you, Junior, I been better."

"You shoot the ol' lady?"

"Uh, no sir. She's all right."

Haskins hurled his cap to the ground in frustration. "By God, I'm sick of this. Where's the tear gas, Grady?"

The new arrival looked sheepish. "In the cruiser. I'll get it. Who is she, anyways?"

"My great-aunt," I responded, still rankling at Jay being written off as a crazy old bat.

"You're Miz Burdette?" Haskins demanded. "Whyn't ya say so? Grady, will you please haul your ass back to the car and get the damned tear gas? Bring the bullhorn, too. I'll give you five minutes to talk some sense into her, ma'am, and then we're flushing her out."

Officer Grady squatted and duckwalked his way back to

the cruiser as yet another man, tall, distinguished in his dark blue suit, and well set-up, as my mom would say, sprinted from the doorway of an office building across the street. Even after that forty-yard dash not a single silver hair was out of place.

He glanced at me for as long as it took for his baby blues to focus on me, then glared at my companion. "Haskins, what's going on? Did I hear gunfire?"

Officer Haskins grimaced. "Sorry, Your Honor. Things just got out of hand. This . . ." His eyes flicked to me, then away. "This lady's great-auntie showed up this morning saying she was turning herself in for murdering somebody back when Hector was a pup and—"

"Her again!" His Honor exploded, aquiline features suffused with vermilion. "By God, I warned her, must have been a couple of years ago, that if she came back talking that foolishness again, I'd have her arrested for trespassing." Alarm flared in his eyes. "She's got a gun?"

Haskins appeared to have trouble meeting the man's gaze. "She must have. We didn't pat her down. No reason to. Even after we realized she didn't have both oars in the water—'scuse me, ma'am, but it's the truth—we didn't think there was anything to worry about. I found Miz Burdette's phone number and called her. She said she'd come take Miz Wingate home, so all we had to do was find some way to keep the old lady here until Miz Burdette arrived."

"Why didn't you just pretend to arrest her?" I asked.

"Why indeed?" Mr. Silver Hair demanded. "Forgive my manners, Ms. Burdette, is it? Leland Spates, mayor of this fair island." He extended a hand and shot me a politician's smile that had the life span of a flashbulb. "Thank you for coming," he added. "Back to the question, Junior. Why didn't you pretend to arrest Miss Wingate?"

"We were about to, but she had commenced to make such a fuss about how dirty things were that I found a mop and broom and let her supervise Ficker while he played janitor. All that cleaning took a couple of hours. Then I decided to go get something t'eat for ever'body, only the Deli was jammed, so I went to Binnie's and you know how slow they are and when I get back, the door's locked. She calls out that we haven't fooled her for a minute. She is going to jail for murder or else and I reckon it don't make no difference to her if it's for the man back in '43 or for Ficker today. Grady here's got the tear gas." He gestured at the second officer, who'd returned with a canvas bag and a bullhorn that looked as if it too was a retiree. "Like I said before, Miz Burdette, you got five minutes and then we're smoking her out. She's dangerous." He extended the bull-horn to me.

"Keep it," I said, making another of those split-second decisions that defy logic. With no further explanation, I headed across the street.

"Hey!" Mr. Haskins bellowed. "Get back here! You wanna get yourself killed?"

I ignored him. I wasn't sure what the gunplay was all about, but I couldn't imagine the woman I knew taking aim at me or anyone else. Behind me, Mr. Haskins launched into some very imaginative swearing concerning the mule-headedness of females in general and Aunt Jay and me in particular. Approaching the building at a leisurely pace, I took a deep breath, stopped at the door and rapped at it, eyeing the Binnie's Burger bag and the three styrofoam cups left on the bench. My stomach growled. There hadn't been time for me to finish eating before I'd left home, and the fare on the plane hadn't been worth the effort. "Aunt Jay, open up," I said, just loudly enough to be heard.

At first nothing. Then, disbelieving: "Troy? Is that you?"

"Yes. Come on, honey. Let me in."

"Wade with you?" she asked.

"No, I'm alone."

Locks clicked. The door was opened a crack and one whiskey-brown eye peered out at me. "Do, Jesus," she murmured. She unlocked the screen and pushed it ajar just wide enough for me to squeeze through. "What in the world are you doing here, daughter?" To a certain extent, the term defined our relationship, even though we weren't related.

"Later," I responded, looking her over carefully. She'd clearly meant to be arrested in style. She wore a navy suit I would normally be drooling over, her favorite pin, a simple gold circle, and low-heeled navy pumps. Snow-white hair was captured by a mother-of-pearl barrette atop her head. There were rings on each of her fingers, thumb included. And in her left hand, the biggest, ugliest revolver on the East Coast.

"What are you doing with that?" I asked, as casually as I could manage.

"This?" She looked at it as if surprised to be holding it. "Oh. Just making sure this child doesn't shoot himself in the foot again." She jerked her head toward the rear, where an officer young enough to be her great-grandson sat in the corner of the room, his head in his hands. He wore a crew cut, his hair so fair it was almost as white as Jay's. "You feeling any better, Leon?" she asked. "Say hello to my grand-niece-in-law, Troy Burdette."

"Ma'am." He rose from his chair just enough for his butt to clear the seat, then plopped back down, as miserable a specimen as I'd seen in a long time. Under more normal circumstances, he was probably a model officer, his brown uniform as crisp as burnt toast, the crease in his pants sharp enough to draw blood. His shoes glistened a shiny black and would have passed muster were it not for the fact that one of them was open-toed. Just at the right of the desk was a jagged hole in the floor. If it and the officer's shoe were related, he was lucky he still had a foot. I saw no blood, so I assumed his toes had survived the encounter.

"Put that thing down, please, Aunt Jay. We've got to talk fast. They're about to lob tear gas in here. What's going on? What are you doing way down here, anyway?"

"Way down here is where I was born and raised," she said, with great dignity. "Not that it's anything like the way it was when I was growing up."

"I bet. Are you really holding this poor man hostage?"

She grunted. "Of course not. That was the other one's, Haskins', idea, not mine. I just didn't tell him any different. But I let him know that he wasn't getting back in until he stopped treating me like some feebleminded old fart. I came here to be arrested and I won't take no for an answer."

With surprising expertise, she emptied the cylinders and dumped the bullets on the big battle-scarred desk, the only furniture aside from a couple of folding chairs. Henry had been right; it was a sorry excuse for a jail—one fair-sized space, a corner of it enclosed with floor-to-ceiling bars. The cell door was open. It held a folding cot, a wooden stool, and a plastic bucket with a mop standing in it. If there was a bathroom, I didn't see it. The whole place smelled of furniture polish, disinfectant, pine-scented cleanser, and gunpowder. The only thing still in need of attention was the window Officer Haskins had been trying to peek through.

"Aunt Jay," I said, sitting her down. "Listen to me closely. This is serious. Did you really kill someone a long time ago?"

She sighed deeply, the rich brown of her skin suddenly sagging. "Troy, it's haunted me for years. I've prayed for forgiveness and tried to live like a good Christian to make up for it. But it comes down to this: the sun is setting on my life. I don't want to stand before my heavenly judge until I've stood before an earthly one and paid for my crime."

I felt a chill. "Are you sick, Aunt Jay?"

"Oh, for pity's—do I look sick to you?"

She really didn't. A trifle thinner, perhaps, but her eyes were bright, her skin as clear and unlined as I'd ever seen it. And there were no signs of the mental deterioration I'd expected. "You look okay to me," I admitted. "Love your suit."

"Do you? End-of-season sale. I sort of like it myself. Now, will you please go tell Haskins I'm not loony? He keeps saying they don't have any record of a murder that year. I don't give a kitty what the records show. I didn't mean to, but I killed that man and I've got to pay. They've got to arrest me."

"I should think that's not a problem any longer," I said. "Now, don't you move." I picked up the gun gingerly and handed it to the young officer. "Will you please take this thing out to Officer Haskins? Aunt Jay and I will wait in here. Quickly, before we wind up with tear gas canisters in our laps."

"Yes, ma'am," he said, rising. He took the revolver and, looking as if he was going out to be shot at dawn, opened the door. "Hold your fire, Junior!" he yelled. "I'm coming out!" Squaring his shoulders, he left.

"It's a shame he's white," Aunt Jay said. "He'd make a nice beau for you. Have you talked to Wade recently?"

I nodded. "That's why I'm here instead of him. He's finally a father, Jay. Latrice just had twins, a boy and a girl. They're premature, so they'll be in the hospital for a while. He can't leave right now, so he asked me to come."

"Twins. Bless his time." All the wisdom of her seventy-five to ninety years was reflected in her eyes. "And you. Are you all right, baby?"

"Fine," I lied. "I'm happy for him, really I am."

"Uh-huh." She lifted one pale brow in response just as the door was thrown open with a bang. The only thing that appeared was an enormous revolver, even bigger than the one I'd sent out, held by a pudgy, sun-freckled hand. It hovered there for at least ten seconds before Officer Haskins stepped into the room, gun still at the ready. His young companion followed, face rosy with embarrassment. The mayor brought up the rear, face rosy with anger.

"All right, lady," Haskins roared, "assume the position!"

Aunt Jay smiled with grim satisfaction. "That's more like it. Where do you want me?"

"Hands flat on the desk. Spread 'em."

"Aw, Junior, cut it out." Leon Ficker grimaced, as Haskins patted her down. "I told you that shot was an accident. Heck, it was your gun. You went out and left the thing on the desk under today's paper. I bumped the paper with my elbow and it started sliding off and I tried to stop it and hit your dad-jim gun underneath. It went skittering off the edge of the desk, and when I tried to catch it, my finger hit the trigger and it went off. She didn't have anything to do with it."

"She wound up with it, didn't she? And she wouldn't unlock the damned door. Miz Wingate, I'm arrestin' you for unlawful imprisonment."

"You could have saved yourself a lot of trouble if you'd just done that when I asked you to the first time," Aunt Jay said grumpily. "Now read me my rights so I can go sit down. These shoes are starting to pinch."

Officer Haskins obliged and when he'd finished, she turned around and walked into the cell, closing the door firmly behind herself. After a second, it swung open again slowly.

"Get the key and lock that thing!" the mayor ordered.

Haskins and young Ficker exchanged a look. Ficker cleared his throat. "No key, Your Honor."

"No key! What kind of jail is this anyway?"

Haskins sat down and laced his fingers across his ample tummy. "The kind of jail you and the city council haven't seen fit to put in the budget for the last seven years, that's the kind of jail it is."

Aunt Jay had perched on the cot and was removing her shoes. "No need to worry. I'm not going anywhere."

Mr. Spates glared at her. "Oh, yes, you are." He turned back to Haskins. "Judge Craymore'll take care of this. As soon as she's formally charged, she's heading over to Innocence General for psychiatric evaluation. You can bet they have locks on the doors over there."

Aunt Jay hopped off the cot and stormed to the opening of the cell, but did not step out. "I'm as sane as you are, Leland Spates! Maybe saner, if there's any chance you take after your Aunt Minnie."

His Honor paled, staring at her intently. "Who are you?"

"Nobody you'd remember, since I grew up on the wrong side of the island, so to speak. I'm from North End, which may not even exist anymore, from the little I've seen."

"It doesn't," the mayor said tersely.

"That figures. Regardless, you're the last person who should be recommending psychiatric evaluation for anybody, considering the number of loonies you had in your family. My memory may not be what it was, but there's nothing wrong with my mind."

The mayor's chin came up. "Obviously there is. I've lived on this island all my life. We've never had a murder on Innocence. Never. And I won't have you saying there has been." Suddenly, he switched tactics, softened his tone. "Look, Miss Wingate—"

"Mrs." Aunt Jay snapped.

"My apologies. Look, Mrs. Wingate, this is a different place from the one you used to know. We're a nice quiet community, completely crime-free, and we're very proud of that. It's one of our most valuable assets."

"Make your point, man." Aunt Jay had reached the outer limits of her patience.

"What I'm saying is that perhaps we're being a trifle hasty here. Except for a bruised ego or two, no one's been hurt. You're talking to a man who'll celebrate his sixty-seventh birthday next October, so I know too well how easily the mind plays tricks on us when we get to a certain station in life. Why don't we simply forget today's little misunderstanding? Your niece is here to see you home, and after you've had a chance to reflect, you'll realize—"

"Leland." Aunt Jay held up a hand to silence him. "I can't tell you how much it pains me to disrupt the serenity of your sweet little community, but, as my nephew used to say, tough noogies. I killed a man back in Nineteen and forty-three and nothing you can say's gonna change that."

The mayor's face closed up. "Have it your way." Turning on his heel, he strode to the door. "Junior, get those barricades off the circle so traffic can get back to normal. And don't forget. You and Grady are to be waiting to meet the governor's limo when it crosses the causeway. Escort it to Dozen Pines with your chase lights going. It's only nine holes of golf, but we want him to feel important."

"Yes, sir," Haskins said, practically tugging on a nonexistent forelock.

"I'll send the judge over here so we can dispense with whatever legalities are necessary to take care of your prisoner. It's obvious she needs professional help and as long as she insists on staying on Innocence, she's going to get it whether she wants it or not." And out he went.

Inexplicably, Officer Haskins began to chuckle, then to giggle, his stomach dancing. Finally he burst into laughter, bent double in his chair. "By God," he said, slapping his thigh, "I remember my pop talking about a woman named Minnie who used to dance down the road in her birthday suit every Tuesday night the Lord sent. She said she just couldn't resist the tootlin' of the Tuesday fairies. That was the mayor's auntie? And him always comin' off as if he's got royal blood flowing through his veins!"

"This ain't funny, Junior." Ficker went over to peer out of the window. "I've never seen His Honor that mad. Sure you won't change your mind about all this, Mrs. Wingate? He's a big man on this island and he can be awfully vindictive. He can see you wind up on the psychiatric ward until the mortar around the bricks crumbles."

Aunt Jay fixed him with a steely eye. "Listen, son. I have no intention of spending the rest of my days in a loony bin. Jail, yes. Considering what I did, that's a fit place for me to be. But I will not have them writing me off as a senile old woman."

"Aunt Jay," I said, hoping she'd listen to reason, "if there's no record of an unexplained death, you must have been mistaken. The man must not have been dead."

She propped her small fists on her hips. "Please! I admit I wasn't the brightest young woman, but I knew dead when I saw it and that man was well and truly dead. I killed him. This is where I belong and this is where I stay." Reaching out, she shut the door of the cell. Wouldn't you know, for some reason, this time the damned thing stayed closed.

3

"Hey, Junior." Officer Aaron Grady peered into the room through the screen door. "Gimme back my gun so I can get on over to the golf course. What you want me to do with the tear gas?"

Haskins, still in a good humor thanks to the mayor's Aunt Minnie, leaned forward, elbows on his knees, and smiled at Jay. "You of a mind to take any more hostages, Miz Wingate?" he asked.

She smiled back. If he'd known her better, he'd have realized he was about to hang himself with an invisible rope. "Don't get too full of yourself, Marion Haskins."

"Marion?" Officers Ficker and Grady yelped in concert. Clearly their co-worker's first name was news to them.

Jay ignored them. "Not only do I remember you in short pants," she continued, "I remember you in no pants at all."

"What?" His head shot forward.

She began to sing, a wicked gleam in her eye.

"Wee-wah-wee pot that grunt,

Wee-wah-wee pot that grunt,
Wee-wah-wee pot, pot, pot . . . "

For the first few notes, Officer Haskins watched Aunt Jay as if she really had gone around the Horn. Gradually, however, his expression changed, eyes narrowing and gazing off into the middle distance.

Suddenly his mouth dropped open. He stared at her, saucer-eyed, rising slowly to his feet. "My God! You're Miz Lena's girl. Julie, that's it! That's the song . . ." He stopped, flabbergasted, and dropped heavily onto his chair again. "How could I have forgotten you?"

Jay's smile was angelic. "Because that was nigh unto sixty years ago. And you were just a little tyke."

He shook his head in astonishment. "Lord, Julie Brownlee. Who'd have believed it."

"You know Mrs. Wingate?" Ficker asked, his glance darting from one to the other.

"Do I!" Haskins started to elaborate, then thought better of it. "Get outta here and change those shoes. Did you remember to put gas in the motorcycle this time?"

Ficker winced. "Yes sir. I'll meet you at the causeway." Taking the gun from Haskins, he crossed to the door and handed it to Grady. "Nice meeting you, Miss Burdette. Mrs. Wingate, you take care, hear?"

Jay's eyes warmed. "I hear. You do the same." She watched with a wistful smile as he left. "Such a shame," she said, with a sigh. Julia Wingate, frustrated matchmaker.

As soon as he'd closed the door, Haskins pulled his chair over to the cell. "Listen, Miz Julie, my mama used to say that if it hadn't been for that little ditty you taught her to sing to me, I'd have been in diapers until I was five. She used it to help potty-train my kids, and my daughter's fixin' to try it with her youngest. So I'm gonna tell you something for old time's sake. All ol' Leland's got on his mind right now is butterin' up the governor this afternoon and getting ready for the big golf tournament week after next. He don't want to be distracted and that's what you are, a distraction. If I was in your place right now, when Judge Craymore shows up I'd pretend I don't know what he's talkin' about. Act a little addled and he'll chew us out for wastin' his time with someone who's . . . well, not quite responsible, okay? We'll just forget that unlawful imprisonment charge. I was just blowing off steam anyhow. Do like I say and you'll be on your way home in no time."

Jay reached through the bars and patted his shoulder. "You don't understand, son. I am home. I came home to atone for my sins and to make amends."

"But I keep telling you, there's nothing to atone and make amends for, Miz Julie. I checked. Nobody found a corpse. Nobody reported nobody missing. You've been beating yourself over the head all these years for something you didn't do. Stick with that story and you're gonna wind up in the booby wing, sure as shootin'."

Jay's face was a mask of sadness, "So be it. What kind of place is this Innocence General they might send me to?"

"Well, if you gotta go to one, you couldn't ask for a better hospital. The best geriatric doctors in the state. Food's good, too. Folks go over there to eat just like it's a regular restaurant."

"But it's still a hospital." Jay shook her head. "Well. You go on and get spruced up for the governor. Troy and I will wait here for the judge."

"Well, now, about that." He hitched his chair even closer. "Judge Craymore's gonna be playing those nine holes with the mayor and the governor. And the judge, he takes his golf seriously. He meditates before he plays and not even Lord High Mayor Leland Spates is gonna make him cut that short to deal with you. You probably won't come up before him until tomorrow morning."

"So?" Jay's complete lack of concern reinforced her intention to stick it out.

"So you and Miz Burdette could probably go get yourself something to eat and relax a little. Nobody would even know you'd been gone, 'cause the whole town will be out at Dozen Pines watching the governor play. You could come back tonight, tomorrow even, whenever you've a mind to."

"This child needs to find herself someplace to stay," Aunt Jay said, echoing my thoughts. "Ya'll got a decent hotel here?"

"Plenty of 'em. I'd recommend The Haven. Nice big rooms with balconies overlooking the ocean. Cable, too. And their restaurant serves the best seafood. They got a shrimp dish . . ." He shook his head, practically salivating. Even without his girth as evidence, it was obvious the part food played in his life. "The Haven's on Main Street, right-hand side," he finished. "You can't miss it."

"Do they allow pets?" I asked, remembering belatedly that I was not alone.

"Pets and kids. For pets they tack ten dollars more on the cost of the room. Don't know about how much they charge for kids."

Jay peered at me from beneath lowered lids. "You brought the demon with you?"

"On such short notice, I had to."

Haskins checked his watch. "I've got to skedaddle."

"You haven't fingerprinted me yet," Jay reminded him.

He looked at me in frustration. Do it, I mouthed, knowing he would not change her mind. He sighed and mopped his brow. "Best we get on with it, then. Some forms to fill out, too. Make yourself comfortable, Miz Burdette."

Wishful thinking. So while they took care of legalities, I

excused myself, hoping that Henry and The Deacon hadn't succumbed to heat stroke. I'd even left my purse in his car.

The street was practically empty except for a few who appeared to be going about their usual business, whatever that was. Henry, however, was precisely where I'd left him. He got out as I approached.

"Everything all right in yonder? What was the shootin' about?"

"The gun went off accidentally," I said truthfully. "Everybody's fine. I'm so sorry to have kept you waiting like this. I'll take my suitcase and the carrier so you can be on your way. And I'd like to give you something for your trouble."

"No'm." He gazed at me mournfully. "It's like this, Miz Burdette. I can't tolerate air conditionin' in the car but so long or it locks my knees up something fierce. Arthuritis, don't ya know. So I turned it off and opened up all the windows, let the breeze blow through. Only it must have been hotter than I'd thought, 'cause all of a sudden your cat starts actin' funny. I jump out and go back there to see what's wrong and he's all hunched over."

I stepped around him and looked in the back seat. No cat. No carrier. "Henry, where's my cat?"

"It's like this. I was worried what was ailin' him, so I opened the cage so I could see him better. And, well . . ."

"Where's my cat?" I asked again, wondering how long this saga would continue before I'd get an answer.

"The last I seen him he was headin' across the street like greased lightning. He ran behind the bank, but when I went back there, he was nowhere in sight."

"Oh, God." Heaven knew where he might be. And as much as that flea-bitten feline meant to me, I couldn't abandon Jay to search for him. Thank God we were on an island. As much as he hated water, he'd be going only so far. Besides, if he made his way to the beach, he'd be in cat heaven. It would be the biggest litter box he'd ever seen. "Does Innocence have a dogcatcher?" I asked.

"No'm, because we don't have any strays. I wouldn't worry overmuch. Mabel Potee was standing beside the car, watching all the excitement. She saw your cat light out, so she grabbed the carrier out the back and took off after him. Mabel's a fool for animals. She'll find him. All we have to do is find her." He opened the door for me.

I refused his offer and explained why, deleting certain details. All of Innocence would know them soon enough.

"Well," Henry said, still chewing a cud of guilt, "at least let me take you and your auntie to The Haven so you can get yourselves a room. While y'all are gettin' settled, I'll hunt down Mabel. If she didn't catch him, I'll ask around. Somebody's bound to have seen him, big as he is. If he doesn't turn up tonight, I'll call my grandchildren—they live over on Hilton Head. We'll all start lookin' for him at first light and turn this island inside out. I'm really sorry, Miz Burdette. Now, let's go get your auntie."

Julia Wingate, however, had other ideas. Refusing Henry's services as a chauffeur, she asked him to transfer my suitcase from his back seat to the trunk of her Buick, which she'd parked behind the courthouse. Henry, at first hurt by her rejection, took one look at her car and fell in love. "By Gawd, she's a beauty! What is she, a '39? No. Thirty-eight, right?"

Other than her rings, there was nothing more dear to Jay's heart than that Buick. Big, bulky, and as shiny as polished coal, it was the first car she'd ever purchased and she'd never given it up. It had outlived the three husbands she'd buried even though she swore she'd taken almost as good care of them as she had the Buick. It was now an antique, of course, with all the rights and privileges thereto, and anyone who showed genuine appreciation for it became her friend for life. Henry had hit the year on the nose, confessing wistfully that he'd owned one himself a century ago, an admission that immediately levered him up a couple of dozen notches in Jay's estimation.

"Then you know what a fine machine it is," she responded, her eyes lighting up. "Wait."

My spirits sank as she opened the hood to expose the works. If she got really wound up, we'd be here until the judge arrived. I decided I'd give her ten minutes for Show and Tell. If she hadn't run down by then, I'd excuse myself and use the time to search the area for my errant pussycat.

"By Gawd, Julie," Henry said, the car having put them on a first-name basis, "this engine's so clean a body could eat off it. Who takes care of it for you?"

This response alone could take a half an hour. I swallowed a groan as she launched into an explanation of the care and feeding of her pride and joy, and prayed that for once she hadn't stashed two pairs of coveralls in the car, one for herself, a second for the occasional admirer who just had to see what the thing looked like from underneath. Fortunately, she'd had other priorities when she'd left home; I'd spotted only one small overnight bag in the trunk. She'd probably packed what she thought she'd be allowed to keep in jail.

"Bernice—that's the baby's name—and I will be around for a spell," she was saying as she closed the hood, "so you'll have a chance to get a better look at her later. Right now we need to hurry on to the hotel so we can eat and get back before Judge Craymore does."

"If you've got business with the judge," Henry said, "why not see him now, so you won't have to rush through your supper? He's right upstairs. Saw him go in while I was waitin' for your niece. This time of day, he's probably in his chambers."

My spirits sagged. I had to sidetrack Jay. "Mr. Haskins says he meditates before playing," I reminded her. "It might not be a good idea to interrupt him."

"If he's meditating, we'll let him be. Run back and see if Junior Haskins has left yet. Henry can show me where the courtroom is. We can meet up there and get this over with. Hurry, daughter."

From the determined glint in her eye, I knew there was no discouraging her, so I sprinted back around to the front of the building and caught Mr. Haskins just as he was pulling away from the curb. His reaction to the unexpected appearance of Judge Craymore was a heartrending groan.

"Miz Burdette, all Miss Julie's gonna do is aggravate the judge before he gets on the golf course. If she irks him now and he doesn't play well, there's gonna be hell to pay."

"I've tried, so have you. She's being muleheaded about this."

"Muleheaded ain't the word for it. Where is she now?"

"On her way inside. She'll meet us in the courtroom."

"Well," he said, getting out and hitching up his pants, "let's see if we can get through this without Miss Julie windin' up in the hoosegow. If I have anything to do with putting that little woman in jail, every mama on this island who's ever sung that potty song to her young'un will string me up by my . . . never mind. I'll do the best I can, Miz Burdette, but I swear 'fore God, as stubborn as Miss Julie's bein' about this, I got a feeling my best will be a long way from enough."

We found Henry waiting for us just inside the door of the courtroom, a far smaller and austere space than I would have expected, with seats for perhaps fifty or sixty people.

The blinds were closed, the lights off. It was obvious no business was scheduled today.

"Where's Miss Julie?" Mr. Haskins asked.

"She just now went back to talk to Judge Craymore. It's all right. Whatever he's doing back there, it's not meditating."

"What do you mean?" Mr. Haskins asked.

His question was answered by a thump and a roar of pain from beyond the door to the left of the judge's bench. He snatched his service revolver from his holster.

"Y'all stay here," he said, his voice taut with tension. Moving with surprising speed and agility, given the tummy suspended above his belt, he stopped at the door, his back against the wall. Gingerly he reached for the knob, threw the door open, and stepped into the room, gun at the ready.

There was a moment's silence. Then: "Junior Haskins, what the hell do you mean, busting in here like that? Who you plan on shooting?"

We were too far away to make out Mr. Haskins's response, but from what little I could hear, he was doing some fast talking. We waited for several minutes, during which I prayed that the reason for the judge's shout was in no way related to Jay's presence in his chambers. Finally, however, I couldn't stand it any longer. If I was to protect her, I'd better get moving.

My first glimpse into the anteroom stopped my heart in midbeat. Wade's great-aunt stood before a monk-tonsured man, wiping blood from the top of his head. He was perhaps a quarter inch taller than she was, dressed in red and green plaid plus fours loud enough to halt rush-hour traffic in midtown Manhattan. Jay passed the bloodstained tissue to Officer Haskins and took a second one, folded it into a small square, and plastered it to his head.

"Aunt Jay, you hit him?" I blurted.

"Of course not. He was under the desk when I came in. I startled him and he hit his head on the bottom of the drawer."

"Feel downright foolish," Judge Craymore said, with an air of distraction. He fingered the tissue. "Thank you kindly, madam. Now, forgive me, but I'm rather pressed for time. Since Junior says he's dropping the charges against you and that it was all a big misunderstanding, you have our apologies, Miss Winthrop. You're free to go." He turned away from her and peered around the room, clearly looking for something.

"The name's Wingate," Jay corrected him. "And it's Mrs. But what about the other?"

"Come on, Miz Julie," Officer Haskins said. "We already told you there's nothing we can do about that."

"About what?" the judge asked, crossing to an open closet door. His top half disappeared into the enclosure as he stooped to paw through the items on the floor. "This is the last straw," he said in a growl. "I've told Dora time and again not to move my putter!"

"Benton!" a familiar voice called from the courtroom. "What are you doing back here? You're supposed to be out at the golf course!"

"Oh, hell," Officer Haskins muttered, as Mayor Spates strode into the room, saw the assemblage, and scowled. I moved to Jay's side and gave her a gentle nudge toward the door. She gave me a sharp elbow back and stood her ground.

"What is going on in here?" he demanded. "Why are you wasting time on this woman? You can handle her case after we play. We've got to go."

A kelly green and white golf cap sailed out of the closet and dropped to the floor. "Keep your britches on, Leland," the judge snapped, disappearing into the walk-in altogether. "This lady's not responsible for the delay. She and I have finished our business."

"Capital. So what's the holdup?"

"Can't find my lucky putter," came the muffled response.

"Just a minute." Jay held up a hand like a cop directing traffic. "I'm sorry, Your Honor, but you and I won't be finished until we've dealt with the murder charge."

"The what?" Judge Craymore's head appeared from around the door.

"Murder?" Henry said, turning cookie-dough pale.

Officer Haskins groaned. "Aww, Miss Julie."

The mayor slammed his fist down onto the desk. "Damn it, woman, why are you so determined to make trouble?"

"I killed a man back in '43," Jay persisted. "I'm pleading guilty, Your Honor. Do I still have to stand trial or can you just sentence me and tell me where I'm going to be sent?"

"She's not responsible, Benton," Spates pronounced. "Lack of oxygen to the brain or something. This young woman—" he jerked his head in my general direction— "she's her niece, come to take her home. Let her. Now will you get a move on? We're going to be late."

The judge came out of the closet and closed the door behind him. "What do you know about this, Junior?"

"Nothing, Your Honor. I mean, she told us the same thing but there's nothing to back her up, no records or anything, or we'd have brought her up on charges, since there's no statue of limitations on murder."

"Statute," the mayor corrected him. "Benton—"

"In a minute, Leland." Suddenly Judge Craymore was no longer a balding little man in ridiculous-looking red and green plaid knickers and a Kleenex plastered top center of his head. He seemed taller, with an unmistakable air of authority. For the first time I could envision him, gavel in hand, looking down from his bench.

"Have a seat, Mrs. Wingate," he said, and pulled over a big mahogany armchair for her. Seeing my last chance to get Jay off this island tonight exiting stage right, I gave up, headed for the sofa, and plopped down onto it.

"This happened here?" he asked, moving to sit behind his desk. "On Innocence?"

"Yes, sir, it did, in Miss Lucy Stokes's rooming house. The man was one of her boarders."

"Why were you there? In as few words as possible," he added, glancing at his watch.

"My mother took in washing. She sent me over to collect Miss Lucy's. Miss Lucy told me to strip the bed in the back bedroom upstairs because the boarder wouldn't be staying another night. He wasn't in the room but his valise was on the bed and I had to move it to get the linens off. I was tugging at it when all of a sudden it comes open. I was trying to close it when the boarder walked in and started accusing me of going through his things. Before I could explain what had happened, he hit me. We tussled some, then he threw me across the bed so hard I rolled off it onto the floor on the other side in a space hardly big enough for me to sit in. I was trapped with my back against the wall and he kept hitting me, saying he would teach me a lesson. I had to do something, so I grabbed the only thing close to hand to protect myself, a . . . well, a piece of heavy crockery. I swung it with all my might and caught him right above his ear. He went flop across the bed and that was that. I'd killed him."

"You're sure the man was dead?" the judge asked.

"He never took another breath."

"What was his name?"

Jay shook her head. "I don't know. I got out of there as fast as I could and ran home. My mother packed a few things for me and I left that night. It was wrong. I should have stayed and confessed."

"Why didn't you?" the judge asked, his tone gentle, encouraging.

"He was a white man and it was a different time. I figured I'd get hung for it. I'm not much for heights so I ran."

"Your mother, is she still with us?"

"You mean, alive?" Jay shook her head. "She died in '47."

"Did you tell anyone else about it?"

"No, sir. I didn't dare."

The mayor sighed. "Damn it, Benton, I was sixteen back in '43. Nothing much ever happened around here, so if somebody had turned up dead at Miss Lucy's—who, by the way, went to her reward long since—I'd have remembered it. This woman is clearly delusional."

"She seems lucid enough to me," the judge said. "But you do see, Mrs. Wingate, that there is no basis on which to pursue this further. We have no name, no body, no witnesses, nothing. I'd hazard a guess you simply stunned the man. When he came around, he was probably too embarrassed to tell anyone he'd had his bell rung by such a little snip of a girl. I bet he closed that valise and went on about his business." Getting up, he came from behind his desk, helped Jay to her feet, and with a gentle hand on her elbow, escorted her to the door. "I think it's time you put this out of your mind and consider the matter closed. Now," he said, turning away from her, "where in God's name could Dora have hidden that putter?" Jay, it appeared, had been dismissed.

Henry backed quickly out of the room and Mr. Haskins, looking much relieved, crossed to the door, beckoning me to follow.

"I've got a putter you can use," the mayor said. "Considering how many holes you bogeyed day before yesterday, seems to me you'd want to try a different one anyway."

Judge Craymore pulled himself to his full height. "I bogeyed four holes day before yesterday, Leland Spates. At least I own up to all my bogeys on my scorecard!"

"By God, somebody had better listen to me!" Jay roared.

Riveted on the juvenile display of the two men, I'd momentarily forgotten her. So had the others. She had everyone's attention now. "I am not some addlepated old fart who's lost her senses! I know dead when I see it and that man was deader than last week's news! I came back to see justice done, and I won't see it denied!" Then, as suddenly as she'd exploded, she seemed to implode, folding in on herself and slowly, like a silk scarf slipping through one's fingers, drifting silently toward the floor.

I wasn't sure whether Jay was faking or not, she'd done it so gracefully. If she'd been performing the death scene in *Swan Lake*, her audience would have been on its feet shouting "Brava!" And she came to quickly enough, brushing off the helping hands that had caught her and maneuvered her into the nearest chair.

"Are you all right?" I asked, on my knees in front of her.

Judge Craymore gestured for Henry to get a cup of water for her from the cooler. "Junior, maybe you'd better drive her over to the hospital, let them take a look at her."

"I'm fine," Jay insisted, her expression best described as sheepish. "Just embarrassed. I haven't eaten since dinner last night. I just assumed I'd be having breakfast in jail, so I didn't bother to fix anything before I got on the road this morning."

The mayor sighed, eyeing her solicitously. "I owe you an apology, Mrs. Wingate. You came back in good faith and we've treated you with appalling insensitivity."

"Speak for yourself, Leland." Judge Craymore took the

tiny cone of water from Henry and placed it in her hand. "But you must understand, there's nothing we can do. Until Junior has some evidence that a homicide occurred, he has no grounds on which to arrest you."

"My word's not enough," Jay said.

"I'm afraid not. Bring us proof and we can proceed from there. Even then, I wouldn't count on spending any time in jail. Sounds to me like a clear case of self-defense. But without evidence, what we have is nothing at all. You can see that, can't you?"

Jay nodded. After a second, she rose, steadied herself, and with Henry on one side and Junior on the other, headed for the door. She stopped beside the coat tree just inside the doorway. "I'm sorry to have wasted your time. By the way, Your Honor, is this what you've been looking for?" Reaching under one of the robes hanging from the coat tree, she withdrew her hand. In it was the putter, which she flipped toward the judge in a perfect, spiraling arc. He caught it with a squeak of surprise. "Now, you folks had better hurry," she said dryly. "The governor's waiting."

"Jesus!" the mayor exclaimed. "Bet he's sitting at the gatehouse right now, waiting for an escort. Move it, Junior! Come on, Benton!"

Judge Craymore slapped the plaid cap atop the Kleenex still stuck to his head. "Ladies," he said, doffing it in a gesture of farewell, and scurried out of the room, the mayor in hot pursuit.

"Miz Julie." Haskins sidled toward the door. "I hate to leave you like this, but you gotta understand, it's my job. It's been a pleasure seeing you again. Nice meetin' you, Miz Burdette. Henry, I'm deputizing you to see to these ladies. Whatever help they need, give it to them. I'm counting on you, y'hear?" Without waiting for a response, Officer Haskins hurried off.

Jay took a deep breath and straightened her shoulders. "Well. I guess we'd better go, too." She opened her purse as she walked slowly out of the door, removed something, and slipped her hand into her pocket. Then, stopping, she stepped back into the judge's chambers and peered around anxiously.

Henry, leading the way, glanced back, and stopped, too. "You forget something, Julie?"

"My keys. They aren't in my pocketbook. See if I dropped them somewhere between here and the car, please, Henry."

"Sure." He scuttled down the side aisle and through the double doors at the rear of the room.

As soon as he was gone, Jay opened the hand in which she had palmed her keys. "I hated to do that, but I wanted to speak to you alone. I need you to do a couple of favors for me and I want your promise you'll ask no questions and do them without making a lot of fuss."

Against my better judgment, I nodded. "You've got it."

"Dump Henry, nicely, but dump him. That's number one."

It wasn't quite what I'd expected, but I'd promised no questions. "That's easy enough. All I've got to do is hint that I'm worried about The Deacon. Henry sort of lost him for me."

She gave me a wry look. "You don't know when you're well off."

"Stop casting aspersions on my cat. What's favor number two?"

"Don't forget, no fuss. You promised. I need you to get me to the hospital. Now."

4

"Ms. Burdette?"

"Hmp?" I came awake with a hiccup, horrified to realize I'd been nodding, and faking a yawn, swept my fingers across my lips and chin. To my relief, my skin was dry. Years before, Wade had told me I drooled in my sleep and I'd lived in terror of dropping off in public ever since. Blinking, I sat up straight, and found myself the focus of a sympathetic gaze emitting from the most astonishing green eyes. Sort of charcoal green, really, or maybe heather, and astonishing because the face of which they were a feature was the color of teak. It was an exotic combination. And even with the dark smudges of fatigue under the eyes, damned attractive.

I glanced at the clock; then, certain that it was wrong, my watch. They read the same. Three-plus hours had elapsed since we'd arrived at the Emergency Room of Innocence General!

"I'm Dr. Baskerville," he said, extending a hand. "Sorry

to keep you waiting so long, but things have gotten complicated. Mrs. Wingate is being admitted. She's down in Radiology at the moment, but they're almost through. They'll be taking her to her room from there. She'll be in 3E118."

His words sent an arrow of panic down my spine. "What's wrong with her?"

"Well . . ." His hesitation panicked me even further. "What is your relationship to Mrs. Wingate?"

"She's my ex-husband's great-aunt," I said, deciding to be truthful, then wished I hadn't emphasized the "ex" part quite so much. I hate to be that obvious.

Taking the chair at right angles to mine, he leaned forward, elbows on his knees. The short sleeves of his lab coat exposed well-muscled biceps and forearms. "Does she have any children?" he asked.

"No. My ex is her only remaining relative. And before you ask, he lives in California, which is why I'm here and he's not, and you haven't answered my question. What's happening with Jay?"

He sat back and sighed. "Bear with me. Has she complained of any pain in her stomach or abdominal area?"

"Not to me, and knowing her, not to Wade either. We've kept in touch with her by phone, but today's the first time I've actually seen her in a couple of years. What's wrong with her?"

He eyed me warily for a moment and finally shrugged broad, high-set shoulders. "I suspect an aortic aneurysm. When I palpated her abdomen, I detected a very strong pulsation, which means—"

"Wait a minute!" I was having trouble keeping up. "I thought the aorta was up around the heart."

"That's where it begins." He pointed at his chest. "It arches up from the left ventricle, curves behind the heart, and runs down from there through the chest and into the abdomen, where it forks, each branch running through the pelvis and on down. There are several different types of aneurysm but to keep it simple, it's a weakness in the wall of an artery, and under pressure, the wall begins to balloon. Undetected, it gets larger and weaker and will eventually rupture. It's a life-threatening condition, so we'll need to get to work on her immediately."

"Hold it." This wasn't quite what I'd counted on when I'd answered the phone this morning. "Aunt Jay lives in North Carolina. She must have a doctor up there. He may be treating her already."

"Nope. The last time she saw a doctor was fifteen years ago when she broke a toe. She says she's experienced occasional discomfort so she's been dosing herself with over-the-counter antacids. The fact that she has been bothered is not a good sign."

"Are we talking surgery?" I asked.

"Definitely, and soon."

"How's she taking all this?"

His brow furrowed. "Well, to be honest, her reaction threw me, something about this place certainly being a step up from our jail, and as long as we didn't send her to our booby hatch—that's a quote—she wouldn't mind the stay. So I need to know: is she competent?"

I decided to give the question serious consideration, especially since I was on this island because of her obsession with a fifty-year-old murder that might not have occurred. So the answer to Dr. Baskerville depended on whether I believed that what she said happened actually had. Whereas I was pretty sure she hadn't actually killed the man, I had no doubt that the incident had occurred.

"She's competent, Dr. Baskerville."

"Well," he said, "we'd best get on with it, then. Dr.

McCall—he's head of surgery—is on his way over from the mainland. By the time he gets here, we'll have finished with all the preliminaries—EKG, blood work, X-rays. McCall will also want angiographic studies for a definite diagnosis and to pinpoint the precise location. That's the story. Rest assured, she's in good hands. Do you have any questions?"

"The obvious," I said, rising with him. "Is she going to be all right?"

He hesitated. "It's too early for me to say. I'll be able to tell you more after I've seen the X-rays. But I won't deceive you, Ms. Burdette. An aneurysm is bad enough. An abdominal aneurysm is a time bomb. The only question is how long the wick is."

That put things in perspective as nothing else could have.

I watched as he strode across the waiting room and disappeared behind the swinging doors, the hem of his lab coat flapping against his long legs. Despite the circumstances, I found myself taking inventory. Five-ten or -eleven, on the lean side, dark curly hair cut fairly short, broad, high-set shoulders, good arms, nice hands, nicer fingers—no ring on them, no pale band where a ring might have been. And green eyes, for God's sake. My mother's voice whispered in my ear. *Child, this one looks like a winner, so if he's unattached, you'd better strike while the iron's hot. Plug the thing in and if it heats up, start pressing.* From somewhere deep in my center, however, another voice responded. *I don't think so, Mom. I'm damaged goods, remember?* Shushing them both, I crossed toward the elevator, and debated whether I should call Wade now or later. By the time I got to the third floor, I'd decided. Definitely later. Besides, the intriguing Dr. Baskerville just might be wrong. But deep down in my heart, I didn't think he was.

The bed in 3E118, a cozy private room done up in mauve and gray, was empty. I deposited my purse on the dresser just as the door opened and was filled by an elderly woman with skin the color of a Hershey's Kiss. She wore a pink and white striped uniform she must have made herself because I doubted seriously they came in her size; she was at least six-three. If she'd been forty years younger, basketball coaches across the nation would have been drooling into their whistles just looking at her.

"If you're the patient, honey," she said, in a contralto as smooth and dark as her skin, "let me in on your secret, 'cause you're the best-preserved senior citizen I've ever seen. I'm the P.H., which stands for Patient Helper. Used to call us Candy Stripers until they realized it was ridiculous to call somebody seventy-something candy anything. The name's Mabel, by the way."

"I'm Troy Burdette," I said, liking her immediately. "And I'm not the patient. I guess they'll be bringing her up soon."

"They already did," Jay's voice sounded from the bathroom. "Oh, just damn it."

"What's going on?" I asked. "Do you need any help?"

"I can pee by myself, thank you."

"Cantankerous, ain't she?" Mabel said, grinning. Striding to the bathroom door, she tapped at it. "You doing all right in there?"

"If you call trying to catch your water in a bottle the size of a thimble without dribbling all over your hands doing all right, I'm doing just fine," Jay responded. "I hear a touch of Gullah sing-song in your voice. Who're you?"

"Your Patient Helper, here to get you settled in. Take your time. She sounds familiar to me, too," she said to me, and moved to the bed to fold back the covers.

"Daughter," Jay called, before I could tell her that Jay

was a native. "I'm going to need the overnight case from the car. My robe's in it."

"Okay." I'd won a protracted argument with her back at the courthouse over which of us would be driving her to the hospital in the Buick, and once we'd arrived, I had dropped the keys into my purse. Since it was the size and shape of a Clydesdale's feed bag, the keys were now somewhere in the bottom, arm's-length deep with assorted earrings, jumbo paperclips, small change, and other junk. I dumped the contents onto the dresser, retrieved the keys, and began tossing everything back in.

The P.H. watched, shaking her head in wonder. "Everything but the kitchen sink. And cat yummies?" she said, spotting the small plastic bag of Meow Mix. "Got the cat in there, too?"

"He's too big. And, at the moment, lost somewhere on the island."

She eyed me with speculation. "A big gray mouser with the temperament of Attila the Hun?"

I stopped what I was doing. "You've seen my cat?"

"Seen him and caught him, and I've got to tell you, honey, that's the meanest damned feline I've met in a long time. You were Henry's passenger?"

"That's right." I laughed, relieved. "Of course. You're Miss Potee. Henry assured me that if anyone could catch The Deacon, you would."

She snorted. "Wasn't all that hard. He wanted out because he had to go. So he was kind of busy when I sneaked up on him. I left him with my son. He's a vet, owns the Island Animal Clinic at Main and Palmetto Street. I'll call and tell him you'll be by to get the monster sooner or later. There's no hurry."

"Troy, my robe, please?" Jay called. "I'd just as soon not come out of here with my rear end exposed."

"I'm going, I'm going. Thanks for rescuing The Deacon. Will you stay with her, just in case?" I asked Miss Potee.

"Sure, honey," she said, plumping a pillow. "I'm not going anywhere. Neither," she added, jerking her head toward the bathroom door, "is she."

I thought it an intriguing response and wondered if Dr. Baskerville had put out the word to keep a close eye on Jay in case she decided to fly the coop.

When I returned with Jay's small Samsonite case, not much had changed. Miss Potee stood, arms folded, her back against the dresser, patience personified as she focused on the bathroom door.

"She's still in there. I tried to tell her I've seen more backsides than I care to count and one more wouldn't send me over the edge, but she wasn't impressed. Is she always this stubborn?"

"Only on her good days," I said, removing the robe from the case. "On her bad days, there's no describing her. Open the door, Aunt Jay." I handed the garment through when a six-inch gap appeared, and she emerged a minute later barefoot, blouse and skirt draped neatly over one arm, her underwear folded in a neat square in her hand.

Miss Potee stepped forward to take the clothes, then, inexplicably, stopped, her eyes slowly narrowing to slits beneath a frown that etched deep ridges across her broad forehead. "Little Bits Brownlee," she said, her voice hoarse with amazement. "Damn it, Bits, where have you been? We thought you were dead."

"We who?" Jay asked, examining the woman's features intently. "As much of you as there is up and down, along with the trace of Gullah I hear, and I figure you've got to be a McKee, but which one are you?"

"Don't recognize me, huh?" Miss Potee grinned. "I've grown some since you left. Broke my brothers' hearts because they couldn't call me runt anymore. And my best friend wasn't around to help me feed them fricaseed crow."

Watching Jay's baffled expression segue through recognition, astonishment, and elation was like witnessing time-lapsed photography of the blooming of a giant peony. "Mabel Lee," she said, as the clothes on her arm dropped to the floor. "Mabel Lee McKee."

They came together like a pair of magnets, Jay practically disappearing into the woman's bulk. All I could see of her was her small brown hands struggling to close around Miss Potee's waist. They stood locked together for a full minute, rocking like boats in the wind, while I rescued Jay's things from the floor, and placed her undies on the bed. By the time I'd gotten her blouse and skirt on hangers, they had separated, tears glistening in their eyes.

"Lord, let me sit," Jay said, backing up to the bed. "I can't believe it. I just . . ." She ran down, at a loss for words, her hands trembling as she grabbed her slip and dabbed at her tears with it. "I swear, the island's so different now, and it's been so long, I was sure all the colored people from North End were dead and gone."

"Well, hell, they are," Miss Potee said, blowing her nose. "Practically, anyway."

"So who's left here now?"

"I'm it, the last North Ender on the island. Where have you been, anyway? One day you were here and the next gone without so much as a see-ya-later or kiss my butt. Why, Bits?"

Jay settled back on the bed, kneading her slip. "It's a long story, Mabel Lee."

"I got time," Miss Potee said, snatching the slip from Jay's hands, "and you owe me, Bits. I thought we were better friends than that."

"We were. I did what I thought was the best thing at the time. Do you remember Miss Lucy Stokes?"

"Miss Lucy? Of course. Why?"

"Anything unusual happen at her place after I left?"

"No'm, except of course when they found her dead. You'd been gone awhile by then. Found her stiff as a board in that ol' big tester bed of hers."

"Heart attack?"

Miss Potee's bark of laughter echoed around the room, as she pulled a chair to the bedside. "Hell, no. Drank herself to death."

"You never heard of a problem with any of her boarders?" Jay persisted.

"No. Why?"

"Because I killed one of them. That's why I left. I came back to confess and take my punishment. Only now it looks like I'm the only person around who knows I killed the man."

Miss Potee got up and moved to my side. "Is she all right?" she asked, sotto voce. "You her caretaker or something?"

"I was married to her great-nephew," I said quickly, seeing Jay about to blow. "And she's fine. Honestly."

"Well." Miss Potee returned to the chair. "Let's hear it, Bits."

Jay groaned. "Seems to me I've told it a dozen times today already. It all started when Mama sent me to Miss Lucy's to pick up her laundry."

I tuned out at that point, having heard it in the judge's chambers. There were further decisions to be made and this might be the only time I'd have to consider them. The first was how much to tell Wade when I finally called him. Letting him in on the crisis of the moment would put him in a worse bind than he was in already.

He would want so desperately to come. Looking at it objectively, however, there was nothing he could do once he got here, whereas back there he was contributing to the well-being of his children. And if things weren't as serious as Dr. Green Eyes thought, I would have put Wade through hell for nothing. So it would make sense to wait, not only for the final diagnosis, but also to find out whether they'd have to perform any surgery and what her chances were.

That hurdle behind me for the moment, I moved on to quandary number two: what was *I* going to do? There was no question of my leaving. As relieved as I was that she'd found an old friend, the reality was that for the moment, I was all Jay had. And I owed her. She was the only one I'd been able to talk to during the dark days while I waited for the divorce to become final, the only one who could understand why, in spite of everything, I still loved Wade. She'd listened, never judged. She'd kept me sane. I could not abandon her. That was that.

By the time I tuned in on the narrative, Jay had begun her description of her struggle with the boarder.

"He pinned me against the wall beside the dresser with one hand and locked the door with the other, and shoved the key in his pocket. He said he was going to show me what they did to thieves up in Charleston and he hurled me onto the bed." She paused, the memory in her eyes.

Miss Potee's expression was murderous. "He rape you, Bits?"

"Thank the Lord, no. He clamped his hand over my face and I bit him, and took a hunk out of the edge of his palm. He whacked me one and flung me across the bed so hard I landed on the floor between the bed and the wall. I was trying to back my way out when he hit me a real ear-ringer with a look in those scary light eyes that let me know he was enjoying the whole business. I knew if I didn't do something fast, he might just beat me to death. I grabbed the only thing to hand, the thunder jar under the bed, and slammed it against the side of his head with all the strength I had. He collapsed on his stomach and I ran for it."

"Good for you!" Miss Potee exclaimed.

"But don't forget, he'd locked the door. I had to get that key from him before he came to. I can't tell you how much I hated having to squeeze into his pants pocket. That's when I realized he was way too still. I took a close look at him. That man was dead. I'd killed him."

"Bits." Miss Potee held up a hand. "You're saying you killed a man with a slop jar? A slop jar?"

She tried, I'll give her that. Biting her lips, she lowered her head. Then she lost it, simply exploded with laughter, lolling to one side in her chair, completely helpless to stop herself.

The charge nurse popped in, her expression horrified. "Mabel! Hush that racket this minute! Mrs. Wingate is not to be upset! Doctor's orders!"

"I'm all right, honey," Jay assured her, scowling at her friend. "If anybody's going to bust a gut, it's her."

The nurse's white cap quivered with indignation. "Mabel, folks can hear you clear down to the end of the hall."

Gradually Miss Potee wound down. "Sorry, Reggie. I'll shut up, I promise."

"And I'm holding you to it. I'm serious, Mabel. This patient needs rest."

"Yes, ma'am." Miss Potee managed a meek expression, which lasted until the door had closed. She flashed a grin at Jay. "Bits, you are a caution."

"I don't see a damned thing funny about what I told you," Jay snapped.

"Aunt Jay," I said. "The man probably died of a coronary or something. You couldn't possibly have hurt him that badly with a hand-sized jar."

"He wasn't old enough to have a coronary. And chamber pots aren't hand-sized."

Miss Potee gave me an indulgent smile. "Let me explain it to her, Bits. We didn't always have indoor bathrooms, baby. When I was a girl, a pot like that in each bedroom saved you a trip to the outhouse in the middle of the night."

"Oh," I said, belatedly getting the point. Nana Webster had had one, pink and white with a fluted edge, big purple flowers on the sides and matching top.

"We are not talking bone china here," Miss Potee continued. "They were good thick stoneware, had to be, to support a body's weight. But, swear to God, this is the first time I've ever heard of one being used as a lethal weapon." She chuckled. "Slaughtered by a slop jar. Leave it to Bits. What was his name?"

"I don't know. I'd never seen him before. Mama usually picked up Miss Lucy's laundry, but she didn't know his name, either. She just knew he'd been there awhile and that Miss Lucy had said he was trouble. When she sent me upstairs to strip his bed, she said she'd warned him it was going to be his last night under her roof."

"Sounds like it sure as hell was," Miss Potee remarked.

Suddenly the hall door moved inward and a lean, ascetic face peered in, sort of like an Abe Lincoln with graying blond hair. "Afternoon, ladies." He was a basso, sub-basement deep.

Miss Potee, her expression softening, stood up and smiled. "Afternoon, Reverend."

He stepped into the room and the comparison to Lincoln became even stronger. He was tall and beanpole lean, with dark, deep-set eyes that brimmed with warmth and concern. "Just ministerin' to the sick," he said. "Thought I'd check to see if there was anyone desiring a word of prayer."

"Maybe later," Miss Potee said quickly. "Mrs. Wingate just got here. Hasn't had a chance to get settled yet."

"Ah." He nodded thoughtfully, reached into his pocket and laid a bookmark on the bedside table. "I'll come back, then, but in the meantime, I'll leave this for you," he said to Jay. "It has a few verses of Scripture on it. Some patients find it offers a measure of comfort. Keep up the good work, Mabel. Ma'am." He bobbed his head in farewell and left the room as quietly as he'd entered.

"Whew!" Miss Potee exhaled gustily. "He's a sweet man, Reverend Allenby, but his word of prayer is more likely to be a couple of thousand. Now, where were we?"

"Look, Aunt Jay," I said. "It's time to let go of the past and concentrate on your health so you can get out of here. You've got a brand-new great-great-nephew and -niece to help spoil. Wade's counting on you."

Her startled expression told me I'd hit home. "Lord. I'd forgot all about the new babies." Lowering the head of the bed, she sighed. "Mabel Lee, go tell that bossy nurse that if she doesn't come take my history soon or whatever she's supposed to do, I'm going to be asleep and it's going to be Kitty-Bar-the-Door if anybody wakes me up. Shoo, Troy. Go check in at your hotel and get some rest. I'll see you tomorrow."

I let her think she'd talked me into it and was about to kiss her goodbye when the door opened and Dr. Baskerville came in. The news was bad; it was written all over his face.

"Evening, Mrs. Potee," he said. "I think Reverend Allenby's waiting to speak to you, so if you've finished in here . . . ?"

Miss Potee hoisted one brow. "For God's sake, Davey, if

that's a hint that you'd like to talk to these folks in private, whyn't you just say so?"

He managed a tired smile. "Can't get anything by you, can I?"

"Wait a second, Mabel." Jay held up a restraining hand. "Just so you'll know, Dr. Baskerville, Mabel and I go back to caveman days. She's practically family, so anything you need to say to me you can say in front of her."

If he was surprised, he hid it well. "Fine with me."

Miss Potee's expression was pained. "Wouldn't you know? As much as I'd love to stay, Bits, I can't. The Reverend's waiting and I've got a couple of other patients checking in. I'll stop in and see you later."

Jay took her hand. "I can't tell you how glad I am you're still around. You be sure and come back. We've got a lot to catch up on."

"Fifty years' worth." Miss Potee bent down and planted an eardrum-shattering kiss on Jay's cheek. "Troy, baby, I'll be seeing you."

I thanked her and walked her to the door, almost as grateful for her presence as Jay seemed to be.

"Now," Jay said to Dr. Baskerville when the door closed behind Miss Potee. "Let's hear the bad news."

He looked very stern. "The first thing I want to do is preach a sermon. It is vital, Mrs. Wingate, that from this point on, you are completely open with me. I was about to order an MRI for you and the fact that you hadn't told me everything I needed to know might well have cost you your life. How long ago were you shot, Mrs. Wingate?"

Jay's eyes became mere slits. "How long ago was I *what*?"

He gazed at her long and hard. "Mrs. Wingate," he said, slowly, "for your information, you've been walking around, for some time, obviously, with a fragment of a bullet in your back."

5

Jay tossed the covers aside and sat up. "Daughter, get my clothes. I admit I haven't had a whole lot of education, but you don't even have to graduate kindergarten to know whether or not you've been shot. I haven't."

"Mrs. Wingate," he said firmly. "I spent two of the longest years of my life at Harlem Hospital. I've seen more bullets and fragments of bullets on more X-ray films than you could ever imagine. There's a fragment that's probably the nose of a small-caliber bullet lodged near the top of your left deltoid."

"I am not a doctor!" Jay snapped. "Use words I can understand."

"Sorry. The big muscle at the top of the shoulder. The fact that it didn't become infected at the time was pure luck. Since it hasn't presented a problem, we'll leave it there. But the MRI is out."

"Wait a minute," I said again, my head reeling. "I know it's possible to live a more or less normal life with a bullet in you. I've got a student . . . never mind. But how could she have been shot and not know it?"

"It happens, not often, but it does happen. Tell me how you got that scar on the back of your shoulder, Mrs. Wingate."

"I fell."

"Describe precisely how it happened, please."

Inching back onto the bed, Jay frowned. "Well, you know, I never really figured it out. I was moseying along the end of the pier, just enjoying the sunset and trying to figure out what to do, since nobody would listen to me. The next thing I knew I was face down, peering between the boards, and had one whale of a pain back there. I don't even remember falling, but it was right after a thunderstorm and the pier was wet, so I figured I must have slipped. There was blood back here and a knot, so I must have whacked myself on the edge of the bench going down." She pursed her lips. "That was right curious. I wasn't all that close to the bench, but it was the only thing that made sense at the time."

"You didn't have a doctor look you over?"

"What for? It hurt like blazes, but it didn't bleed all that much. I certainly didn't feel a hole or anything. I stopped in the drugstore and got some peroxide and a Band-Aid and cleaned myself up in the Ladies Room. When I got home I put an ice pack on it and that was that. You think . . . ?"

Baskerville nodded. "I definitely think. The only logical reason you weren't seriously wounded was that the caliber was so small and whoever pulled the trigger was so far away that by the time the bullet reached you it had lost most of its momentum. You were lucky it wound up where it did. How long ago was this?"

"Has to be three years back. That's the last time I tried to turn myself in."

Something quivered at the nape of my neck. "It happened here, Aunt Jay?"

"Just a second." Baskerville's eyes widened. "Turn yourself in for what?"

"That's a dead issue," I said quickly and winced at my choice of words. "So what happens now?"

He gave me the kind of look that made it perfectly clear he was aware I hadn't answered his question. "The X-rays show a calcified mass in your abdomen, Mrs. Wingate, which confirms my diagnosis. It's possible it may be a dissecting aneurysm."

"What's that mean?" Jay asked.

"A hemorrhage into the vessel wall that causes the wall to split and widen. It's a life-threatening condition and it's important that you understand that. If the wall ruptures . . . well, rupture of an aneurysm is almost always fatal. We'll schedule an angiogram so we'll have the precise location and size of the damaged area. But it has to be repaired, Mrs. Wingate. As soon as possible. Dr. McCall will go over the procedure with you. He'll perform the surgery."

"I'd rather you did it," Jay said, her features expressionless.

"I'm not a surgeon, Mrs. Wingate. Lincoln McCall is— the best."

"All right, son." Jay pinned him with a look. "Just answer me one question: Is there any chance I might not survive this operation?".

His eyes changed, softened. "That possibility exists with practically any surgery."

"But my chances would be better if I weren't older than water. All right. If surgery's what I need, fine. Just don't count on getting me on the table anytime soon."

"Mrs. Wingate." Dr. Baskerville's tone was patient, rife

with reason. "We have a day, maybe two. Beyond that, you're living from moment to moment."

"Well, that's my decision to make, don't you think?" Jay demanded. "Since it's my life, my moment to moment?"

"But it's imperative that we do it immediately. I can't stress that strongly enough. Consider the episode you experienced in the judge's chambers a big red flag. I hate to sound like a walking cliché, but time is of the essence."

"Too bad. There's something I have to clear up first."

An alarm went off somewhere deep behind my eyes. I sensed another Mack truck on my horizon.

Baskerville rubbed his forehead, as if fighting fatigue. "I can't see what could possibly be more important than your life."

"Nothing is," Jay said. "But your definition of life is different from mine, because you've got a lot more in front of you than behind you. Me, I'm flirting with eighty and life to me is my past, whether the way I've lived and the decisions I made were done for the right reason. When I know that, you can cut away."

A muscle in his jaw moved rhythmically, as if he was clenching his teeth. "If that's the case, I would advise you to find out as soon as you can. You're running out of time."

"I tell him I'm almost eighty and he tells me I'm running out of time," Jay said, settling her shoulders against the pillow. "Troy, I want the truth. If I didn't kill that man—"

"Excuse me?" Baskerville croaked.

"—what happened to him? If I did kill him, what happened to him? I want to know that, Troy. I *need* that answered before I die. I'm not going into that operating room until I know."

✧   ✧   ✧

I left Jay, feeling much like Atlas with the world on my shoulders, and after a conference with Dr. Baskerville, realized that trying to find Jay's alleged victim wasn't the only problem I had to worry about. The X-rays he showed me left little room for doubt. Not much of the shadowy images made much sense to me but I would have to have lived my whole life in a cave not to recognize the dark, clearly defined shape he pointed out. It was definitely a bullet.

"You didn't believe me, did you?" he asked, as he escorted me out of the conference room.

"I didn't want to. The implications are scary. Why would someone shoot at her? She said she was standing on the pier at North End. Where is that?"

"To the right outside the front door, just beyond the traffic circle."

"Is there a shooting range nearby?" I asked.

"No, and there's no hunting allowed on the island either. I can't imagine how it happened."

"How are race relations on Innocence?"

Baskerville looked surprised at the question. "No problems I've ever heard of. Look," he said, exhibiting impatience for the first time, "this place is really unique. It's a throwback to a different time, when people took being a neighbor seriously. We don't even lock our doors. Can you imagine what an adjustment that was for me, after two years of living in New York City? It's a never-never land, and no one would shoot at Mrs. Wingate simply because she's black."

Then why would they, I wondered.

Officer Haskins's reaction was puzzling when I called him from the hospital later that night to report the incident. "So she really was here before. Well, the only thing I can figure is that she must have been on the pier the time somebody reported kids taking potshots at seagulls. Grady kicked 'em off the island right then and there and gave their grandparents a warning. Imagine kids dumb enough to do something like that when there were people around they might shoot by accident."

He'd been on Innocence too long, I thought, and decided to let him keep his illusions.

Then his first comment registered. "What did you mean, she really was here before?"

"Well," he said, sounding oddly reticent, "it's just that . . . wait a minute, Miz Burdette. How long ago did she say that happened?"

"The last time she was here, three years ago. You talked as if you believed her this morning. What happened in the interim to make you doubt it?"

He didn't answer at first. After a lengthy silence, he cleared his throat. "We've got us a routine here. Everything that happens goes into a daily log, no matter how trifling it seems. We stop a citizen for riding his bike on the sidewalk instead of the bike lane, it goes into the log. A lady comes in wondering if anybody turned in a lost earring, it goes into the log."

"Sounds very efficient," I said, wishing I'd picked a telephone nearer a chair. My foot was going to sleep. I wiggled my toes and turned so I could see the door of Jay's room. Dr. McCall was due any time and I didn't want to miss him.

"About a month ago," Haskins said, "I had to go back through the daily logs for the last five years—we were tracking somebody's driving record—and I didn't see nothing about Miz Julie coming in then. I went through them again after I got back from the golf course this afternoon. There's nothing there, Miz Burdette, no record of her coming in at all. So I'd begun to wonder. Now you tell me somebody shot at her then. And I'm back to believing she's tried to turn herself in before. But who'd she talk to and why didn't they put it down?"

"It couldn't have been Officer Grady," I said, thinking aloud, "because he didn't act as though he recognized her, and she certainly didn't react to seeing him."

"He swears he'd never seen her before. He ain't a liar and he's a stickler for writing things down. Now, three years ago I was out having my double bypass, so I kind of lost track of what was happening in the station for a while. But for there to be no record about Miz Julie being here, that's a serious matter."

"And," I reminded him, "no record of the . . . the death she says she caused." I was still uncomfortable with calling it a murder.

I assume he went into a deep thinking mode, because there was another lengthy silence before he spoke again. "Something about this don't feel right, Miz Burdette."

"What if the shooting wasn't accidental, Mr. Haskins?" I proposed, voicing the unthinkable. "What if Aunt Jay really did kill the man and somebody, for whatever reason, covered it up? If that person was still around, they wouldn't exactly be happy about Aunt Jay coming back and yanking off those covers, would they?"

"No'm, but that person would have to be about Miz Julie's age, give or take five years in either direction. There ain't all that many who lived here back then. And none of them have ever been on my police force. You see what I'm saying?"

"You're saying something stinks."

"Yes, ma'am, that's exactly what I'm saying. I'd appreciate it if you'd find out who she talked to before. Is she gonna be all right?"

"I don't know," I said, watching Baskerville as he leaned over the counter of the nurses' station. A very nice heinie. Distracted by it, I turned my back and concentrated on answering Officer Haskins's question. "They need to operate as soon as possible, but she won't agree to it until she knows what really happened back in '43. She's asked me to look into it, so I'd appreciate any help you can give me. And is there any possibility of posting one of your men outside her room, just in case? People come and go at will. The way things are stacking up, her life's still in danger from whoever shot at her."

"The best I can do, Miz Burdette, is ask Norm Cheek—he's in charge of security at the hospital—to have one of his men keep an eye on her. There's only four of us on a shift and I just can't spare anyone. Besides, the mayor would wet his pants if he found out I'd assigned someone to protect Miz Julie."

What could I say? A hospital security guard would have to do.

"As for helping you," he continued, "Hizzoner's got us hoppin', getting ready for that stupid golf tournament, holding meetings about crowd control and traffic detours and such. It's his top priority and he ain't gonna want to hear about us working on nothin' else, especially something that happened three years ago, much less fifty. I know what he'd say: it's waited this long, it can wait ten days more."

But the way things looked, Jay didn't have ten days. I thanked him, told him where he could find me, and hung up. The weight dropped around my shoulders again.

"You want Troy to do *what*?"

Miss Potee looked from Jay to me and back again, her eyes and mouth perfect O's of astonishment. I'd tracked her down to request her help in making Jay revise her priorities. Even though there was little chance of unearthing the identity of someone who'd visited the island fifty years ago, I was more than willing to go through the motions to put her mind at ease. Given how long it might take, however, she might be dead and buried before I got to first base. It was imperative that she have the surgery first. I had talked, whined, cried, cajoled, and had even exploded with exasperation. It had gotten me exactly nowhere. Jay was unmoved. I'd even threatened to call Wade.

"No, you won't," she'd responded with utter lack of concern. "You still love him enough that you wouldn't for the world put him in a position where he'd have to choose between those babies and me. You divorced him because you knew how much having children meant to him. Now he's got them and they need him and I don't. If he walked through the door this minute, he wouldn't be able to change my mind. So don't waste your breath talking about calling him. Don't waste your breath, period. I'm not going under the knife before I find out once and for all about that man."

"Julia Eliza Brownlee Wingate," Miss Potee said now, "have you got cracks in what marbles you've got left? You need that surgery like yesterday! And it's not fair to this child to have your life hanging over her head."

"The name's Julia Eliza Brownlee Morgan Jones Wingate," Jay said. She reached for the bowl of grapes Miss Potee had brought her and popped one into her mouth. "And the only head my life's hanging over is mine. Troy, I wouldn't ask you to do it if I thought you couldn't. You know how to find out things. You used to make a living at it."

"Come on, Aunt Jay, I worked part-time evenings as a

skip-tracer for a bail bondsman to help pay for grad school. That was years ago. And we had access to computer systems that are off-limits to me now. I'm a private citizen from out of state, with no resources at all."

"Well, now, I wouldn't say that," Miss Potee countered, her focus somewhere in the middle distance. "Bits, are you bound and determined to have your way? Even knowing what you're risking by putting off the surgery?"

Jay simply gazed at her friend, chewing on a grape.

Miss Potee rolled her eyes in disgust. "Lady Nero yonder, chompin' on Concords while her life goes down the tubes. Troy, considerin' this hard-headed old bat used to be my best friend, the least I can do is try to line up some ree-sources that might be able to help. Give me tonight to think about it and make some calls. I've got a patient to see to at Azalea House first thing in the morning, but I can pick you up at around ten."

"What's Azalea House?" Jay asked.

"A hospice for the terminally ill," Miss Potee snapped, "which if you don't come to your senses soon, will be holding a bed for you. Except if what Troy says is true, you won't even be there long enough to get the sheets warm."

The door swung open and a petite blond nurse came in. "Time for your medication, Mrs. Wingate. And it's long past visiting hours, ladies."

I gathered my things. Visiting hours had ended at eight and it was nearing eleven. It felt as if days had passed since Dr. Baskerville had caught me napping downstairs.

"Lord, I almost forgot, Troy," Miss Potee said. "I've got your demon cat in my car. But first, stop at the nurses' station and ask for a voucher so you can get yourself a room across the street at Hospitality House. Anybody can stay there, but it's especially for family of patients. Good rates, too, and they allow pets. Bits, I'll stop in tomorrow to see if you survived the night. Troy, I'll wait for you outside."

"Good night, Miss Mabel," the nurse said pointedly. She watched as Jay swallowed the pills she'd given her, then left, nudging Miss Potee out into the hall.

I stalled for a moment longer, pawing through my brain for something to say in a last-ditch effort to make Jay see reason. As usual, she cut me off at the pass.

"Daughter," she said, beckoning me to her bedside, "I wouldn't ask you to do this if it weren't more important to me than anything else in the world. Promise me you'll see it through, even if I die before you finish the job. Wherever I am, playing a harp or stoking a furnace, I'll know. That's all I want: to know."

What could I say to that?

The room rate at Hospitality House across the street was one even Scrooge wouldn't have objected to. I claimed The Deacon from Miss Potee's back seat and the two of us moved into a very comfortable single on the sixth floor. A bonus for The Deacon was the room's tiny balcony. It overlooked a rear garden with enough distractions to keep him from becoming bored: fishponds, fountains, a gazebo, and dozens of chattering birds. I knew he'd be fine. The Deacon was mean, but he wasn't dumb enough to take a flying leap from six stories up.

My next chore was a call to Wade. I gave him a sanitized version of the truth. "She thought she'd killed someone years ago, but the authorities are convinced she didn't. Since we're here, we're going to stay for a few days."

"What was she doing there in the first place?" he asked. "I've never heard of it."

"This is where she grew up. I assumed you knew that."

"Oh. I guess I forgot. Put her on. Let me speak to her."

I did some mental footwork. "She's not here. I wanted to call you when she wasn't around. You'll be hearing from her soon. She's delighted about the twins. I've got to run. I'll check in with you from time to time. Regards to Latrice. And kiss the twins for me."

He cleared his throat. "You really are a very special person, Troy. You know that, don't you?"

Just not quite special enough, I thought, and hung up. The Deacon, always supersensitive to my moods, stropped my leg and propped his chin on my knee, his iridescent eyes peering up at me quizzically. I scratched him behind his ears in gratitude. He was a sorry substitute for my ex, but the way things were stacking up, he might be my only source of male companionship and moral support for some time to come. Under the circumstances, I would need all the moral support I could get.

I woke from a sound sleep at two in the morning and realized I'd forgotten to ask Jay about the policeman she'd confessed to three years ago. I got up and called the hospital, just to ask how she was doing.

"Resting comfortably," an unfamiliar voice said.

"Is someone from Security on the floor?"

"Just a minute, I'll check." The phone was put down with a bang. After a long two minutes, the woman returned. "Yes, ma'am. Vickery's down the hall. Did you want to speak to him?"

I was tempted, but what could I say to him? He took his orders from his supervisor, not me. "Thanks, I won't bother him."

I replaced the phone and tossed and turned until four-thirty, when fatigue finally won the fight. By then I'd I made a decision. I would give myself a couple of days to find out what I could about Jay's mystery man. If I failed, I would go to Jay and lie like a fine Oriental rug and tell her I'd found out what she wanted to know. I'd give her man a name, a brief history, and kill him off a couple of years after she thought she had. A rotten trick? Mayhap, but better than having him kill her off fifty years later.

6

The second morning of my first vacation in three years had an even less auspicious start than the first because I began it by falling out of bed. I tend to migrate from one edge to the other in my sleep and I guess I wandered an inch too far. I lay there feeling sorry for myself. As far as I was concerned, I was entitled. I'd deliberately made no plans for my vacation, intending to go—wherever—if the spirit moved me or stay put if it didn't. But never in my darkest nightmares did I think I'd wind up on a two-by-four island charged with learning the identity of a man who was supposed to have died fifty years ago and having to ferret him out in time to save the life of my ex-husband's great-aunt, the same ex-husband who wasn't around to do it himself because he was on the opposite coast nurturing his newborn son and daughter, the ones I was supposed to have had with him and hadn't been able to because of fibroids in all the wrong places. I was just about to go skinny-dipping in a bottomless pool of self-pity when The Deacon must

have decided that enough was enough. He pounced
from wherever he'd been sleeping onto my midsection.
A sixteen-pound pussycat in the solar plexus tends to
make one forget everything else except the basic need
for oxygen. So there I was, flat on my back gasping for
breath, and my damned cat was kneading my pecs and
purring like an Evanrude running wide open.

I rolled over, dislodging him, got up, and was immediately assailed by the need to get going and do something,
anything to clear up the mess Jay had dumped in my lap.
Unfortunately it was only seven-forty-five and I wouldn't
be meeting Miss Potee until ten. I was on my own. I called
Innocence General.

A different voice from that of the previous call informed
me that Mrs. Wingate had spent a good night and was resting comfortably. There was no one from Security on the
floor at the moment, but I shouldn't be concerned. During
normal visiting hours there would always be someone at the
nurses' station who'd be keeping an eye on 3E118. It was
only overnight, when there was reduced staff, that Security
would be needed. Yeah, right.

I opened a can of beef and liver mush for the cat,
spent twenty minutes in the bathroom doing my morning ablutions, dressed, and went out on the little balcony
to get the lay of the land in daylight. Hospitality House
was a U-shaped affair and the Japanese-styled garden
nestled between its wings was charming, complete with
glossy lily-padded ponds stocked full of Koa so big, they
were easily visible even from six stories up. Paving stones
marked pathways that wound past plots of delicate yellow
and orange blossoms, and diminutive bridges arched over
the ponds. The flowers were alive with a bumper crop of
white butterflies, and birds zipped through the trees,
making the leaves quiver. The Deacon would have plenty

to occupy his waking hours, what few of them there'd be. He was already yawning, in preparation for his first post-prandial nap of the day.

I was just about to step back into the room when a split-second flash of light, like a sunbeam momentarily captured on the surface of a mirror or perhaps a pair of eyeglasses, seared my corneas. I squinted at the rear of the house directly opposite. Peeling white clapboard and three stories high, it was old, slightly seedy, and smacked of New England Gothic, curiously out of place next to the redwood A-frame on one side and the neat little stucco bungalow on the other. It had the aura of a house still asleep, but I couldn't be sure. The rear windows faced east and the morning sun painted each of them in a wash of gold. The two tiny openings in the attic, shuttered by wooden slats, were the only ones untouched by the morning light.

I lollygagged for a moment or two longer, when something about the small, screened rear porch drew my attention, a shade or shadow far enough back in the enclosure so that I couldn't even be sure it was anything more than that. The longer I stared at it, the more uneasy I became. The shadow seemed to have taken shape, to have grown a head, shoulders, a torso. It didn't move and neither did I, paralyzed by the willies and an unreasonable conviction that whoever it was had been watching me.

A head-butt against my calf by The Deacon jolted a little sense into me. Short of going down there to see, there was no way to prove there was anyone there at all. "Even if there is," I muttered, "how can I gripe about him looking at me if I've been standing here looking at him?" I stepped back into the room, leaving the sliding door open pussycat-width, and packed up to go.

I stopped in Hospitality House's dining room long enough to grab a couple of bagels and a bottle of orange juice, then hit the streets. Jay's Buick and I were becoming more comfortable with each other, so I drove around for the next hour, during which I stumbled upon a well-camouflaged supermarket and picked up more cat supplies, then headed north to find the pier where Jay had been shot.

Innocence is shaped like a shrimp with a glandular condition, the commercial section occupying the head at the southern end, the residential section the body. Traffic circles fit neatly in the narrow passages between head and body, body and fan-shaped tail. The tail, it turned out, was North End, where the black population had lived years before. It was far larger than I'd expected, in fact broad enough to support a golf course on the east side and a driving range on the west. A no-man's land separated them, a pale sea-oats-strewn strip of sand which sloped down to the ocean. On the very tip of it I found Jay's pier, well within view of both the hospital and Hospitality House. I'd driven all over the island when my goal had been a five-minute walk away.

Perhaps because of its position between the golf enclaves, the pier had an air of isolation and serenity about it. Benches lined its edges and despite the early hour, most were occupied by people watching the gulls swoop and turn above the ocean, and the pelicans bob like giant rubber ducks on the waves.

Turning my back on the water, I leaned against a piling and looked around. If the pier had been deserted when Jay was here, she would have been perfectly visible. Whoever shot at her might have been on the golf course or the driving range, but I doubted they'd have risked it. The hospital sat just on the other side of the traffic circle, a couple of hundred yards away from the pier. Anyone looking out a hospital window would have seen both the assailant and Jay.

But the miniature jungle in the middle of the traffic island, a grove of palmettos and assorted oaks and shrubbery that I fought my way through just to check, was thick enough to have made an effective blind. I headed back to Hospitality House still wondering how the shooting could have been an accident. If it had been intentional, the next question was whether she'd been a target because she was there or because she was who she was and back on Innocence to confess to murder.

I got back to my room, having left just enough time to call Jay and to freshen the litter in The Deacon's portable potty. Opening the door, however, I was confronted by a faint scent, familiar yet too elusive for me to identify at the moment, and a very agitated cat. The Deacon stood, back arched, tail fluffed to feather-duster dimensions, whipping from side to side.

"Good grief, what's eating you?" I asked. Pupils fully dilated, he fussed, tail still lashing, before he finally leveled his spine and stropped my legs a couple of times. Heaving my supermarket loot onto the dresser, I stooped, smoothed his fur, and added a thorough scratching behind both ears as I assessed his behavior. The only times I'd seen him in this state were after he felt his territory had been invaded. Perhaps someone from Housekeeping had come in to straighten up and change the towels. But the bed was still unmade, the towels I'd used this morning precisely where I'd left them. And the aroma I'd detected was so faint that I wondered if I'd imagined it.

"Look, honey," I said to The Deacon, now busy giving himself a thorough cleaning, "we've got to come to an understanding about the people who work here." Locking him on the balcony, I went looking for the woman I'd seen earlier pushing her linen-laden cart into the room next door. I found her at the end of the hall, but a few moments of conversation with her left me genuinely puzzled.

"No'm," she said. "I haven't got to 622 yet. I heard you moving around in there so I was gonna wait."

"How long ago was that?" I asked. "Before or after you did the room next door to mine?"

"After, I think, but I wouldn't put my hand to the Bible about it. I can do your room now if you want, but I'd 'preciate it if you'd put your cat out on the balcony. I heard him cussin' up a storm in there a little while ago."

I assured her the monster was out of the way and she followed me back. While she cleaned the bathtub, I looked around the room, but as far as I could tell, nothing was missing. The contents of the dresser drawers and the bathroom countertop appeared undisturbed.

I moved to the closet. The doors were bi-fold and, like mine at home, jumped the track if you didn't handle them just so. I'd had problems with the one on the left when I'd tried to close it, but had finally managed it. Now, however, the left side was not only open a few inches, it was out of its track.

There was a distinct possibility The Deacon was responsible, since nothing bugs a cat more than a closed door. The space between these was about his size. I widened the gap slowly. The items I'd put on hangers were all there, my carry-on still on the shelf. Since it was empty, I didn't bother to check it.

Pushing the right-hand door aside, I glanced up at Jay's little overnight case. I'd brought it back with me because the nursing staff had insisted she remove her rings and watch. She had put them in her overnight case and had asked me to hold on to it because she hadn't been able to find the keys and couldn't lock it. When I'd placed her bag on the shelf last night, I could swear I'd shoved it back against the rear wall. It was now aligned with the front edge of the shelf. A finger of panic brushed the back of my neck. If her rings and watch were gone . . .

They were exactly as I'd placed them on the ring-holder in the satin-lined compartment of the lid. I counted them twice. Ten rings, one watch, one pair of tiny gold hoop earrings. I put them back and pushed the case against the rear wall, envisioning doing exactly the same the night before. While the cleaning lady made the bed, I sat out on the balcony with The Deacon and tried to convince myself that I had jumped to conclusions because of his earlier behavior. He'd snookered me and I'd fallen for it. Score one for The Deacon.

Once the lady from Housekeeping had finished, I let The Deacon in from the balcony so he could satisfy himself that nothing of his had been disturbed. Before leaving to meet Miss Potee, I did that dumb James Bond trick with the strand of hair across the closet bi-folds and the dresser drawers. If I didn't find out something about Jay's mystery man soon, not only would she be in critical condition, yours truly would be completely bald.

"Where are we going?" I asked as I secured the seatbelt of Miss Potee's big silver Lincoln Town Car. It, like her, had some years on it, a throwback to the days when most American luxury cars were the size of aircraft carriers. It felt heavy and solid, its engine purring seductively.

"Around the corner to Palmetto Arbor. Blanche Lacey lives there. Elva Peterson, she's driving over to meet us. They've lived here all their lives and knew everybody—all the white folks, anyway. Blanche used to put out the newspaper."

"Did they know Jay?"

"Probably. Won't matter to them whether they knew her or not. There's so few of us left that we kind of watch out for one another, call ourselves the Old Timers Club. And, praise God, we've lived long enough that finally color doesn't make any difference."

"How can they help?" I asked.

"Well, Elva lived kitty-corner from Miss Lucy's and Blanche lived directly behind her on Carolina Street. They might remember something. Fair warning: Elva has a thing about bows."

"Bows."

"In her hair, around her waist, on the toes of her shoes. Never knew there was anything like a bow fetish, but there must be 'cause Elva has one. Here we are."

"Here" was a complex of single-storied town houses in a T-shaped cluster of fours around a community center. And Blanche Lacey was waiting for us. There was no missing her in her iridescent purple sweatsuit, sturdy walking shoes, abbreviated dutchboy haircut and bangs. She was tiny, perhaps five feet tall, if that, with a bright, inquisitive gaze behind silver-framed, wire-rimmed glasses. She sat perched on a paisley-cushioned recliner, a newspaper in her lap, and yoo-hooed, beckoning us to the diminutive front porch of an end unit with gleaming white shutters and window boxes, and pink stucco exterior walls. It reminded me of a gingerbread house slathered with strawberry icing. Considering her size, the place fit her to a T.

"Mornin', Mabel," she chirped.

"Mornin', honey. Meet Troy Burdette."

Miss Lacey dimpled at me and patted the cushion beside her. "Call me Blanche. You're mighty pretty to have a boy's name."

"My dad's the first Burdette to father a female in three generations," I explained, sitting next to her. "They'd already picked the name before I was born, and couldn't agree on one for a girl once I surprised them, so Troy it remained."

"You wear it well," she said, bobbing her head. "Not everyone could. Mabel, this seat good enough for your back?"

"And my backside." Miss Potee lowered herself gingerly onto the sturdy captain's chair.

"Don't y'all dare start without me," a voice called. It belonged to a statuesque redhead rushing up the ramp to the porch, her hair new-penny bright. No sweatsuit and Nikes for this one. I'd been warned, but there was no way I could have been prepared for the reality. Miss Peterson's dress was lime-mint green, and frothy as cotton candy, its V-neck and the hem of its full skirt adorned with a three-inch ruffle of dotted Swiss. At the back was an enormous green bow. Her shoes were white patent leather pumps with tiny white fabric bows across the instep and heels high enough to be declared lethal weapons. Seventy-plus or not, she had the feet and ankles to wear the heels. Her hair pouffed around her face in a variation of a pompadour, with the remainder captured by a pale green ribbon tied high on the back of her head in a loose ponytail. Elva Peterson was a Southern belle who wore the title like a badge.

"Hey, everybody," she said, plopping onto the other end of the recliner, sandwiching me in the middle. "I'm Elva. You must be Troy. Sorry I'm late. Had aerobics first thing and then dropped off the quilt I made for Reverend Allenby's guest bedroom. That's the cutest little house. I know he'll just love it. How's Julia this mornin'?" She squinted nearsightedly at me. For some reason, I got the impression that she was edgy. I couldn't be sure whether it was me or her normal condition.

"Aunt Jay's holding her own," I responded. At least I

assumed she was. What with the foolishness about an intruder in my room, I hadn't gotten around to calling the hospital again.

"This is so exciting," Blanche twittered. "An old mystery on our own little island. A murder mystery at that."

Miss Potee frowned. "How'd you know about that? I didn't mention it when I talked to you this morning."

"Well, shoot," Elva said, rooting into her fabric tote bag for a fan. "Everybody knows about it. And let me tell you, I ran into Leland at the Reverend's new house and he is not a happy camper about Julia and all the publicity about her."

"What publicity?" I asked, wondering what I'd missed.

"It's all in here." Blanche shoved the newspaper at me. "About how Julia came back to confess and locked herself in the jail with young Ficker because nobody would arrest her—"

"And how she wants to know what really happened," Elva finished.

"They let a reporter in to talk to her?" I said, hackles rising. Jay had made the front page: Local Woman Returns to Confess to Murder. So had I. The photo of the two of us leaving the jail took up the top half of the page. I hadn't noticed a photographer yesterday, but probably wouldn't have anyway. I'd had other things on my mind at that point.

I scanned the article and found it surprisingly accurate. The reporter had paraphrased the sworn statement Jay had insisted on making to Mr. Haskins, and had countered it with a quote from Leon Ficker that there were no witnesses and no evidence to support the event. "We're sure Mrs. Wingate is relating what she remembers," he'd told the reporter, "but without some kind of proof or evidence, we have to assume she only stunned the man." My buddy, Mr. Haskins had contributed far less, to wit: "No comment." I liked him more and more by the minute.

The mayor, however, had had plenty to say, his quote an impassioned defense of the island, its trouble-free history, and his hope that Jay's unsupported claim would in no way blemish Innocence's stellar reputation, especially when there was so much at stake, to wit: its appeal as a crime-free place to live, and the Dozen Pines golf tournament. The article ended with the ubiquitous "Mrs. Wingate was unavailable for comment." I passed the newspaper to Miss Potee, making a mental note to phone the hospital and make sure that Jay remained exactly that: unavailable for comment.

"Well, the reason we're here," I said, to get the ball rolling while Miss Potee was reading, "is that the doctors say Aunt Jay needs an operation as soon as possible. She refuses to have it until she finds out whether the man she thought she killed really died."

"Well," Elva said, fanning up a gale, "I don't see a problem. There's no way anybody could have been murdered at Miss Lucy's without everybody finding out sooner or later. Miss Lucy couldn't have kept it to herself, even if the prize for doin' it was a fifth of liquor. I lived right across the street, so I know. Tell Julia to go ahead and have her surgery."

"She won't listen. She wants me to find out what really happened. If the man was alive, she wants proof, which means I've got to find him—or his relatives—and I don't have a lot of time to do it."

"This was when, in 1943?" Blanche asked.

"July fourth."

"Oh, my God," Elva groaned. "Then it could have been anybody. Every summer during the war we threw a big Fourth of July picnic and invited any of the boys stationed nearby who wanted to come. They came in droves."

"This was a boarder," I reminded them. "Perhaps someone in town on business."

Elva responded with a peal of laughter. "Business! There wasn't any business on Innocence back then—unless you count fishing. I can only remember one or two traveling salesmen staying at Miss Lucy's. It must have been a soldier. She'd pack them in for the Fourth, even kick little Nathan out of his room and put a cot on the back veranda for him."

"Nathan." Blanche's eyes became saucers. "Lord love a duck, I'd forgotten all about Miss Lucy's son. He couldn't have been more than maybe eleven or twelve back then. Big for his age, though, and he had some sort of problem. Retarded, maybe, I don't know, except that when she died, they packed him off to an institution. Haven't seen him since."

"Even if we found him," Elva said, "what would we ask him? 'Do you remember a man who boarded at your mama's house fifty years ago?' We don't even know what he looks like, except that he was white."

"He probably used his leave to come spend a few extra days," Blanche said. "A lot of them did. Others just came for our Saturday night dances at the town hall. Innocence lost a lot of its young ladies to the sailors who came to those dances."

Elva snorted. "You've got that ass-backwards, honey chile. A lot of our young ladies lost their innocence to the sailors who came to those dances." She chuckled, pleased by her clever reversal of Blanche's comment. "Anyhow, what we're saying, Troy, is that Miss Lucy stacked them to the rafters every Fourth, but they all must have gone back when they were supposed to because we never had any MPs show up looking for AWOLs."

My spirits began a downhill plunge. It must have shown, because Blanche squeezed my hand. "Don't give up hope yet. I have an idea. Do you think Julia would recognize a picture of the man? If he was one of the boys in the service, I just might have one."

"You're kidding."

"We took photos at the picnic," Blanche amplified, "a special issue full of nothing but Fourth of July activities."

It was a long shot, but worth trying. "How long would it take to find them?" I asked.

"About as long as it'll take to walk to my kitchen. The new people who took over the paper were going to trash all the old glossies. It would have been like seeing my life's work tossed in a dumpster. So I took them," she finished, a defiant tilt to her chin. "I pulled them out after I read the article this morning, to reminisce a bit. But who knows? He just might be in one of those pictures."

"That's him," Aunt Jay said, a trembling finger glued firmly under the handsome face of a man on the very edge of a photo. Had he been a foot farther to his right, the camera wouldn't have caught him. He stood apart, watching a group of sailors and girls hang tiny flags from the branches of an enormous tree.

"You sure?" Miss Potee asked.

I could understand the reason for the question. Blanche Lacey had loaded me down with four large envelopes dated July 4, 1943. They contained over sixty eight-by-ten glossies and Jay had gone through practically all of them before she had hit pay dirt.

"Am I sure?" she snapped irritably. "I may feel like hell, but there's nothing wrong with my eyes. That's the man. I told you he wasn't a sailor or a soldier. See? He's wearing a suit."

That was no guarantee he wasn't in the service, but I didn't have the nerve to say so. Miss Potee did.

"Then why'd he have a suitcase instead of a duffle bag?" Jay responded. "And when the top popped open, I don't remember seeing a uniform, just underwear way too fancy for Uncle Sam to have issued it to him."

I took a closer look at the photograph and began to think she might be right about his status as a civilian. His hair was considerably longer than that of the boys in uniform. His most noticeable feature, however, were his eyes. His hair was very dark, but his eyes were startlingly light, perhaps pale gray or blue; in a black and white photo, there was no way to tell. But I could understand now how Jay would not forget his face. This man had lady-killer written all over him.

"So what now?" Jay asked.

"I'll find a photo shop and see if they can enlarge just his face. You do have a one-hour developer on Innocence?" I asked Miss Potee, remembering the 1950s nature of the island's commercial section.

"A couple of them. We'll show the copies to Elva and Blanche first. A man this handsome? Elva's bound to remember him, big a flirt as she used to be. But if we strike out there, I'm willing to show the enlargements to other old timers to see if they remember him. There are a couple of dozen white folks who were here during the war. I'll get to everybody, one way or another. If you want to stay and visit, I can go to the photo shop for you, Troy."

Jay shook her head. "As much as I love you, daughter, all I want is to be alone."

"You and Greta Garbo," I said, pecking her on the cheek. "By the way, Officer Haskins wants to know who you talked to when you tried to turn yourself in the last time?"

"A policeman, of course," she said, obviously nearing the end of her patience. "I didn't catch his name. On the tall side, maybe fifty, in plain clothes. Had a beard that needed trimming, I remember that. Why?"

"Officer Haskins forgot to ask, that's all. You're sure you don't need me here?"

"I'm sure." She still held the photo of him, her eyes glued on his face.

There was a tap at the door, unnecessary since it was already open. Reverend Allenby, followed by a Gene Hackman look-alike came in, the former smiling beatifically, the latter with a canyon-deep scowl.

"Oh, Lord," Jay muttered, and inched down in the bed.

"Morning, Reverend," Miss Potee said, moving aside. "Morning, Dr. McCall."

Dr. McCall crossed to me as the minister moved to the bed to talk to Jay. "Ms. Burdette, sorry I missed meeting you yesterday," he said, pulling me to one side. "I was in surgery over on Hilton Head longer than I expected. But I had quite a conversation with Mrs. Wingate late last night and wasted a lot of breath. I brought Reverend Allenby in, hoping he can make her see reason. Delaying her surgery is akin to suicide. You'll never find out what she wants to know in time."

"Well, we've had a little luck," I said. "We have a picture of the man. All we have to do now is find someone who remembers him." I nodded toward the bed where Jay was showing the photo to Reverend Allenby.

"I'm delighted to hear it, but you must understand, an abdominal aortic aneurysm is nothing to play with. She's been asymptomatic until just recently but now that she's experienced discomfort, that's a sign that the clock's ticking. We need to get her into surgery as soon as we've completed angiographic studies. She's on borrowed time, Ms. Burdette. The longer the wait, the greater the possibility that the aneurysm will rupture. There's almost no chance she'd survive that."

I felt sick, but there was nothing I could say. I'd done the best I could to change her mind and hadn't made a dent. I thanked him and consigned Jay to the Reverend's expert hands.

Miss Potee and I headed for Main Street, Dr. McCall's clock ticking in my head, marking the hours before the alarm went off and Jay ran out of time. Even with the photo in hand, I don't think I've ever felt more helpless in my life.

I didn't want to delay passing along what Jay had said about the officer she'd talked to before, so Miss Potee waited for me in her car while I dashed into the police station. I found Mr. Haskins elbow-deep in dusty three-ring binders.

"So what did Miz Julie say?" he asked, after I reported on her condition. I launched into the description she'd given me, but he began shaking his head before I was halfway through. "Uh-uh. No, ma'am. He wasn't one of ours. I've checked the roster to see who worked while I was in the hospital. The youngest one, Jesse Primo, is black and only forty-one or so. You saw Aaron yesterday, and Ficker replaced Rathbone, who died last year. The problem is, there's only two men on each twelve-hour shift so it ain't that unusual for the office to be empty if both of us are out on a call. Anybody could walk in, 'cause we don't lock the door."

"Then who could it have been?" I asked.

"I don't know, but whoever it was was passing himself off as an officer of the law and that's illegal. Like I said yesterday, Miz Burdette, this is gettin' smellier by the day."

"Smelly enough for the mayor to let you spend some time on this?" I asked.

He grunted. "If we were dealing with a fresh corpse, he'd have to, but not one that's fifty years old. Shoot, he come stormin' in here this mornin', raisin' hell about the story in the paper, as if there was anything we coulda done to stop it. Well, he can tell me what to do when I'm on duty, but he ain't got nothin' to say about what I do on my own time. Here's my number at home," he said, handing me a card. "If you and Miz Mabel come up with anything I can use, you call me. And if I were you, I'd drop off one of those enlargements at the Innocence *Daily*. See if they'll run it with one of those 'Did You Know This Man?' headlines. Couldn't hurt, and God knows it'll sure as hell get Hizzoner's goat. Run one by here, too. And tell Miz Julia we're prayin' for her, ya hear?"

When we returned to Blanche's, the only indication that she and Miss Peterson had moved in our absence was the empty pitcher of lemonade on the kitchen table and the high-heeled shoes parked in the corner beside the pantry. They grabbed the enlargements and a quiet descended on the room as they stared at the photos.

"Handsome, wasn't he?" Blanche said finally with a pointed look at Miss Peterson. "You'd think we'd remember him, wouldn't you? Especially you, Elva."

"Why me?" Miss Peterson was on the defensive. "You talk like I met the boat and saw every Tom, Dick, and Harry that set foot on Innocence. There were hundreds of them. I didn't know them all."

Blanche held the picture at arm's length. "Notice how he seems to be on the outside of the group looking in, as if he doesn't belong? And what's this light blotch at the bottom of the picture?"

"The top of the head of a girl standing a little ways in front of him," I said, sliding the original from the envelope. "They could have cropped it higher and cut her out altogether, but I thought it was important to show as much of what he was wearing as possible."

Blanche bobbed her head. "Smart, Troy. Quite a dandy, wasn't he? But those eyes. Cold as a Vermont January." She shuddered, and squinted at the original again. "And look at whose head was in the way," she said, shoving it across to Elva.

Elva's eyes welled with sudden tears. "Angel. Lord, we were so close back then. I still miss her sometimes."

"The Reverend does, too," Miss Potee said. "Poor man."

"All the more reason for him to move out of that house," Blanche said. "I hear tell he hasn't changed a thing of Angela's since she left. Won't even let the cleaning ladies from the church flick a duster in her room. Closed off the upstairs altogether. Keeps the place like a shrine."

She began gathering the glossies we hadn't needed, the swollen joints of arthritic fingers making it awkward for her. "Well, let's be honest. He's to blame for her running away the way she did. There's such a thing as holding a body on too tight a leash and that's what he did. And he's still waiting for her to come back. All his good works, even helping raise an orphan or two, couldn't fill the gap Angel left."

"Well." Elva folded her fan and got up. "I'll take one of the copies and show them to Ardella, Josephine, maybe Ronnie U. His memory comes and goes these days, but it won't hurt to check. In fact, I'll stop at anyone else I think of in my neighborhood."

"'Preciate it," Miss Potee said and reached for her purse. "Time's a-wastin'. Blanche, are you sure you're up to getting out today?"

"I want to help," Blanche said, collecting the remaining photos lined up around the edges of the table. "Elva, don't forget this." She handed her the slip of paper with Miss Potee's pager number.

"Luck, ever'body," Elva said, tucking it into her tote.

"See y'all later." She stepped into her shoes. Then, with a toss of her head, ribbon ends flying, she swished out.

Blanche watched her go with an expression I found difficult to read.

"Is something wrong?" I asked.

"She took a picture. She slipped one of the glossies into her bag. There were fifteen photos in this envelope. The number's written on the outside. Now there's only fourteen. She took one."

Miss Potee cocked her head to one side. "Am I the only one who noticed that, for the longest time after we showed y'all the enlargements, Elva never said a word? She just sat there and stared at that man's face and didn't open her mouth."

Blanche frowned. "Elva used to be a shameless flirt. There's no way under the sun she'd have missed batting her lashes at a man as handsome as this one. She wouldn't have forgotten him either. I think seeing his face again shocked her speechless. I think she remembered something."

"Then why didn't she say so?" Miss Potee asked.

Blanche's small face sagged with concern. "I don't know, Mabel. I don't know. But suddenly I'm very uneasy about her. I have a bad feeling. Really bad."

7

Miss Potee started the engine, put the gearshift in Drive, changed her mind and yanked it back into Park. "Sorry, honey, but I just reached my geezer threshhold. The thing about old folks: ask us how we feel and by God, we'll tell you. One more recitation of the misery of the day without some reinforcement and I will be plumb suicidal. I could use a drink. Since I don't drink and drive, either you take the wheel or we walk the rest of the way."

I chuckled, knowing exactly how she felt. The three we'd visited so far had told us everything, except what we needed to know. "Sure, I'll drive. Do you want me to take over now?"

"Not yet. You don't know the way to the watering hole and I do. Besides, I need to make a thirty-second stop on the way." She shifted gears again and pulled into traffic just as the pager clipped to her waist beeped to life. "Oh, damn it." She snatched it off and handed it to me. "What's the number?" When I read it off to her, she frowned. "I don't recognize it. I'll call in from the restaurant."

She drove south and I found myself paying closer attention to the wide variety of housing, a comfortable blend of old and new on tree-shaded lots of differing sizes. Palmettos, scrub pine, and live oaks lined Oceanside, Central, and Western, three broad north-south boulevards that began at the traffic circle at the neck of the shrimp and ended at the one near North End. Thirty-odd streets ran east and west, with flowering trees and bushes in riotous bloom. Clearly the planners and developers had left untouched as many of the indigenous plants and trees as possible. It gave the island a lushness and a permanence that contributed greatly to Innocence's aura of serenity. But how much of that serenity was illusion?

We were very near the southern traffic circle when Miss Potee turned east toward the ocean on Sixth Street and slowed in front of a charming little cottage of gleaming white stucco.

"This is gonna be Reverend Allenby's new place," she said, peering past me. "I just wanted to make sure my son had planted the azaleas my church group donated. The house is a surprise. They're gonna present it to him this Sunday."

"Who? His church?"

"Everybody. He's still living in New Faith's old manse. New Faith outgrew their first church years ago. They put up a new one and bought another house for the pastor who took over after Reverend Allenby retired. Reverend Allenby was so attached to the old house that they let him stay on in it."

"I get the impression he's very special to the people here."

"Yes, ma'am. He helped make this place what it is today.

Old-fashioned as all get-out, but he's got a good heart. After his daughter, Angel, left home, and he was all alone—his wife died when Angel was a baby—he helped raise a couple of orphans, sent them to private church schools and everything. Hear tell one's a preacher over up in Charleston. But the homeplace is so old now, it's falling down around his ears and New Faith can't afford to keep it up any longer. Yet and still, nobody wanted to see the Reverend kicked out on the street. For once, ol' Leland came through, twisted a few of the right arms, and they bought this house for him. Then the whole island got in on the act. We've been cleaning and painting and raisin' money to furnish it ever since."

"And he doesn't know?" I asked.

"Best-kept secret on the island," she said, pulling away. "Like I told you, us old timers take care of our own. And we're gonna find out about Little Bits's man or die trying."

If we didn't find him soon, I reflected, it wouldn't be the old timers doing the dying. It would be Jay.

I'd taken Miss Potee figuratively when she said we were heading for the watering hole. She'd meant it literally. The Watering Hole was a combination restaurant and bar on a side street off Main. She led me toward the rear of the dining area to a pair of telephone booths with folding doors. Just as she squeezed herself into one, her beeper went off again. "Oh, Lord," she said, squinting at the display. "This time it is the hospice." She closed the door of her booth and I slipped into the other to call the hospital. A nurse answered and told me that Jay was on her way down to Radiology again. "You just missed her. She's going to be a while. I'll tell her you called."

I hung up just as Miss Potee tapped on the door of the booth.

"That first page was Elva, calling from Ron Unthank's house," she said. "This thing must not be working right; she says she's been trying to get me for a couple of hours. No luck with the picture, but she found out where Miss Lucy's son is."

"What good does that do us?" I asked.

"Well, he's in a group home called Safe Harbor. I know the place; a college friend of my son works there. If Nathan's a resident it means he must be in a lot better shape than he was when he was a kid. It might be worth talking to him. The problem is, I have to get back to the hospice. Callie Drew is dying and I promised her I'd be there when her time came."

"Then by all means go. Just tell me how to get to Safe Harbor and I'll be fine."

"That's simple enough," she said, as we hurried out to the car again. "I'll give you my map. And I'll call Danny so they'll be expecting you. There's no guarantee you'll learn anything from Nathan, but face it, honey, it would be criminal not to ask. If you're antsy about going by yourself, I'm sure Blanche would go with you."

But Miss Lacey wasn't home and her minivan, which had been parked out front earlier, was gone. I went alone.

In some previous life, Safe Harbor had been a motel—sixteen small cabins horseshoed in two rows around a larger building which appeared to be for administration, recreation, and dining. It was a miracle I found it. I'd been driving around the area and had asked directions several times before stumbling on it by accident, on a cul-de-sac behind a long-defunct gas station.

The receptionist was clearly on her way to the Ladies when I caught her. "My goodness, Mr. Stokes has been popular today," she said, jiggling in place. "No visitors in over a year, then two in one day. He's in Cabin Eight. Stop by Cabin Six and his counselor will go with you.

Excuse me, I've gotta go." She darted down the hall and I left.

Whitewashed clapboard with decorative black shutters, each of Safe Harbor's cabins had a tiny patch of grass in front edged by a length of white plastic fencing. It still looked like the kind of motel you'd find off a two-lane highway going nowhere, but I had to give them credit for trying.

I hesitated in front of Cabin Six, then decided against involving the counselor unless I had to. At Number Eight, I tapped on the door, which was not quite closed.

"Mr. Stokes?"

No answer. I called again. Still no response. Nudging the door open a little farther, I stuck my head in. The cabin was perhaps fifteen feet square, furnished simply and sparely with a neatly made brass bed, an old-fashioned chifferobe, its top aligned with framed photos and postcards, two cane-bottomed chairs, and a bedside table of unvarnished wood. The floor was covered by a large braided rug. Now what? I wondered. Ask the counselor next door where to find Mr. Stokes, of course.

I was just backing away, trying to leave the door as I'd found it, when something stopped me. There's no point in my trying to describe what that something was because it's beyond intuition or anything else I can think of. The bottom line was that I was sure something wasn't right.

I nudged the door open, my antennae fully extended, and stepped into the room. Technically I was trespassing, but even that was no deterrent. I gazed around, seeing nothing new, except the closet and bathroom doors which had been beyond my field of vision before. I moved to the bathroom; its door was slightly ajar. Tapping on it and praying I wasn't intruding at the worst possible moment for either one of us, I called out just in case.

"Mr. Stokes?"

No response.

I pushed at the door with one finger. It opened easily, giving me a view of the washbasin and the toilet, but it stopped at the halfway point, thanks to a sneaker-clad foot.

I stepped back quickly, horrified that I'd almost walked in on him. "Oh, Mr. Stokes, I'm so sorry. I did knock. I guess you didn't hear me. I'll just wait out here for you."

No response. No flush. No running water. Nothing.

I leaned to my left, puzzled. Why didn't he answer? For that matter, why didn't he shut the damned door, now that he knew I was out there?

The foot hadn't budged. "Mr. Stokes?" I rapped on the molding. "Uh . . . Mr. Stokes?"

Still, nothing. This was scary.

I inched closer and closer, took a deep breath, and peered around the open door. Head thrown back and eyes fixed toward the ceiling, Nathan Stokes sat, his back against the tub, his knees raised so that his feet were flat against the floor. I'd never seen a dead body without benefit of a coffin and makeup and the rest of the trimmings, but peeking around that door I understood as I couldn't have before precisely what Jay had meant when she said she knew dead when she saw it. Even without the anguished expression on his flushed face, and the open mouth, bits of mustard yellow on the tip of his tongue and lips, there was no doubt.

I stood frozen for an eternity, my brain absolutely empty of thought. Finally something kicked me in the mental can and I tossed my bag aside and edged carefully around the door, squeezing past his legs.

It was hard to tell what he'd looked like alive; his skin was mottled, his features distorted. He had a head full of thick dark hair with very little gray. The expressionless eyes were large, protruding now, and dark with long lashes.

It was a futile gesture and the hardest thing I'd ever had

to do, but I slipped my hand into the hollow of his neck to feel for a pulse. His flesh yielded under my fingers but with no life, no resistance from the muscle and tendons. But his skin was still warm. Perhaps it wasn't too late. A few yellow bits clung to my fingertips and I cringed, uncertain what they were. I scrubbed my hand against my denim skirt and got the hell out of there, dashing over to Cabin Six and banging on the door. It was opened immediately by a tow-headed young man in a *Cheers* T-shirt with "Phil" embroidered on the sleeve, cut-off jeans, and bare feet. He glared at me with annoyance.

"Mr. Stokes," I gasped. "Dead. Bathroom."

His face paled. "You're shittin' me." Stepping to one side, he snatched off the handset of the phone mounted on the wall beside the door. Punching the zero, he jiggled with impatience until someone answered. "Phil," he barked. "Medical emergency, Cabin Eight. Ambulance." He slammed the phone onto its cradle and darted past me, reaching the cabin next door in five strides.

I hurried after him but left the scene in the bathroom to him.

"Jesus," he said from behind the door. I heard him moving around, grunting with effort. "Lady," he called, "I could use some help. I need to move him so I can start CPR. There's not enough room to work on him in here."

I took a deep breath and went in. Phil had maneuvered around behind Mr. Stokes and held him under the arms.

"Grab his ankles," he directed. With a new appreciation for the meaning of dead weight, I helped half drag, half carry the man from the tiny bathroom. As we crossed the threshold, something slid from Mr. Stokes's pants pocket. Phil stepped on it and swore. "What the hell . . . ? Right here's fine," he said, once we'd gotten our burden clear of the door. Dropping to his knees, he placed one hand behind Mr. Stokes's neck, tilting his head backward, and probed for a pulse. "Nada," he muttered, and pried the man's jaw open, to scoop out more small yellow lumps. "What the hell was he eating?"

"Whatever it was stuck to your heel." I examined the crumbs and bits clinging to Phil's bare foot as he pinched Mr. Stokes's nose and knelt to blow four hard breaths into the man's mouth. "Just crackers." I held the corner his heel had missed. "It fell out of his pocket."

"See if he's got any more," he said grimly and began the first series of compressions. "Maybe he's allergic to something in 'em."

I couldn't figure any way to get out of it so I jammed my hand into Mr. Stokes's left-hand pocket and came away with a sandwich bag half-full of the crushed remnants of what had been thin golden crackers with a pale yellow filling. "I recognize these," I said. "They cost a mint. Give me Cheez-Its any day."

Phil's head snapped around to me. "They're cheese crackers?" I held up the sandwich bag and he exploded. "Goddammit! Nathan's on Nardil. He's not supposed to eat cheese! He knows that! Look, do you know CPR?"

I nodded. "Uh—yes."

"Terrific." He bent over, pinched Mr. Stokes's nostrils and blew twice. "Get ready to take over after I finish this next cycle. I need to check on the—" The rest of the sentence was drowned out by the wail of an ambulance screeching to a stop in front of the cabin. Footsteps pounded on the porch and through the door. I scrambled backward out of the way and claimed a corner by the window.

"What we got, Phil?" an attendant asked, dropping to his knees.

An old-model squad car sped across the lawn and

stopped, chase lights whirling. A gangly young man in civvies practically fell out of the cruiser and raced inside. The cabin was beginning to feel claustrophic. I inched my way toward the door and went out onto the porch, remembering at the last minute that my purse was still inside somewhere.

Behind me, the residents of Safe Harbor gathered on the lawn, huddling together, their expressions of anxiety running the gamut from a rhythmic rocking in place to gnawing on fingernails. Most, however, stood quietly and watched, arms around one another's shoulders. One man hovered near the corner of the main building, hand over his mouth, eyes wide with fright, yet he rejected the support offered by the person nearest who'd reached to take his arm.

After several minutes, Phil came out, glanced at me and shrugged helplessly before hurrying to each group to reassure them with a touch here, a hug there. The crowd gradually grew until Nathan Stokes was taken away in the ambulance, his features hidden by an oxygen mask. The grim expressions of the attendants and the young officer's taut shake of his head to me as he left made any questions I might have asked unnecessary. I knew from what I'd heard from the porch that they'd managed to resuscitate him. They seemed certain, however, that they'd simply delayed the inevitable.

Phil worked his way back around to me. "I'm going to the hospital, see if there's any paperwork or questions to be answered. I just wanted to thank you for your help." He turned to look back at the residents still milling around the open area. "I've got to find out where those damned crackers came from. He knew cheese was one of the things he was not supposed to eat."

"Why not?"

"He was on an MAO I, shorthand for monoamine oxidase inhibitor. It's an antidepressant. While you're taking it, foods containing tyramine or dopamine are strictly verboten—stuff like salami, yogurt, cheese; the list is as long as your arm. Eat any of them and your blood pressure skyrockets out of control and before you know it you're dead. His diet was closely monitored by the staff, so the crackers had to be brought in from outside."

"Check with your receptionist," I said. "She said something about me being the second visitor Mr. Stokes had today. Whoever was here earlier might have given it to him."

Phil's blond brows took an elevator up. "Someone else was here? Damn it!" He whacked the porch railing, clearly agitated. "I'm responsible for six residents. They can have visitors anytime but I'm supposed to be notified first, so I can make sure they understand the rules, one of which is no edible goodies for any of our people unless our dietition okays it first."

"Then I owe you an apology," I said, to get the receptionist off the hook. "The lady at the desk suggested I stop at your cabin, but I didn't realize it was a prerequisite."

Phil managed to be gracious. "Apology accepted. And thanks for the info about the other visitor. I'll check on it. I'm really sorry about Nathan. He was a special guy. Did you know him well?"

"I'd never met him," I confessed. "To be honest, I came hoping he could identify a man who lived in his house a long time ago. Someone's life depends on it."

"Geez." His pale-lashed eyes were troubled. "Then I really am sorry. Nate would have tried to help you, I know that. Even if he couldn't remember the man's name, he'd have made one up just to be helpful. That's how anxious he was to please." He blinked rapidly, his eyes suspiciously wet. "I'd better put some shoes on and get to the hospital.

Nice meeting you and thanks again," he said, shaking my hand before dashing to his cabin, then sprinting toward a battered Volkswagen Beetle with a purple flower painted on the hood. After a few seconds of coaxing, it started with a clatter. He sped away.

I sat, unable to move as the image of poor Nathan Stokes flashed through my mind. If it hadn't taken me so long to find this place, I might have been able to save him. I squeezed my eyes closed, trying to blot out the picture. But Phil's brief description of the kind of person Mr. Stokes had been had made him as real to me as if I'd known him.

There was another part of the equation to deal with as well: the niggling suspicion that what had happened to Mr. Stokes had not been an accident. What were the chances that Mr. Stokes, who according to the receptionist hadn't had a visitor in a year, would have two on the same day and that the first would bring Mr. Stokes something that would make it impossible for him to answer questions the second visitor planned to ask?

Won't wash, I told myself. The only people likely to have known what kind of medication Mr. Stokes was taking, along with what he could and couldn't eat, were on the staff. I doubted they'd breach client confidentiality by yakking about it to an outsider. It had to have been plain bad luck. I couldn't even nitpick about the fact that visitor number one hadn't announced himself to Phil. I'd done the same thing. Then why was I having such a hard time quashing the notion that someone had tried to put Mr. Stokes out of action?

I'd call Phil later to see if they'd identified the first visitor. God willing, it would turn out to be a well-meaning friend who had no idea the harm the crackers would cause. Otherwise I'd have to face the possibility that my coming here had served as Mr. Stokes's death sentence.

My purse was still in the cabin, on the floor where I'd dropped it. It had landed upside down and now half the contents were strewn across the room. I gathered up all my junk, hunted on all fours until I found the keys to the Buick peeking from behind a leg of the chifferobe. As I stood up again, I found myself a nose away from the things on top of the chifferobe. The arrangement intrigued me. Mr. Stokes had evidently worshipped at the altar of symmetry.

There were eight postcards from Hawaii, matted and framed, four on the right, four on the left. Between and slightly in front of them were six Polaroid photographs similarly framed, probably fellow residents, since Phil appeared in two of them with several faces I'd seen outside.

At the very front of the grouping on the left was a faded eight-by-ten of an apple-cheeked woman with laughing eyes, her fair hair piled high in a pompadour, which in combination with the tweezed brows betrayed the age of the picture. The handwriting angled across the bottom right corner was faded but legible: To my Nathan. Mom. This was Lucy Stokes. And each item on the dresser top had a mate in size and placement, except the photo of his mother. It wasn't centered, yet had nothing to balance it.

I glanced at the wall between the closet and bathroom doors. Four more framed postcards, two small photos, two small prints of kittens, in a maddeningly symmetrical arrangement. Given Mr. Stokes's mania for precise order and balance, there should be an eight-by-ten on the right side of the dresser to match the one of his mother. Even if he had removed it or placed the mate somewhere else, he would almost certainly have moved his mother's photo to the center. As it was, the arrangement was out of kilter. Someone else must have removed the second photo recently enough for Mr. Stokes not to have noticed it was gone. His earlier visitor?

Curiosity propelled me toward the wall placement. More Hawaii postcards—Waikiki Beach, the Pearl Harbor memorial. The prints of the kittens were pure five-and-dime quality, cute and kitschy. The small photo on the left was a less flattering sepia of Miss Lucy Stokes. Its mate stopped my heart midbeat. It was Jay's mystery man, a good bit younger than he'd been in the Fourth of July picture, his handsome face a little fuller with the baby fat he'd have yet to lose. But the thick dark hair with the lock falling onto his forehead was the same, the angle of the brows, the line of the jaw.

He stood with one arm around the shoulder of a woman almost as tall as he was, her hair braided into a crown above her oval face. Her age was difficult to guess but she was definitely older than he was. The facade of a building made of rough logs dominated the background, a large hand-painted sign above their heads announcing its name: Taine's General Store. The front half of a car protruding from the left edge of the picture confirmed the era in which it had been taken: the late Thirties.

What I did next was unpardonable, but I had to. I removed the photo from its hook, pried up the tiny nails that anchored the cardboard backing, and hit pay dirt. Written on the back in a spindly handwriting that also confirmed the age of the photo: Estelle and Vinnie, 1939. I had a name!

I compared the smaller image with the larger one from Blanche's photo. The young man in the snapshot looked like a Vinnie, the man in the enlargement did not. The nickname didn't fit him. He seemed harder, colder. I had a sense that in the years between the two pictures, Vinnie Whatsisname had changed a good deal. He'd lost his innocence. So now I knew for certain that Nathan Stokes could have given me the man's full name and might also have been able to tell me what had happened to him. And now because of some fancy cheese crackers and the length of time it had taken me to find Safe Harbor, he would probably never be able to tell anyone anything ever again.

I sat down in one of the cane-bottomed chairs and debated what to do. I had the man's nickname and the name of the woman with him. Neither was worth much unless I could find out where the snapshot had been taken. Was Taine the name of the town or the name of the owner of the store? I sat for a moment longer, trying to adjust to this turn of events. I'd promised Jay I'd give all this a try, but it never occurred to me I might get lucky so soon. Even if this turned out to be a dead end and I had to lie to her about the results, I had a first name I could use for the man she thought she'd sent to his eternal reward.

I rooted out my pad and pen and scribbled a note for Phil, to let him know that I had borrowed the photo and would return it as soon as I could. I slipped the note under the door of his cabin and headed back out to the street, where I was almost creamed by an idiot in a big old Lincoln in a hurry to get to wherever it is people who drive twenty-year-old gas guzzlers go these days.

I'd parked the Buick in front of him and as I rounded the front of Jay's behemoth to get in, he pulled away from behind me and gunned his engine as if he was at target practice and I was the bulls-eye. I plastered my carcass against Bernice's front fender so hard I could have been a second coat of paint. The Lincoln flew past me in a gust of wind, dirt, and gravel flying from under its tires like shrapnel.

I cussed at him under my breath and climbed into the front seat, legs shaking. I wasn't sure whether or not to take the incident personally, hadn't even gotten a good look at the driver; I'd been too busy hugging metal. That's all I needed, to be knocked ass-over-teakettle in the middle of a two-lane highway out in the middle of nowhere. If I didn't survive, neither would Jay. Considering the nasty suspicions I'd had about what had happened to Mr. Stokes, that was not a comforting thought. If someone wanted to make sure Jay didn't find the answers to the questions she had, all that someone had to do was get rid of me.

Puh-lease, I chided myself. I was becoming paranoid. I gave myself a good talking-to, then went to find the nearest library.

8

"You're right, that is him," Jay said, a perceptible tremor in her fingers as she held the photo. "Miss Lucy's boy had it? I don't know what to make of that."

"Me either," I confessed, doing my best to hide my alarm at how lethargic she seemed. It was almost six, long past the time I'd agreed to meet Miss Potee, Elva Peterson, and Blanche to compare notes, but I'd felt compelled to stop at the hospital. Now that I had, I had serious misgivings about leaving. Jay was so apathetic. Even the fact that we now had a second photo and a name of sorts for the man whose alleged death had haunted her for years hadn't lifted her spirits. Perhaps its memory was eating into her soul. Fear of failure was eating into mine.

I'd been so sure I could find the answers I needed at a library. My mother was a retired librarian. All through my elementary and junior high school years, Mom had insisted that after school I come to whichever branch she was working in and spend the time there until the end of her shift.

That's where I'd learned to read books far beyond the comprehension and interest of my classmates. It's where I'd done my homework for years. And I'd come to the conclusion that librarians were the smartest people going. It wasn't that they knew everything; it was simply that they almost always knew where to find everything. And this was before computers, thank you very much. So it never occurred to me that they wouldn't be able to help me pinpoint the town where the photo had been taken.

They'd tried, I'd give them that. They'd even turned me loose with one of the computers only the staff could use and a set of compact disks that listed every city, town, and one-stop-sign hamlet in the state, and every man, woman and child who had a published telephone number. Taine did not exist, at least not in South Carolina. Unless Blanche or Miss Peterson or Miss Potee had come up with something, I'd reached a dead end.

"Daughter," Jay said now, returning the photo to me, "don't look so discouraged. You're doing fine." She took my hand. Hers was dry and hot, her skin parchment thin. "You made me a promise you'd go on trying, no matter what, so I expect you to stick to your word. And you won't get anywhere sitting here with me. Shoo. Go meet the others like you're supposed to. Give me a call later and let me know what's happening."

"You're sure?" I asked. I was still afraid to leave.

"Positive. By the way, I talked to Wade and got him off your back. I lied, told him we were visiting my old haunts and moving around a lot, so he shouldn't worry if he didn't hear from us."

I was relieved. I'd felt so guilty keeping the truth from him. I knew he'd want to know how sick she was. On the other hand, he was under enough stress already. There was no point in making it worse. Still, I was glad it was Jay who'd done the lying. Wade and I had promised we'd never keep secrets from one another. We'd even pricked our fingers to seal the vow in blood, a big deal since we were eight and ten years old at the time. As far as I was concerned, the promise still held, and it bugged me that I'd had to mangle the truth when I'd talked to him the evening before. Jay's big fat lie had bought us some time, but unless a miracle happened, there wasn't much time left. How would I make him understand if Jay died before we had a chance to tell him everything?

"While we're on the subject, daughter, there's something I want to say to you." Jay pulled herself a little higher in the bed. "I know what it's like to long for a child. I could have had babies. I decided not to because I was terrified that one day a policeman would knock on my door with a warrant in his hand to arrest me for killing this man. I couldn't stand the thought of being in jail and my children growing up without me. That's why I chose the kind of work I've done, helping mothers behind bars and their babies on the outside."

I was speechless. It had never occurred to me to wonder how she'd become involved with women in jail.

"When you and Wade split up, I swore I wouldn't take sides, but there's a part of me that will never forgive him for choosing divorce over y'all adopting a child. There was no excuse for it, especially since he was adopted himself."

"What?" For the second time that day I felt as if I'd had all the wind knocked out of me. "Wade was adopted?"

"That poor, stupid child didn't tell you? Lord, Troy. I thought you knew. As much as Carrie and Doug loved that boy, deep down inside he never got over the fact that his real mother gave him away. I guess he didn't want to adopt a child who might always feel the way he did."

"He never told me any of that," I said, stunned that he'd kept it from me.

Jay pulled me toward her and kissed my forehead. "I'll always love you for loving that fool enough to let him go. You got the piece of paper that made it legal, daughter. It's time to do it in there," she said, placing her hand over my heart. "Let him go, Troy. He didn't deserve you, so let him go. Now, scram. I'll talk to you later." She closed her eyes, lowering the head of the bed slowly, and was asleep by the time it was horizontal.

I watched her for a minute, loving every ounce of her, then slipped from the room. I managed to get all the way outside with the Buick in sight before the full implications of the conversation with her snuck up on me from behind and hit me with the force of a wrecking ball. I collapsed on one of the benches under the portico over the front walkway, and sat, head back, eyes closed.

Wade, adopted. How could he not have told me? We had been friends from the day he and his parents had moved into the house across the street, had been inseparable all through high school and college. We were married before the ink on our bachelor's degrees had dried, with everyone saying it had to be because we were meant for each other. Yeah, right.

We'd always talked about the kind of parents we'd be one day. After five years of marriage and a sixth spent trying to conceive, we learned that it wasn't in the cards. That's when I began to realize just how important having children was to Wade. I'd felt so guilty that I was the problem—fibroids, lots of them in all the wrong places. The prospect of adopting had been my emotional salvation, except to my surprise Wade had freaked out when I'd proposed it, wouldn't even discuss it.

And like a fool, I'd felt so noble when I'd broached the subject of divorce a year later, and so devastated when he'd agreed to it. It had never occurred to me that sharing a life with me, even a childless life, wouldn't be enough for him. It would have been for me; I loved him that much. To find out the real reason for his attitude from someone else destroyed the last of my illusions about our relationship. Not only had I not meant enough to him, he'd broken the blood vow we'd made. Okay, it was childish of me, but I'd always taken it seriously. Wade hadn't been honest with me. I hadn't known him at all.

"Ms. Burdette?"

I recognized Dr. Baskerville's voice immediately and opened my eyes, struggling to arrange my face in a semblance of a smile. Not only did I fail, the tears dammed up behind my closed lids began to slide down my cheeks.

"Oh, hey now," he said, sitting down beside me. "Things are bad but they could be a lot worse."

"How would you know?" I snapped, and then lost it completely, the tears coming full force.

"Come on," he said, pulling me to my feet. He walked me to the reserved-for-doctors section of the parking lot and opened the passenger door of a blue-green Honda Accord. "In," he ordered. He slid behind the wheel, starting the engine even before he'd closed and locked his door. Pulling out of the lot, he turned right and eased into the traffic around the circle.

From that point, I have no idea which direction he went. I was too busy bawling my head off. It was disgusting. I was one great, sobbing mess, blubbering as if I was being paid a thousand dollars a teardrop. I couldn't seem to stop. The harder I tried, the harder I cried. At some point, Dr. Baskerville crammed a wad of tissues into my hand. I jammed them against my face and kept right on boo-hooing.

I'd rather not think about how I looked when I finally ran dry. By that time I had a sense we had gone quite a distance. Seeing that the flood had run its course, he took the next exit and pulled to a stop in the parking area beside a smallish lighthouse. Beyond it was a deserted stretch of shore that sloped gently down to quiet, blue-gray water. I had no idea where we were, and didn't really care. Embarrassed and thoroughly ashamed of myself, I wiped and sniffed and blew, putting the absorbency of the tissues to the test, then sat there, trying to figure out what to say to him.

"When's the last time you cried?" he asked, surprising me.

I thought about it. "Nineteen eighty-seven, when my last grandparent died."

"You were way overdue." He released his seatbelt and shifted so he could lean back against the door. "Feel better now?"

I nodded. It was simpler than trying to explain that it wasn't that I felt better; I felt nothing at all. I was empty.

"What just happened wasn't solely about Mrs. Wingate, was it?" he asked gently. "That explosion came out of a whole closet full of pain, things you've been cramming in there for years. What finally sprung the lock?"

"Dr. Baskerville," I said, about to tell him it was none of his business, as kindly as I could.

"The name's David," he corrected me. "Look, forget I'm your aunt's doctor and consider me a friend for the time being, okay? If that's too much of a stretch, consider me a sympathetic ear, someone willing to listen. You're getting a pretty good deal. Therapists charge seventy-five dollars an hour and up to do what I'm offering to do free."

He really was making me feel better. "Are you in the habit of spiriting away the families of your patients and taking them off to . . . where are we, anyway?"

"One of those dots of land with no name sitting in the

middle of the Intracoastal Waterway. And I'm not in the habit of spiriting away the families of my patients or anyone else, for that matter. I rarely have the time, even if I wanted to. For once I do, and do."

It took me a moment to figure out that last bit. "I'm glad. Thank you. The change of scenery is just what I needed. I've been on Innocence less than two days but it feels more like a month."

"A variation of cabin fever. You haven't answered my question." Green eyes regarded me with a steady gaze. "What triggered the deluge? It might help if you talked about it."

Opening up to other than family had always been difficult for me, but I felt an urge to respond to avoid hurting his feelings. I flipped through the three-by-five cards in my mind in search of a safe and easy subject and was halfway through the stack when he interrupted the weeding-out process with a question.

"You said Mrs. Wingate is your ex-husband's great aunt. If I talked to him and explained the urgency of the situation, would he be able to influence her decision? Or will he be coming soon?"

"Uh . . . he's not coming," I admitted. "We haven't told him."

"Why the hell not?" he demanded, his eyes widening. They really were the most amazing color.

"Well, his wife just gave birth to twins yesterday. They're premature, two pounds each, something like that. He's needed there."

"Ah," he said quietly. "The light dawns."

"Excuse me?"

"I just got a glimpse of one of the items in that closet of yours. Did the two of you have any children together?"

I winced, wondering how to get off this topic. "No. And I'd rather not discuss it."

The silence in the car spun itself out for over a minute, an uncomfortable silence for me. His gaze, intense and probing, seemed to peel away layer after layer of my facade. I felt like a damned onion.

"Okay," he said finally. "Consider the subject dropped. Back to our problem. I read the story about Mrs. Wingate in the morning paper. How's the search going?"

Breathing was a little easier now that we'd moved to a safer topic. "We have a photo of the man taken in '43 and another taken several years earlier." I reached for my purse, but hesitated in midthought, distracted by the image of Mr. Stokes's face.

"What is it?" David prodded. "Tell me, Ms. Burdette."

"Troy," I said, and told him about my afternoon. "I feel so rotten about it. I keep thinking that I'm responsible somehow."

He shook his head. "How could you be? Sometimes you have to accept the fact that there's nothing more you could have done. It's hard, believe me, I know. But you have to do it, if you want to hold on to your sanity."

"It's not that." I struggled to put my thoughts into words. "I know it's a reach to link my going there with what happened to him before I got to him, but it's too much of a coincidence for me to ignore. I keep thinking it was done to get Mr. Stokes out of the way. Someone knew he'd be able to identify Aunt Jay's mystery man."

"What makes you think he could?"

"This," I said, handing him the snapshot. "It was hanging on the wall of his room. Their names are written on the back, along with the year." I passed the enlargement so he could compare them.

He peered at both photos intently. "Certainly looks like the same man. And that's Taine's General Store! I had no idea it was that old."

"You've seen it?" I asked, my pulse quickening. "It still exists?"

"Are you kidding?" He laughed, fatigue disappearing from his face. "The family name was originally de La Fontaine, and the nickname is Taine. They sell the best pralines in the state . . . hell, in the South. And you're talking to a man whose roots are deep in N'Orleans mud, so I know whereof I speak." He looked ten years younger.

"Where is that store?" I prodded him. "There was no telephone number listed for it. Please don't tell me it's in Louisiana."

"Jacques Landing? It's spittin' distance, as the locals say, two islands over. Another one of those dots in the Intracoastal Waterway. And the phone's listed under Jacques Landing General Store. The sign's so old, nobody wants to take it down. What's your interest in the Landing?"

"I thought if it's a small enough place, I might be able to find someone who recognized them. Then if I had their surnames, I could look for phones listed to people with that name, call, and ask if they are related and if they had known a man called Vinnie."

He fastened his seatbelt and started the engine. "I guarantee you, you'd get nowhere on the phone. Talk about family business? Not on your life. Your chances are better—not by much, but a little—if you take the trouble to go to them. It's about an hour away. I'll take you if you like. It's up to you."

"Oh." His offer caught me off guard. "I don't want to mess up any plans you might have had."

He smiled and I had a sense that he could see right through me. "I had no plans except to get away from the hospital for a while. There's no one waiting at home for me, so my time is my own. Besides," he continued, sobering,

"Mrs. Wingate is my patient. Whatever I can do to help save her life, I'll do."

I figured a little graciousness wouldn't hurt about now. "Then thank you. I might have more luck if I could talk to people face-to-face."

"That's another reason for me to take you," he said, maneuvering off the tiny parking lot. "Jacques Landing people give new meaning to the definition of insular. If I'm with you, there's a better chance that they'll open up. At least they've seen me there before."

I had to ask. "What were you doing there?"

He eased into traffic on a two-lane highway. "Looking for distant cousins. My ancestors were Creoles named Basquevilles. Somewhere down the line the spelling was anglicized. According to my grandmother, her grandfather left Louisiana with the law on his heels for smuggling slaves out of the state. The story goes, he hid out on one of the islands along here and started a whole new branch of the family. When I started working on Innocence, I figured since I was in the neighborhood, I'd see if I could find them."

"Did you?"

"Not yet, but I have my suspicions." He flashed a grin in my direction. "Especially since my triple-great grandfather's first name was Jacques. Maybe one day they'll tell me the truth."

I was not encouraged. If the people on Jacques Landing wouldn't open up to David, who I was beginning to suspect could talk a clam out of its shell, I doubted seriously they'd be any more forthcoming with me. I might be wasting valuable time. If it were mine, I'd be far less concerned. It wasn't. It was Jay's.

9

David was right; Taine's General Store looked exactly as it had fifty years before. The sign had been repainted but other than that I saw little difference from the photograph. David parked the Honda and escorted me inside, greeting by name a couple of elderly men in rocking chairs on the front porch.

The interior of the store was a complete surprise. I'd expected something reminiscent of the Olesons' store on *Little House on the Prairie*, complete with bolts of fabric and pickle barrels full of dried goods. The reality was more like a super Seven-Eleven, clean and brightly lit, with aisles of soft drinks and baked goods, general household needs, a deli counter, and refrigerated compartments for frozen foods and dairy products. The only departure was the glass-fronted candy counter, its shelves lined with boxes of pralines, taffy, and caramels. There wasn't a single clerk in sight. Perhaps the place worked on an honor system. Serve yourself and put the money in the cash register.

"He must be in the back," David said and led me through a storeroom and into a rear hall, calling, "Mr. Fontaine?"

"Who's that?" A prototype for Santa Claus appeared from a door on our right. "David!" The lips under the snow-white beard stretched into a wide smile. "What a surprise! And with company!" He stepped out into the hallway to greet us, a hearty handshake for me, a pat on the back for David.

David introduced me and we were ushered into an office that, like the store, was strictly twentieth century, with mauve carpeting, Scandinavian-simple desk and chairs, and top-of-the-line computer equipment.

"Sit, sit," he urged us, directing us to a sofa of leather so butter-soft it was like being swallowed by a kidskin cloud. "So solemn," he said, pointing to David's face. "You've made your decision? You've left the hospital?"

I pulled a poker face, hoping my surprise didn't show. Our conversation during the drive to Jacques Landing had focused on Jay and, to a lesser extent, David's experiences at Harlem Hospital. At no time had I gotten the impression that he'd be leaving Innocence General.

"No, I'm still there." He leaned forward, elbows on his knees. "Mr. Fontaine, we're here hoping you can help us save the life of one of my patients."

"Oh?"

David nodded at me and I took the ball. "We need information about the people in this snapshot," I said. I pulled it out and passed it to Mr. Fontaine.

Reaching up under his beard, he retrieved a pair of glasses and scrutinized the picture, his blue eyes widening. "Well, Lord, will you look at this? This must be forty, fifty years old."

"It was taken in 1939," I responded. "The woman's name

was Estelle. The young man's nickname was Vinnie. Do you recognize them?"

His eyes, shuttered, flicked to mine, then down again. "How would it help this patient of yours?"

David started to speak, then stopped and sighed. "Look, Mr. Fontaine, I've been coming here on and off for the last three years. I've eaten at your table and treated members of your family. In spite of all that, you've done a masterful job of not answering the questions I've asked about the early settlers on Jacques Landing."

The older man flushed. "Well—"

"Let me finish, please, because in the scheme of things, not getting those answers hasn't mattered all that much. The information about these two people, especially the boy, does matter, enough so that, if you insist, I'll tell you how it would help my patient. But after all this time I shouldn't have to, should I?" He folded his hands, held Mr. Fontaine's gaze and waited.

Mr. Fontaine leaned back in his chair and peered over his glasses at him for a long, tense minute. He pursed his lips, moved his mouth from one side to the other. "No, reckon you shouldn't. You've been a good friend to us, David. I recognize these faces like I seen them yesterday. Let me get my magnifying glass." David and I exchanged relieved smiles as he went to his desk and returned with a magnifying glass that would have done Sherlock Holmes proud. Cradling the snapshot in his hand, he peered at it, moving the magnifier back and forth until it was a comfortable distance for him.

"Cousin Vinnie and Aunt Estelle. Last name was Quarles."

"He was your cousin?" I couldn't believe it. We'd hit the jackpot.

"Four or five times removed. Used to be that everybody

on the Landing was related somehow or other. Anyway, Aunt Estelle died years ago, while Vinnie was overseas. He came home on one leg looking for her, found her buried out yonder behind Our Lady of Peace."

"About what year did he come back?" I asked, wondering how Jay could have failed to notice a limp. Had he had an artificial leg long enough to have mastered a natural gait?

"Poor Aunt Estelle." Mr. Fontaine's eyes were still focused in the past. "It was a different time then, not like now, when nobody turns a hair if you have a baby and no ring on your finger. I remember my Mama talking about how Aunt Estelle went off to work in the city and came back with Vinnie in her oven. Raised him all by herself."

"Mr. Fontaine." David interrupted his reveries. "Vinnie Quarles was down on Innocence Island July of 1943. What we're trying to find out is, did he come back here after that?"

"Well, let me think. Aunt Estelle died just before I got married the first time, so that's Christmas of 1942. Vinnie—his full name was Vincent William—came home soon after that because he was at the wedding. Then I got shipped out, so the rest of it is all secondhand. The only reason Vinnie didn't wait to be drafted was that Aunt Estelle had come down with TB and he wanted the best care for her. He figured she'd get all his soldier's pay and that would be enough to keep her in a decent sanitarium. That's where they sent folks with TB back then. And he put her in a good one, too. But after a time she came home. Seems the money he was sending her wasn't enough anymore. Then he was missing in action for a time, too. Anyhow, Aunt Estelle got worse and worse and finally died. Vinnie pitched a fit when he got back and found out what had happened to her. He was a wild man, carrying on about finding the person responsible for not sending all his pay. He left and never came back."

I'd counted my chickens too soon. All I still had were scrambled eggs. "So there's no evidence that he was alive after July of that year."

"Sure he was. He had a first-class mausoleum built for Aunt Estelle, had her moved from the crypt that Landing folks had buried her in. It arrived just before President Roosevelt died. Everybody always said Mr. Roosevelt couldn't have had any finer resting place than Vinnie set up for his mama."

"Roosevelt died when?" I asked, unable to keep a lid on my rising excitement.

"April of Nineteen and forty-five," Mr. Fontaine responded. "It's one of those dates a body never forgets, like when President Kennedy was killed."

"You're certain Vinnie had it built?" David said, taking the words out of my mouth.

"Who else would have done it? He was the only close family she had. Besides, Cousin Robert worked for Laniard, the undertaker, and took delivery of all that marble. He said Vinnie sent it. We kept waiting for him to come back to see it, but he never did."

All the tension of the last twenty-four hours seemed to drain from my pores like invisible perspiration. We'd done it. Thanks to David, we had all the information we needed. I couldn't wait to tell Jay.

"May I use a phone to call Innocence Island?" I asked, rising, light-headed with relief. "I'll pay for it, of course."

"Appreciate the offer," Mr. Fontaine said, "but there's no need. Glad to oblige."

David, his face creased by a boyish grin, gave me a thumbs-up and I dialed Innocence General, hoping that

Jay was still in the room and able to answer. I prayed my way through four rings before she picked it up.

"Aunt Jay, everything's all right," I said, my voice shaking with emotion. "The man's name was Vincent Quarles. Dav . . . I mean, Dr. Baskerville and I have talked to a distant cousin who says he was alive in 1945. You're cleared, Aunt Jay. Please, have someone notify Dr. McCall. There's no reason to put off the surgery any longer."

"Well, that's good news," she said, sounding like her old self. "I knew you could do it. And it's David, now, is it?"

"Don't you start," I warned her, laughing. "I won't get back to Innocence for another hour or so, but I'll check in with you then."

"Wait till tomorrow, Troy. I have company. She just arrived. But be prepared to tell me every little detail. Daughter, thank you. And thank Dr. Baskerville for me. He's a good man. You'll make a lovely couple." She hung up before I could protest.

"How'd she take it?" David asked, looking more relaxed than he had all day.

"She's very pleased and relieved. She told me to thank you."

Mr. Fontaine fidgeted in his chair. "What's this all about? Seems to me if I just helped save somebody's life, I ought to know how I did it."

David's eyes locked with mine, a question in his. "Be my guest," I said, collapsing in the chair, suddenly exhausted and wobbly-legged. I hadn't eaten since the bagels and orange juice this morning and with nothing to distract me any longer, the hungries had finally gotten my attention. I vowed to reward myself tonight with the thickest steak on the hospital's dining room menu.

"Show him the other photo," he said, jolting me out of my daydream. "Hey, are you all right?"

"Floating on air," I responded, pulling out the enlargements. "This was taken on Innocence in 1943. We don't know what he was doing there. Probably never will. But—" I stopped, brought up short by the stunned expression on his face. "What is it, Mr. Fontaine?"

"This," he said, waving the smaller photograph, "this here is Vinnie Quarles. But this other one, he has Vinnie's face and Vinnie's hair and Vinnie's mouth, but he does not have Vinnie's coal-black eyes. I'm sorry, little miss, but this other man is *not* Vinnie Quarles."

"I should have seen it," I said for the fifth time, pounding on my knee in frustration. "I saw the subtle difference between the two faces, but I put it down to their ages—one was a gangly teenager and the other a mature man. But how could I have missed the eyes?"

"Will you please stop beating on yourself?" David reached over and placed a gentling hand around my raised fist without taking his eyes off the road. The sun had long since disappeared behind the thick foliage of the treetops. We were deep in Low Country countryside headed back toward Innocence, speeding through rural areas in which the only illumination was supplied by a star-strewn canopy overhead and the ricochet of the Honda's headlights off the passing scene. "The features aren't all that distinct in the earlier snapshot. Besides, the sepia tones of those old photos make it impossible to tell much of anything. It was a mistake anyone would have made."

"But what am I going to do, David? Tell Aunt Jay that yes, Vinnie Quarles was alive in 1945; unfortunately, he isn't the white man you bashed across the head in 1943. They just happened to be dead ringers for each other, so you'll have to put off the surgery a little longer?"

"Oh, my God." David slapped himself on the forehead. "I just wasted three hours of your time. I'm sorry, Troy. Vinnie Quarles was black."

"What?"

"All the residents on Jacques Landing are black. I assumed you knew that; I told you they may be distant relations of mine."

"David." I placed a hand on his arm. "My mother's family is not quite as light as Mr. Fontaine's but they're damned close, so it's obvious that somewhere back down the line a Caucasian slipped into somebody's bed, whether by invitation or not. Having a white ancestor's not all that unusual. As for you, how could anybody who's black and has green eyes not have a white wing of the family?"

He laughed. "You have a point. And they're hazel, not green."

"Then you're color-blind. But to backtrack: What should I do about Aunt Jay? Tell her we were wrong?"

David concentrated on the road for the next mile or two. "Under ordinary circumstances," he said finally, "I think a patient is entitled to the truth. But these aren't ordinary circumstances, not by a long shot. Mrs. Wingate's *got* to have that surgery." He bounced his fist against the steering wheel for emphasis. "If you want my opinion, I'd sit on this for the time being. McCall's bound to have her on the table first thing in the morning. Maybe even tonight. You can tell her when she comes around."

"If she survives it."

"If she survives it. Regardless of the outcome, she'll be going into surgery with her mind at ease and that's very important."

He was right. Letting the truth wait a few hours would do far more good than harm. Suddenly I remembered Miss Lacey. "Oh, David, I need to find a phone."

"Be my guest," he said. In a compartment between the seats was a cellular phone.

I found the number I'd scribbled on a Post-It and dialed, hoping Blanche Lacey wasn't the kind who went to bed with the sun. She answered on the first ring.

"Troy, thank goodness! I was beginning to think everyone was deserting me. I know where Mabel is, but where are you?"

"On the way back to Innocence." I broke the news about Nathan Stokes and explained the results of the trip to Jacques Landing. "What about you? Any luck?"

"Nothing that helps. Poor Nathan. I'll have to wire some flowers. But you may have run all over the state for nothing, Troy. Elva decided to come clean. She left a message on my answering machine this afternoon."

"Hallelujah! What did she say?"

"It doesn't make much sense, but then, Elva seldom does. She said it would take some skullduggery but she knew where she could find proof that that man left Innocence under his own steam. I considered calling Julia, but thought I'd better wait until I hear what Elva has to say."

Relief washed over me like a spring shower. "What time are you expecting her?"

"I assumed she'd be here at four. I'm still waiting. But do feel free to drop by, dear. I'll put the kettle on and we'll all have tea. Bye, now." She hung up and I hit the End button.

I threw my head back and closed my eyes. "It's over, after all. Miss Peterson's getting the proof we need. This has been the longest two days I've ever spent. I'm used to stress at work, but this . . . "

"What kind of work do you do?" David asked.

"Director of an adult education community center. And this is the second day of my vacation. But it's really not over yet, is it? There's the surgery to get through first. Will you be assisting?"

"Oh, no," he said, slowing to take an exit that brought us up onto a four-lane highway. "Don't worry. McCall's good, among the best on the East Coast."

I hesitated for only a heartbeat and then asked the question that had been sitting on the tip of my tongue since Mr. Fontaine's remark to David. So I'm nosy. Sue me. "You're leaving Innocence General?"

He winced. "I'd hoped you'd missed that. Yes, I am."

"Why?"

He waited until a sixteen-wheeler roared past. "I came as a favor to a friend who wanted to go back to school for a couple of years. I'm sort of saving his space for him. I could probably stay on permanently, but I don't want to. I want to contribute, make a difference. And I'm not doing it here."

"How can you say that?" I demanded.

"I didn't say I'm not helping, but that's not enough, Troy, that's all."

It was the first time he'd actually called me other than Ms. Burdette, even though I'd asked him to several times today. The fact that he finally had pleased me immensely, enough so I realized how much of a friend he'd become in a little more than a day. I poked at the thought, examining it from various angles, and decided that it was okay. Sure, Wade and I had been friends for years before that changed. In this instance, however, I wouldn't be around long enough for the relationship to morph into anything else. Lord knows I wasn't ready for anything else.

"What would you really like to do?" I asked, curious as to what drove this man.

"I've always wanted to be a family doctor like the one who took care of me and my brothers and sisters, even when we couldn't pay him. Don't misunderstand, Troy. I've thoroughly enjoyed treating the people of Innocence, but they've already succeeded with their lives and are resting on their laurels. My concern is for the ones who're struggling to make their way up, the ones with no medical insurance even though they're working."

I knew precisely who he meant. They were my students. Fortunately, they had my brother, Jimmy, and his neighborhood clinic, which sounded like exactly what David was saying he wanted. I considered telling him about Jimmy's setup, but couldn't bring myself to do it, at least not yet. Perhaps after Jay was out of surgery and recuperating and my mind was clearer. At this point the thought of David in the building next door to the Adult Ed Center day in and day out turned my brain to scrambled eggs.

"So how are you going to work it?" I asked.

"I've already put out some feelers. Once Danny gets back I'll follow up on them. That's enough about me. Are you happy doing what you do? Is it what you imagined yourself doing, say, ten years ago?"

I debated whether to answer him truthfully, then decided that, considering how helpful he'd been, it was the least I could do. "Ten years ago I imagined myself as wife of Wade Prentiss and mother of his children. I envisioned launching a computer-related business from home so I could have the best of both worlds: I could work in a field that interested me and still be home for my children. Now I work with mothers, most of whom have no home at all. It's not what I'd planned, but it'll do."

"I see. You can't have children, right?"

"Right."

"I'm sorry. Really sorry, because I sense you're still in love with your husband, right?"

"No." My answer surprised me. "If you'd asked me that this morning, I would have said yes, probably out of habit. I loved Wade so deeply for so long, enough to let him out of our marriage so he could find and marry someone who could give him the children he wanted so desperately."

"You didn't."

"I did. And I guess technically I do still love him, but it's different now. I'm not in love with him anymore. That concept is so new, I still haven't gotten used to it. But I will. I will."

David shot me an enigmatic look. "Wade was a fool. Where do you want me to take you, back to the hospital?"

I nodded, and mused during the remaining miles about how different he was from Wade, who could talk about himself for hours on end. Fortunately for Wade, I'd loved him enough to listen. But I realized now how often I'd secretly wished he'd been as interested in hearing what I thought as he was in his own ambitions and goals.

As we crossed the causeway, my stomach announced its displeasure with its resemblance to a vacuum. "David, is there anything like a McDonald's on this island? Miss Lacey's making tea but I'm hungry enough to eat the kettle."

He frowned. "When's the last time you ate?"

"This morning. I've been on the run ever since."

"You must think I'm one hell of a lousy date," he said, shaking his head in disgust. "We'll stop at the Hometown Deli. They make a dynamite turkey club. And we can pick up some of those ridiculous finger sandwiches for Miss Lacey. That way you won't be eating alone."

At this point a turkey club sounded like a four-course meal. It also looked like one, since it turned out to be a creation worthy of Dagwood Bumstead. The Hometown Deli was obviously a favorite of the locals; all the tables were full and there was a line at the counter. By the time we left with our two carry-out boxes, it was almost ten o'clock.

We were getting into the Honda, my stomach knotting with hunger, when I heard my name. Henry, on his way into the Deli, had spotted us.

"That is you," he said, peering at me with a squint. "Evenin', Dr. Baskerville. I saw Mabel earlier today. She told me you got your cat back. How's Julia doing?"

"Not well, but she'll probably have her surgery tomorrow morning."

"That's dandy," he said, his wrinkled face crinkling even more with a smile. "So you cleared up that little mystery of hers. No wonder you was hotfootin' it up Central so fast a little while ago. You got to be careful about your speed, Miz Burdette. They'll ticket you in a minute and there's no talkin' your way out of it."

"Thanks for the warning," I said, "but it wasn't me you saw. The Buick's been parked at the hospital since this afternoon."

He frowned. "Is that a fact? Guess I was mistook. Well, my best to Julia. I'll be praying for her."

I thanked him and climbed into the Honda, wondering if I had the willpower to leave the turkey club alone until I got to Miss Lacey's. Unfortunately, once we arrived at Innocence General, I lost my appetite. The slot where I'd left Jay's Buick was occupied by a monster recreational vehicle.

"Wait a minute," David said, as I began hyperventilating. "Just calm down. Are you sure this is where you left it?"

"Positive. Henry was right. It must have been the Buick. Oh, my God, what am I going to tell Aunt Jay?"

"For the time being, nothing. Get the phone out while I park." He zipped back down the row and careened into the doctors' parking lot. Taking the phone from me, he called the police station. "Leon? Dave Baskerville. Look, man, someone's stolen Mrs. Wingate's Buick. We ran into Henry at the Deli. He said he saw it going north on Central. You might check the gatehouse to see if it's left the island. Take my pager number," he said, and rattled it off. "I'm with Ms. Burdette. If you want to reach her, call me. Is that all right?" he directed at me.

"Fine." I was beyond any response requiring more than a one-syllable answer.

"Keep me posted, Leon." He hit the End button and was replacing the phone just as the aforementioned pager went off. He removed it from his breast pocket. "Three East," he muttered. "Guess I'd better get inside. If it looks like I'm going to get hung up with a patient, I'll leave the pager with you. Are you okay?" he asked, releasing my seatbelt.

I nodded, still in shock. Jay's beloved Bernice gone. What else could go wrong?

He cut around the building to the Emergency Room entrance with me trotting behind like an obedient puppy. As soon as we stepped inside, it was obvious that, even though there were no patients in the waiting area, conditions were not normal. The receptionist saw us and froze for a split second before picking up the phone and turning away as she dialed. A nurse I didn't recognize came through the swinging doors, spotted David, and backed through the doors again, shouting, "Dr. Jones, Dr. Baskerville's here!"

A stocky fireplug of a man in a white jacket and granny glasses perched on the end of his nose barreled through the doors. "Dave, thank God. I need to speak to you."

"I'll go on up," I said, and headed for the elevator as David crossed to meet the man. They went into a huddle just out of earshot. Waiting for the next car to arrive, I tried to remember whether I'd locked the Buick. I was certain I had. When you live in a metropolitan area, you lock up automatically. It's habit. To do otherwise is to kiss your car goodbye.

"What!" David's startled exclamation made me look around. He stared at his companion, dumbfounded. "How could that have happened?"

Dr. Jones pulled him away even farther, turning his back to the room as he spoke in hushed tones, his hands flying as he gestured for emphasis.

David stood unmoving for a second, before spinning around and hurrying back to me. The expression on his face was a mixture of anger and concern. "Troy. There's a problem."

"What is it?"

"Mrs. Wingate's gone."

I felt the blood drain from my cheeks. "She's dead?"

"No, no. I meant it literally. She's gone. Zip. Disappeared."

10

"What do you mean, disappeared? How could she simply disappear?" Panic gripped my throat in a choke hold, sending my contralto into coloratura range.

"They don't know how it happened, just when," Dr. Jones said. "They had a Code Blue on the floor, which required everyone's attention for a few minutes. When Maggie went to take Mrs. Wingate's blood pressure and temperature, the room was empty."

"Where was the person from Security who was supposed to be watching her room?" I demanded.

"They could only be spared during the night shift. I guess they thought you understood that. And under ordinary circumstances there would be someone at the desk at all times during the day. It was pure bad luck the desk clerk was in the Ladies when the Code Blue was called. Security's checking the stairwells and utility spaces. Housekeeping's searching all their storage closets. If she's in this hospital, we'll find her."

"It had better be soon." David's eyes seemed to glow with a feral anger. He walked me back to the elevators, an arm around my shoulders. "I'm sorry, Troy. I don't know what else to say."

I had been prepared for a number of different scenarios—working my way through Jay's mystery, not working my way through it and lying as if I had, Jay becoming worse, undergoing surgery, even failing to survive before I could give her the answers she needed so badly for peace of mind. But Jay disappearing? For the second time in one day I felt myself coming unraveled, as if someone had found a loose thread and was pulling, pulling, pulling on it until there'd be nothing of me left.

"Give me a minute," I said to David, as we left the elevator, and disengaged his arm. As comforting as it was, it was also a crutch. I'd spent the three years since the divorce becoming accustomed to standing on my own two feet. I'd learned today that my self-confidence was still a bit frayed around the edges and more fragile than I'd thought, but it was time to get back on track, for myself and for Jay. Wherever she was, she was still depending on me. David waited quietly, watching me curiously. I let him wait, determined to get my thoughts in order.

"Jay had a visitor," I said, my brain beginning to function again. "She mentioned it while I was talking to her from Mr. Fontaine's. No name, though."

David gazed at me intently, as if he recognized that something had changed for me. "Let's go find out if the nurses know who it was."

On the surface, things looked entirely normal on 3 East until we saw the three responsible for Jay's end of the hall. They stood behind the counter at the nurses' station, one in tears, the others hovering nearby looking helpless. Seeing us, they closed ranks, their faces taut with anxiety.

"Relax, everybody." David stepped behind the counter to give each one a reassuring pat. "No one blames you. You can't be everywhere at once. Who was the Code Blue?"

"Mr. Younger," Maggie said, wiping her nose. "He's stable now. But we weren't gone that long, Doctor, I swear we weren't. I don't know how she could have gotten away from here so fast. I'm so sorry, Miss Burdette."

"I'm not blaming you," I said, wanting to get past this stage of the proceedings. "The important thing now is to find her. Are her clothes gone?"

The response was three blank faces. Maggie recovered first. "We didn't think to look."

I headed at a trot for Jay's room, where the sight of the empty bed, the covers thrown back in disarray, brought a lump to my throat. The navy suit and blouse, hanging precisely as I'd left them, and the tiny blue pumps I'd placed on the overhead shelf of the closet sent a surge of panic up my spine. The last time I'd seen Jay she'd been in a hospital gown. Julia Wingate would never have left this room of her own volition with her fanny exposed. I looked at David and saw a mirror of my thoughts. He skirted the bed to pick up her phone. "Leon needs to know about this."

"I talked to Aunt Jay perhaps an hour and a half ago," I said to Maggie. "She had a visitor. Did you notice who it was?"

"I wasn't here then. It was Barbara's shift. I'll call her. The only person I've seen coming out of this room is Reverend Allenby. He's probably in the chapel now."

"Where's the chapel?" I asked.

Maggie followed me out. "First floor, right next to the coffee shop. We'll find her, Miss Burdette. I just know we will."

Wishing I could be as optimistic as she was, I managed a smile for her before skipping the elevator and taking the stairs to the first floor.

The chapel was charming, a small room with five pews on each side of a center aisle. The altar, on a simple raised platform, was covered with white linen and flanked by a pair of fresh floral arrangements on tall, brass pedestals. On the rear wall behind the altar, an enormous stained glass panel acted as focal point of the room, the gleaming white dove in its center almost blinding in the light spilling from a tiny fresnel mounted on the ceiling. An elderly woman, the only person in the room, sat in the rear, her eyes closed, a rosary in her hands.

I was about to leave when it occurred to me that there might be an office behind the door to the left of the dais. I tapped at it, opened it without waiting for a response, and found Reverend Allenby sitting behind a small desk, head bowed, hands folded in prayer, so still that he might have been a statue. Aside from a couple of folding chairs, a coatrack, and a bookcase, volumes neatly aligned, there was nothing else in the room. After a moment trying to decide whether to step outside until he'd finished, it occurred to me that he just might be catnapping. I made one of those self-conscious throat-clearing sounds. He opened his eyes and smiled.

"A wise decision," he said, rising slowly. "But I wasn't asleep, not this time anyway. How can I help you?" He tilted his head to one side. "We've met, haven't we? I've seen you in a patient's room. I'm sorry, I don't remember which one."

"Mrs. Wingate in 3E118." I closed the door behind me. "I understand you stopped to see her a little while ago."

His long, Lincoln-like features cleared. "Of course, you're her niece. Yes, I dropped by to leave a Scripture card for her."

"Was she there?"

Brow furrowed in a quizzical frown, he waved me to one

of the chairs. "No. She might have been in the lavatory. I
didn't wait to see. I try to make myself available here in the
chapel three evenings a week, and I was running late. Is
there a problem?"

"She's disappeared," I said. "They're searching the hospital for her."

"Dear Lord." He came out from behind the desk immediately. "How long has she been gone?" I told him what little I knew as we left the chapel and took the elevator to the
third floor. "So you found out what she wanted to know?"
he asked, taking my arm as we left the car. "She must have
been very relieved."

"It was the wrong man." I had to hurry to keep up with
him. For someone Miss Potee claimed had celebrated his
ninetieth birthday a couple of years before, he was in dynamite shape.

"The wrong man? I don't understand."

"It's too involved to explain right now. The important
thing is that I didn't get a chance to tell her I'd made a mistake. She thought the mystery was solved, so there was no
reason for her to leave."

"I see your point. Ladies," he said, approaching the
nurses' station.

Maggie was hanging up the phone. "Barbara just got
home. She says the only visitor Mrs. Wingate had while she
was here was a lady she didn't know by name. Tall, lots of
dyed red hair tied with a ribbon, on the plump side, in
black."

"The ribbon sounds like Elva Peterson," the Reverend
supplied without hesitation. "I thought I saw her earlier,
but I was mistaken. The woman I saw getting off the elevator was wearing trousers. I've never known Elva to wear
trousers."

Trousered or not, if she had been here, perhaps she'd

felt Jay was entitled to the information she had before she told the rest of us. Regardless, I still couldn't imagine Jay leaving with her without dressing first. "Give me a minute to call Miss Lacey. Miss Peterson may be there."

Blanche answered in the middle of the first ring. "Troy! Where are you? Tea's ready."

I explained the problem. "Did Miss Peterson show up yet?"

"No, and she hasn't called back. Mabel just dropped in and she's worried about her. Mabel, Julia's disappeared."

"Give me that thing. Troy?" Miss Potee bellowed in my ear. "What the hell is going on?"

"I don't know. Aunt Jay's gone. So's the Buick."

"Don't go anywhere. I'll be right there."

I disconnected and called my room across the street, just in case. I'd feel like a grade-A fool if Jay was there and I hadn't checked. I let the phone ring ten times. Jay didn't answer. Neither did The Deacon. I counted my blessings. The Deacon has been known to answer a phone.

"Would it help if I called out the Finders?" the Reverend was asking David as I returned to the nurses' station. The response came from elsewhere.

"Yes, sir, we can use all the help we can get." Junior Haskins, more pear-shaped than ever in jeans, waddled toward us, Leon Ficker, in uniform, on his tail. "Evenin', Miz Burdette. Can't tell you how sorry I am about all this. I saw Norm Cheek downstairs. He says he and his men have covered every inch of this hospital. Miz Julie ain't here. We also checked with the gatekeeper. Her Buick ain't left this island, so she's still around here somewheres. Reverend, if you'll organize the Finders, I'd 'preciate it." For my benefit he said, "Sometimes Alzheimer's patients wander away. The Finders are a volunteer group who search for them."

"Where would you like them to start?" the Reverend asked.

"Ask them to walk Main Street and look in any shop still open. The rest of my men will cover the boulevards."

"I can check North End pier and the shoreline ocean-side," David volunteered.

"Good idea. We'll divide up the residential section and hit every cross street, like we did after the hurricane. I'll take the courthouse area and every parking lot on Innocence. Okay. Ficker's gonna hold down the fort at the jail—"

"Aw, Junior," Leon complained.

"That's an important job, because everybody's gonna be reportin' in to you every hour on the hour."

"Junior." David spoke quietly. "It's imperative we find Mrs. Wingate as soon as possible. Her aneurysm's a time bomb. It could rupture at any moment. If we don't operate soon, we won't need to. Am I clear?"

Grim-faced, Officer Haskins rocked from heel to toe. "Gotcha. Everybody understand what they're supposed to be doing? Then let's hit it. Miz Burdette, if I could talk to you for a minute. In private."

"Use Mrs. Wingate's room," David suggested.

"Be there directly, Miz Burdette. I want a word with Ficker."

I left them with their heads together, and went into 3E118. There wasn't an emptier room in the hospital. I could still detect the faint aroma of Chanel No. 5, Jay's signature scent. Wade always introduced her to his friends as "the best-smelling old lady I know."

My family had fallen in love with Julia Wingate the first time they'd met her, which happened to be at my wedding to her great-nephew. She'd invaded my bedroom as I was dressing and had chased everyone else out, Mom included.

While she hooked me into my bridal gown, she grilled me about my attitudes about myself, life, marriage, children, work—a seriocomic reversal of the father of the bride subjecting a potential son-in-law to the third degree.

When she'd finished, she looked me in the eye and said, "Honey, Wade's smart and ambitious and he ought to make a right good husband. But let me tell you something: that business about marriage being a fifty-fifty proposition is a bunch of bull; it's more like fifty-five/forty-five. Sometime it'll be you that's ten percent up, most times it'll be you ten percent down. But don't you *ever* let your end of it go below that or you'll have me to deal with." When my mother heard that, Julia Wingate became an honorary member of our family.

Until a few minutes ago, finding Jay's phantom had been sort of a bizarre scavenger hunt, and I'd been fully prepared to cheat in order to win, if it would have gotten that old lady's backside onto the operating table. The fact that someone had taken a shot at her had shaken me, the probable death of Nathan Stokes even more so, but on the whole, neither incident had altered my scavenger-hunt viewpoint. That had changed. Now I was mad, terrified for Jay, and dead serious about getting at the truth someone wanted left alone.

Junior Haskins tapped at the doorsill, grabbed a chair on his way in, and moved it to face me. "Miz Burdette, I need to know, do you think Miz Julie left on her own in that Buick of hers?"

"No. Her clothes are still here, all of them. Besides, I've got the keys, and the extra set's in my room in her jewelry case."

His lips closed in a tight line. "So we've got a car thief to worry about, too. Goddammit! Excuse m' French. Hold on a minute." I waited while he used the phone to alert the gatekeeper. "It still hasn't gone by Cable," he said, hanging up. "And won't. But if you don't think she walked out voluntarily, Miz Burdette, you know what that leaves. Somebody abducted her. The nurses mention any visitors today?"

"There's a possibility Miss Peterson was here earlier, and Reverend Allenby, but by the time he came in, Aunt Jay was gone."

"Well, if she didn't walk out on her own, that changes the whole complexion of things. We maybe need to get some big guns in here, the FBI or at least the state. But before I do that I have to make sure she didn't decide she needed some air and will stroll back in here while we're tearing the island apart. Hizzoner would have my job in a minute. 'Course, before long I just might give it to him. You find out anything new since this morning?"

I brought him up to date, beginning at the point when I'd stopped by the station to see him. He listened, massaging his temples, as if trying to calm a headache. "You're telling me you think somebody meant to kill Nate to keep him from talking? With crackers?"

It did sound ridiculous. I launched a defense. "It's just that I can see someone sneaking something like candy in to him. But cheese crackers? Something guaranteed to make him very ill?"

"Seems to me this visitor was probably just bringing something he knew Stokes liked. They would have no way of knowing cheese could kill him. I'll follow up on it, best I can. Anything else I—"

"I don't care who's in there with her, I'm goin' in." Miss Potee's voice echoed out in the hall. "Troy?" The door banged open and her bulk filled the opening. "She's not back yet? Junior Haskins, why are you here jawin' with Troy instead of out there looking for Little Bits?"

"I'll be leavin' directly, Mabel. Me and Miz Burdette have business. If you'll just wait outside—"

"I ain't goin' nowhere." Miss Potee picked up the second chair and put it down with a thump. She lowered herself into it, folded her arms across her chest, and glared at Mr. Haskins. The dare was implied and Junior Haskins backed down. Faced with a woman of Miss Potee's dimensions, bigger men than he would probably have done precisely the same.

"Well, have it your way," he said, "but don't interrupt. You was saying, Miz Burdette . . . "

"David . . . Dr. Baskerville . . . identified the location of the snapshot I found in Mr. Stokes's room and drove me there."

"What snapshot?" Miss Potee barged in. I handed it to her. "By God, this is him!"

"Gimme that," Mr. Haskins said. She passed it over and he blinked once, twice. "Be damned. Where was it taken?"

"Jacques Landing. His name was Vincent Quarles, but his eyes were very dark, not light like the eyes of the man in our enlargement. Plus, Vinnie Quarles was black, not white. He isn't our man."

Miss Potee leaned over to stare at it. "Could have fooled me."

"Me, too," Mr. Haskins said, rising. "Well, for the time being, the most important thing is findin' Miz Julie. And I'll talk to Leland, too. He'll kick and holler about damagin' Innocence's image, but he's got to see that this is serious. And I promise you, if he doesn't cooperate and let us do our proper job, I'm quittin'. Where can I reach you, Miz Burdette?"

I hadn't thought that far and took a moment to decide what was simplest. "If I don't answer the phone in here, try Hospitality House. You can leave a message for me if I'm not in the room."

He crammed his cap on his head. "Chin up, ladies. We may look like Keystone Kops sometimes, but there's a lot of good ol' common sense on our force. We'll find Miz Julie. We have old folks wanderin' off all the time. We've never lost one of them yet." His departing smile was forced, tight.

"A good man." Miss Potee said, getting up and closing the door behind him. "Looka here, Troy, Little Bits pulled a disappearin' act once before. I need to know if she's done it again." Her voice was hoarse, the pain in her eyes raw and gripping. Seeing it grounded me, a welcome reminder that I wasn't the only person on the island who loved Julia Wingate a great deal.

I met her gaze squarely. "I don't know what happened in here," I admitted, "but I'd bet my life that 1943 was the one and only time Julia Wingate ever ran from anything. I have a confession to make, Miss Potee. When this first began, I started out believing that, no matter what she thought, she had probably injured Miss Lucy's boarder, but hadn't killed him."

Miss Potee's reaction was a sheepish grin. "You aren't by yourself, little girl."

"But when she decided to put off the surgery until I'd found out what really happened that night, I made a decision of my own. I'd give it one day, two at the most, and if I hadn't had any luck, I'd tell her whatever I had to so she'd go ahead with the surgery."

"I'm glad to hear it. I'd have done the same thing in your place." She went back to her chair, sat down and began to fan herself with a handkerchief from the breast pocket of her uniform.

"All that's changed. Somebody doesn't want anyone to know what happened that night at Miss Lucy's and it looks like that somebody's willing to do anything to see that no one finds out."

"Why do you say that?"

I began to pace, putting my thoughts in order as I rattled them off. "First, there's no record that Jay tried to confess three years ago. The person she talked to at the police station wasn't even on the force."

"What? Who was it?"

"Don't know. A man with a dark beard, fifty or so. Mr. Haskins is still trying to figure out who it was."

A frown marred Miss Potee's forehead. "What else?"

"She was shot that same day, standing out there on the pier. Let's consider that suspicious coincidence number one. She comes back yesterday and this time manages to confess to Mr. Haskins and also manages to get the whole story printed in the newspaper."

"So now everybody knows we're searching for the man's identity and what happened to him after that night."

"Right. And when I went to talk to perhaps the only person who might have been able to tell us something about the man—"

"Little Nathan. I was so upset about Bits being gone, I forgot to ask you what happened. Did you find out anything?"

"He's dead. Just before I got there, he had a mysterious visitor." I described the scene I'd encountered. "And on his wall I find this photograph that's a dead ringer for the boarder Aunt Jay thought she'd killed, only he's definitely not the same man in our enlargement. The thing is, the snapshot's fifty-six years old, yet Mr. Stokes still had it, so it must have meant something special to him. Either he knew Vinnie Quarles or his mother, or why keep it? How many coincidences is that? I've lost count."

"Me, too. Poor Little Nate."

"On top of all that," I went on, "Miss Peterson leaves Miss Lacey a message that she can get the proof our man

left Innocence alive. Then a visitor who may have been
Miss Peterson comes by here to see Aunt Jay and poof, Jay
disappears."

"What do you mean, may have been?" Miss Potee
demanded. "One thing about Elva, ain't no way to mistake
her for anybody else."

"The nurse who saw her mentioned the red hair and the
ribbon, but this woman was in black and wearing slacks."

"Wasn't Elva then. You couldn't pay her to wear pants.
Says it ain't feminine. But she still hadn't shown up at
Blanche's when I left there. Let me call her."

I went out to the nurses' station while she used Jay's
phone. A distraught Maggie shook her head at me.
"Nothing yet, Miss Burdette. Where could she be?"

I had no answer for her. "It's early yet," I said, and
returned to the room. Even with Miss Potee there, it still
felt empty.

"I don't like this," she said, hanging up. "Blanche still
hasn't heard a thing and says Elva's phone doesn't answer
either. This ain't like Elva. She wouldn't miss a chance to
show everybody how smart she is. I'm gonna go check her
house. Why don't you come with me? We can let the nurses
know you're with me. They have my pager number. If Jay
turns up, they'll get us."

The thought of waiting there alone or across the street in
my room was more than I could tolerate. "You're on." We
grabbed our gear and left.

Elva Peterson, it turned out, lived one short block over
on the street behind Hospitality House, so at Miss Potee's
suggestion, we walked. It was a relief, since I felt as if I'd
been shut up in cars all day, and a challenge, since Miss
Potee's legs were considerably longer than mine. We chatted as we walked. More accurately, she chatted and I
panted. I was getting a serious aerobic workout.

"I'm still trying to figure out why Mr. Stokes had that snapshot," I managed. "Suppose Vinnie had stayed at Miss Lucy's—"

"Uh-uh," Miss Potee said firmly. "He might have visited, but he damn sure didn't stay. A black man boardin' at a white lady's house? No way, José."

"You saw the photo. Vinnie didn't look black. We do know the light-eyed man boarded with her and we also know that Vinnie Quarles looked enough like him to be a twin. If the two of them ran into one another, it might have made them ask a few questions about their respective parentages." The more I thought about it, the more the idea excited me. "What if they were related, Miss Potee? I mean, to look that much alike . . . "

"Even if they were, that wouldn't explain why Little Nate would keep the picture."

"Granted," I said, feeling argumentative, "but I think the resemblance between the two is important. Maybe we need to find out more about Vinnie."

"Couldn't hurt," Miss Potee said. "The problem is getting the people on Jacques Landing to tell you anything. Elva's is the next house along," she said, pointing.

If I hadn't been so preoccupied with our conversation, I might have realized sooner where we were. As it was, I spotted the upper floors of Hospitality House through the trees. We were directly behind it, one street over, in front of the house that had captured my attention this morning. It still looked out of place, as if the owner had New England roots he was determined to plant on sandy Innocence soil, whether those roots would thrive there or not. There was an austerity about the rear view that had fooled me. The street view was an architectural horror, three stories of Victorian gingerbread with a corner tower and a widow's walk around the front half of the roof for good measure. The windows were dark; the house looked empty.

"Who lives here?" I asked, slowing.

"Reverend Allenby. A sad sight, ain't it? It was right handsome in its day. If it was anyone else but the Reverend living in it, the place would have been condemned and torn down years ago. The way I hear it, there's so much that needs fixin', it's dangerous."

"I'm kind of relieved to know it's his," I admitted. "I thought I saw someone standing on his back porch early this morning. I got the impression whoever it was might have been looking over at Hospitality House with binoculars or something."

"Couldn't have been the Reverend. He was with Mrs. Boston most of the night. He had just left there when we saw him at the hospital this morning. One of the boys he adopted stops by most evenings to check on him and bring him something to eat, but he never stays. There's Elva's car. And her lights are on. Good. She's back." Her stride lengthened, and I speeded up even more to stay abreast of her.

We turned into the walkway of a small stucco cottage sitting high on brick pilings, its front door open. A Volkswagen convertible, top down, was parked under the side of the house. Miss Potee took the steps to the porch, all twelve of them, as if she was walking on level ground.

"Elva?" she called, rapping on the screen door and going on in. "You home? Elva?"

It was an old house, built before the days of sheetrock and drywall. The floors felt solid underfoot, with no yield, no squeak. Even with all the lights blazing, however, I had a feeling Miss Peterson wasn't there. I followed Miss Potee's zigzagging path through a furniture-crammed living room, dining room, and kitchen. The decor reflected the personality of its owner, busy and frou-frou times three. Either Miss Peterson was seriously into crafts or was an avid aficionado of yard sales. Despite all the lacquered boxes, doodads and crocheted doilies, there wasn't a speck of dust on anything.

"Bedroom's this-a-way. Elva, you back here?" Miss Potee strode through a hall off the kitchen. "Dammit, Elva, where are you, girl?"

By the time I caught up with her she was in the bedroom, lilac and white, as feminine a space as I'd ever seen—Priscilla curtains, matching spread with a double tier of lace-edged flounces sweeping the floor around the tester bed. The patent leather purse Miss Peterson had carried this morning sat on the glass-topped double dresser, the fabric tote bag against the lamp on her bedside table. A shopping bag lay on its side at the foot of the bed.

I crossed to the dresser and opened the purse. "Wallet, compact, comb, et cetera," I recited, without removing the contents. "She can't have gone far without her wallet."

"Lemme check the back yard," Miss Potee said, and hurried out.

I went back to the hallway and, holding my breath, slowly nudged the bathroom door open. Empty. The dress she'd worn this morning was draped across a wicker hamper, slip and pantyhose on top. Returning to the bedroom, I peered in the shopping bag on the floor. Empty except for a receipt. I fished it out. Elaine's Casuals, today's date. She'd purchased several items, had charged them to her Visa card.

I vaulted through a series of mental hoops and then, feeling more like an intruder by the second, searched until I dug up what I was looking for. Miss Potee found me perched on the edge of the bathtub, a small wicker trash can between my feet.

"What?" she said, cutting to the chase.

I dropped my bounty into her hand. "They're the labels off the things she bought today. A pair of jeans, black, size 14."

"Jesus." She lowered the lid of the toilet and sat down. "The last time I wore a fourteen, I was fourteen."

"A black top of some kind, medium." I fished the bottom of the shoe box out of the trash can. "One pair of black sneakers, eight and a half. One black rain hat."

"Elva in jeans," Miss Potee muttered. "Never seen her in pants and never seen her in black, either. So it probably was her at the hospital. Troy, you figure she sneaked Bits out of there?"

I simply had no answer. If she had proof that our man had left Innocence alive, what reason would she have had to move Jay out of the hospital? It made no sense. Unless . . .

I used the Princess phone in Miss Peterson's bedroom and called Miss Lacey, just in case she'd finally turned up there. "We're at Miss Peterson's. She's not here. Did you tell her that Nathan Stokes was dead and how he'd died?"

"No. She left the message on the answering machine. I never actually talked to her."

Another dead end. I'd thought that if Miss Peterson had found out Mr. Stokes was dead, she might have suspected that whoever had told her where Mr. Stokes was living had hurried to get to him before I could. That might lead her to think that same person could pose a danger to her and Aunt Jay.

"By the way," Miss Lacey said, "I figured out which picture Elva sneaked away with. It was taken at Angela Allenby's Sweet Sixteen party. She's in it, and Angel, of course, so we probably shouldn't make too much of her taking it. Are you and Mabel coming back?"

I made apologies for myself, adding Miss Potee's when she signaled I should do the same for her. "I'll try to stop by tomorrow, but until we find Aunt Jay, I can't make any promises."

"Let's go," Miss Potee said, when I'd finished. "Damn that woman, why couldn't she have spoken up this morning?" Muttering under her breath, she marched out of the bedroom.

As we made our tortuous way back through the maze of living room furniture, I slowed. A small antique trunk sat under a window, its sides decoupaged to a fare-thee-well. The interior was lined with a white piqué fabric and stacked to the brim with photo albums, letters, and news articles in plastic bags, the papers yellowed with age. Three photo albums and two freezer bags, zippers undone, lay on the floor.

"Look." I pointed to the cache. "Looks like she was going through old pictures and souvenirs. Maybe the proof she said she had to get was in here."

Miss Potee eyed the treasure trove. "Troy, baby, this ain't no time to be picky about observin' the proprieties. See what you can find. I'll sit on the porch and warn you if anyone's comin'."

I dropped to my knees and began with the two bags left on the floor. The first, labeled "Bosom Buddies" with a black marking pen, contained snapshots, faded and cracked, of Elva Louisa Sylvester Peterson as a toddler, then as a schoolgirl, in formal poses and white dresses, long ringlets teasing her shoulders, enormous bow perched atop her head. Evidently she'd worn ribbons all her life.

Older sepia photos featured Miss Peterson with Angela Allenby, who couldn't have had a more fitting first name. Lord knows her nickname, Angel, certainly suited her. She had a round baby face, like the cherubs of Michelangelo and Raphael, and a halo of lustrous blond hair. As she'd grown older, she'd lost some of the baby fat, but the aura of purity and naivete had remained in the shy gaze and sweet smile she turned to the camera. She'd have made a perfect model for the Madonna as a young girl, whereas I could almost track Miss Peterson's career as a flirt. The contrast between the two was startling. I was surprised that the Reverend hadn't discouraged their friendship. Since they'd lived next door to one another, there probably wasn't much he could do about it.

Seeing them together in the photos, however, and the camaraderie they'd shared, explained the pain I'd seen in Miss Peterson's eyes this morning. Miss Lacey's glossies must have opened a warehouse of memories for her. Perhaps I'd jumped to the wrong conclusion about her reasons for going into the trunk. That change in attitude accounted for my rather perfunctory examination of the things in the second plastic bag. In other words, I almost missed how important its contents were.

They were diaries, the earliest dated 1939, a present given to her on her thirteenth birthday. Miss Peterson had put Samuel Pepys to shame. Especially in the beginning, she'd recounted practically every minute of her day and all the minutiae that went with it. By 1941, she'd cut the amount of detail by a third, and the size of her writing by half so she could get more on a page about the crush du jour.

Nineteen forty-two had been a banner year; Elva Peterson had been the belle of the Saturday evening dances, pursued by scores of panting servicemen with lascivious intent. In her next diary, she was seriously considering marriage and had narrowed the field to three. She became a blushing bride in 1945.

"What's going on in there?" Miss Potee called softly.

"Miss . . . I mean Mrs. . . . Peterson just got married. Sorry, I found her diaries and . . . wait a minute here." I checked the previous one, which had detailed innumerable near-seductions—1944. Nineteen forty-three was missing.

I flipped through the envelopes in the trunk. No more journals. Either Mrs. Peterson had skipped keeping a diary for 1943—unlikely—or had skipped with the diary for 1943 sometime today. I went outside.

"It looks like she dug out her diary for 1943 and took it with her. I wonder if she went by the hospital to show it to Aunt Jay."

Miss Potee stood up and stretched. "Might have. Best we get back, see if anybody's heard anything."

No one had. I spent half the night in Aunt Jay's room waiting and praying, the other half at Hospitality House with The Deacon, who, bright-eyed and bushy-tailed, ignored me, too busy playing with one of his cat toys. I sat in the dark, listening to his rough and tumble game until he finally fell asleep, his kitty snores a comfort while I dozed fitfully next to the telephone.

It rang at six sharp the next morning. It was Miss Potee.

"Troy, Henry found the Buick. Somebody had run it off the end of the dock at Ingleside Marina. It was in ten feet of water. Henry's practically apoplectic."

"Oh, God. Have they pulled it out yet? Was . . . was anyone in it?"

"No'm. Empty."

I flopped back in bed with relief. "Where are you?"

"Over to the hospital and no, Bits is not back. Why don't you come over and have breakfast with me? They won't be pulling the Buick out for a while yet."

It sounded like an attractive alternative to sitting alone in the room, waiting for a second call. I promised to be there as soon as I'd gotten The Deacon set up for the day.

By the time I'd showered and dressed, it was six-thirty. I taped a note on the door telling Housekeeping not to bother with the room, asked The Deacon to behave himself, left, and locked the door.

The elevator was to the right. Remembering how out of shape I'd felt walking with Miss Potee last night, I went in the opposite direction to take the stairs at the end of the floor. There were only six flights, but it was still exercise of a sort.

I was going past the window on the fourth floor landing when I became aware of unusual activity in the distance. Dozen Pines golf course sat directly opposite this end of the building, North End pier and the driving range off to the right. The hubbub I'd noticed was on the golf course, but after being married to Wade, I knew that people on a golf course this time of morning was an everyday occurrence. Something about the scene made my pulse jump, however, even though it was just far enough away so that I couldn't actually see what was going on.

I ran down another flight and paused at the window on the landing long enough to check on what difference this vantage point might make. Not a heck of a lot. Wasting no more time, I pounded my way down to the first floor, dashed through the lobby and out onto the street. Turning left, I sprinted the half block to the traffic circle, almost got my clock cleaned darting into the beginning of what passed for the island's morning rush hour, and managed to get to the golf course in one piece.

I stopped to catch my breath, but squinting across the greens, found myself even more breathless. The small group of golfers I'd seen from upstairs included two men in the medium-brown uniform of the Innocence Island police force. A cruiser was parked on the golfpath nearby, angled behind a pine green golf cart. Something was definitely wrong.

Officer Grady saw me first and motioned to the second officer, Junior Haskins, who turned, hands out to deter me, his face sagging with fatigue. Officer Grady was standing with one foot in and one out of a water hazard, where something pale was submerged just out of his reach. My heart began to slam against my ribs.

I ran out of steam and courage perhaps ten yards before I reached Mr. Haskins. Stopping under a lone elm tree, I held onto it for support, watching as he came slowly toward me.

"Believe me, you don't want to come any closer, Miz Burdette," he warned me.

"Please," I croaked, "it's not Aunt Jay, is it? Please tell me it's not Aunt Jay."

He took a deep breath. "It ain't. It's Elva Peterson."

Relief surged through me, then shock. "She's dead?"

He nodded. "Looks like she was strangled, then dragged here—she's all scratched up."

"Oh, my God." My knees gave out and I slumped onto my butt under the tree.

"Funny thing about what she's wearing, though."

I tried to sit up straight. "Black jeans and a black top, right?"

"No, ma'am, she's not. What she's wearing is an Innocence General hospital gown."

11

The word of Mrs. Peterson's murder seemed to spread from one end of Innocence to the other at Mach speed. When I'd flirted with suicide darting across that traffic circle, there had been, excluding Innocence's finest, eight people around the water hazard near the eighteenth hole, with another five or six running toward it. Half an hour later, it looked as if the entire population was in attendance, a packed gallery of stunned, frightened expressions. They watched with agitated whispers as the area was taped off and the medical examiner and police photographers arrived to go through their paces.

Mr. Haskins superintended the process with surprising expertise, requiring me to revise my opinion of his qualifications to handle a murder investigation. After all the photographs and measurements had been taken, Officers Grady and Ficker, the latter looking a little green around the gills, gently maneuvered Mrs. Peterson's body out of the shallow pond up onto the grass, positioning it on the far side of a cruiser strategically parked to mask it from the onlookers. A second round of photographs began.

Poor Leon wasn't the only one feeling green around the gills. I watched from my vantage point under the elm, wrestling to keep my emotions at bay. There were so many of them, not all of them quite worthy of me. I was horrified and frightened, yet glad it wasn't Jay on the other side of that cruiser. I was also a little ashamed of myself. Of all the people I'd met so far, I'd liked Elva Peterson the least. Perhaps it had been her manner, coy and slightly flirtatious, even in the company of women, or the stiletto heels and cutsie-pie ribbons and bows. It may have been because the few snippets I'd read in her diary had introduced me to a scheming Scarlett O'Hara determined to enchant and conquer every male who crossed her path, then to leave the poor sap hot and bothered and wondering what he'd done that she didn't like him anymore. Or perhaps it was because she'd known something about Miss Lucy Stokes's boarder and for whatever reason had kept it to herself instead of coming right out and sharing the information on the spot. If she had, she might still be prancing around in her high heels and Jay might be in surgery instead of God knew where. Regardless, nothing she'd done warranted being murdered.

How could something that had happened five decades before cause so much mayhem today? If Jay hadn't killed the man in 1943, what was there about the incident that was worth the lives of two innocent people fifty-plus years later? The same question applied even if Jay had killed the man. One thing was certain: somebody on this island was a murderer. I scanned the crowd, as if "Guilty" might be written across the forehead of the perpetrator. All I saw were people who appeared to be as horrified and dismayed as I was, including Miss Lacey, and Henry, looking mournful.

Probably the last person to arrive on the scene was The Honorable Leland Spates, who, from his demeanor as he hopped off his golf cart, was the only one who hadn't been told what had happened. I heard him before I saw him, his opening shot, projected with all the volume his lungs could provide. "What the holy hell is going on here? You people get off my golf course! You're ruining the greens!" At that point, he spotted Officers Haskins and Grady and turned it up yet another notch as he waded through the crowd, his face the color of a plum tomato. "Junior! Aaron! Why are y'all standing around looking stupid? My God, you parked your cruisers on the fairway? Move them right now!" He turned back to the assemblage. "And if y'all don't get off my golf course immediately, I'm going to send every livin' ass a bill for greens fees, do I make myself clear?"

No one moved. No one spoke. Everyone simply gaped at him as if he'd lost his mind.

Mr. Haskins, it appeared, had had enough. Hooking his thumbs under his suspenders, he waited until Mr. Spates had cleared the crowd, and halted in front of him before he lowered the boom. "Put a sock in it, you pompous jackass," he said quietly. "In the first place, it's not your goddamn golf course, it belongs to everybody. In the second place, take five steps more and I'm puttin' the cuffs on you for crossin' a police line. This is a crime scene, Leland Spates, and it's already been compromised enough without your big feet stompin' all over evidence."

"Crime scene?" For the first time, he seem to notice the yellow tape strung from tree trunk to tree trunk. Because of the cruiser, however, he had yet to see the body. "What's happened?"

"It's Elva Peterson. She's dead."

Hizzoner seemed genuinely confused. "Here? Impossible. Elva doesn't play golf."

"And never will. The groundskeeper found her in the water hazard, face down."

He blinked. "She drowned? How could she? The water's not deep enough."

"I didn't say she drowned," Mr. Haskins enunciated carefully, "I said she's dead. There's a belt around her neck and I'm pretty sure she wasn't wearing it to start a new fashion trend."

The mayor's bottom jaw descended quarter-inch by quarter-inch, in slow motion. "You mean, somebody killed her?"

"That's exactly what I mean. And you show up hootin' and hollerin' about these folk messin' up your grass when Elva's layin' over there growing wings. Don't think folks won't remember that come election time. Now shut your yap, get out of my face, and let me do my goddamn job."

Mr. Spates gaped at him, blinking with astonishment. "You . . . you can't talk to me like that."

"Yes, I can." Mr. Haskins looked the mayor in the eye. "It took that poor woman's death to remind me that I used to be a damned good cop before I accepted your offer to come home and baby-sit the senior citizens on this island. Well, Your Honor, the ass-kissin' stops right here, right now. And before you get on your high horse, it occurs to me to ask how it is that *you* were the only person the day 'fore yesterday who knew that Miz Julie had tried to confess to murder before. It also occurs to me to wonder if that has anything to do with the fact that there's no record of it in the log."

Spates backed up a step. "I don't know what you're talking about. When you said she was confessing to an old murder, I knew it had to be the same woman I'd run into two or three years back. She was sitting on the bench outside the jail that day and I asked her if there was something I could do for her. She told me she was waiting for a policeman so she could turn herself in for murder. When I realized she meant it had happened fifty years ago, and I knew for a fact there had never been a homicide here, I told her she was mistaken and should leave. When she refused and insisted on waiting, I threatened to have her arrested for trespassing. She didn't even have a visitor's pass, for God's sake. I went back to my office and told Sarah or somebody to track down whoever was on duty and have them escort Mrs. Wingate off the island. That's all."

"Well, you can believe I'm going to check with Sarah about that."

"You're doubting my word?" The mayor puffed up, cheeks, chest, and all.

"You should have listened to Miz Julie. So should I. If we had, she might not have a bullet in her—"

"What?"

"—and might not be missing, probably snatched out of her hospital bed, since she was in no shape to leave voluntarily. And Elva Peterson and maybe Nathan Stokes might be alive."

"Nathan . . . ? Miss Lucy's boy? He's dead, too? What the holy hell is going on around here?"

"A good question. So let me tell you what's going to happen now. I'm gonna start being a cop again, the cop I used to be. I'm gonna be investigatin' a homicide that took place on Innocence, *my* turf, on *my* watch. If you're of a mind to fire me to keep me from performin' my duty, you go right ahead. But I promise you if I'm not around to investigate it, I'm gonna see to it that somebody will be, somebody, say, from the county or the state, and you can bet your boots the media will be hot on their heels, setting up microphones and television cameras and tromping all over the place. It's up to you, Leland. Your call. What's it gonna be?"

"Now, don't be hasty, Junior." The mayor, not being one-hundred-percent fool, obviously saw a need for a rapid change of attitude and policy. Hands behind his back, he began to pace, four steps in one direction, four steps in the other, as if wrestling with a weighty decision. "You're quite right. We owe it to the people of Innocence to take care of our own. It's our business, no one else's. You're in charge, Junior. You have carte blanche to do whatever is necessary. Anything you need, you let me know and you've got it. We have emergency funds to cover any contingency. How's that?"

Mr. Haskins just looked at him.

"Excellent. Poor Elva. A good woman. She'll be missed. Well, carry on." He started away, but I guess it was too much for him. Returning he said, sotto voce, "Clear all this up before the tournament, and there's a big bonus in it for you."

The responding fury in Mr. Haskins's eyes sent the mayor scuttling back through the crowd. It closed around him, still silent, and alarmed, and Hizzoner was gone.

An ambulance arrived as one of the photographers approached Mr. Haskins. "All done, Junior. I gave the prints to the youngster. He fooled me. I was sure he was gonna lose his breakfast, but he didn't. He's green, though, don't know spit about crime investigation. You sure you don't want me to ask the boss to send you a couple of men?"

Mr. Haskins managed a grim smile. "Not yet, Roger. Let's leave the sheriff out of it for the time being. But thanks for comin' without tellin' him. I owe ya. I promise, if it looks like I can't handle it, I'll call and ask for help."

"Any time, Junior." The photographer whopped Mr. Haskins on the shoulder in an expression of macho affection, and headed back toward the clubhouse.

Mr. Haskins exchanged a few words with Officers Grady and Ficker, then watched intently as the ambulance attendants removed the body. Once the vehicle had driven back onto the cartpath and the onlookers had begun to disperse, he joined me under the tree again.

"I 'preciate your waitin' around, Miz Burdette. You mind us sittin' in the cruiser while we talk? I'd like to get off my feet for a while."

It was fine with me. My rear was numb from sitting on the ground.

"I'd better warn you, though," he said as he opened the passenger door for me. "Get in my car and your name will be mud. Before the day's over, half of Innocence will be saying you've been arrested for Elva's murder, and the other half will probably be callin' you my chippy and sayin' we ought to be ashamed, carryin' on in the cruiser in broad daylight."

I figured I could live with the former, since once they saw me on the street, they'd know they'd figured wrong. The latter part was so ludicrous that despite the circumstances, I doubled over laughing, precisely what Mr. Haskins had intended because he looked extremely pleased with himself as he closed the passenger door.

Once behind the wheel, however, his manner became grave again. Lips pursed, he took a deep breath. "I want you to know, Miz Burdette, that even though we've got a murder on our hands, that don't mean we'll stop lookin' for Miz Julie. Jesse Primo was on vacation, but I've asked him to come back and take charge of the search. He's got a German Shepherd named Max, with a nose so keen he could track a ghost. He's flying back from upstate New York somewheres, catching the earliest flight he can get. If Miz Julie's still on this island, Max'll find her."

For the first time I was more optimistic that Jay would

be found soon. It was precisely what was needed, a big, wet dog nose.

"Second thing," Mr. Haskins said. "I called a buddy works the Bluffton territory and also woke up a couple of people at Safe Harbor. They're performing the autopsy today. I passed along the word that Nathan's death might have been intentional, so they're dusting his room for prints. They're gonna want yours and a statement laying out exactly what happened after you got there. They also want that picture you took. Better get a copy made before you return it."

I had fully intended to take it back today anyhow, and I'd assumed that sooner or later somebody or other wearing a badge over there would want to talk to me. "What about Mr. Stokes's first visitor?" I asked.

He snorted. "Turns out the only reason anybody knew he had one before you showed up was because another counselor saw the man just as Nathan opened the door to let him in. The counselor mentioned it to the receptionist, otherwise she wouldn't have known either. Unfortunately, the counselor didn't have his glasses on. He can't tell them what the man looked like or anything else."

So the visitor hadn't checked in with the receptionist either. Somehow I wasn't surprised. And unless his prints were on file somewhere, there was a distinct possibility he'd get away with killing Mr. Stokes, whether he'd meant to or not.

"The first thing I've got to do now," Mr. Haskins said, "is get an idea of Elva's movements yesterday. What can you tell me?"

I explained how Miss Potee, Miss Lacey, and Mrs. Peterson had divvied up a list of people who they thought should see the enlargement. "Mrs. Peterson mentioned a few names, but I don't remember who they were. The others might. And at some point after she left us, she went shopping at someplace called Elaine's something or other—"

"Elaine's Casuals."

"That's it. The receipts are in a shopping bag on her bed."

His gaze held more than curiosity. "How do you happen to know that?"

I repeated the message she'd left about knowing where she could get the proof we needed, along with the fact that she hadn't shown up at Miss Lacey's. "And you left last night before I had a chance to tell you I'm pretty sure Mrs. Peterson stopped in to see Aunt Jay last night. She was there when I called from Jacques Landing. One of the nurses saw her and said she was all in black and wearing slacks."

"Ah. So that's why you thought that's what she might be wearing when we found her. Seems to me, though, you didn't answer my question. How'd you know she bought them things yesterday?"

"She was to meet us at Miss Lacey's at four. When she hadn't shown up by ten-thirty last night, Miss Potee and I went around to her house to check on her. She'd been there because the dress and shoes she wore yesterday morning were in the bathroom. The tags off the things she'd bought—a pair of jeans, a top, a rain hat—were in the waste basket. If Elaine's prints the kind of receipts that records the time of purchase on them, that might help you track her movements."

"Elva in jeans. Who'd have thought it?" He shook his head, a disillusioned man. "But since she wasn't wearing them when she was found, it makes me wonder if somebody caught up with her at the hospital, killed her, and put her in a hospital gown to pass her off as a patient. She could have been parked on a gurney somewhere until it was convenient to sneak her out."

It was an unsettling thought, since the same theory might apply to Jay. But why take them both—unless Mrs. Peterson had taken the diary to show her and the perpetrator knew Jay had seen it?

"There's something else you should know," I said. "Mrs. Peterson had a trunk of souvenirs and diaries that she went through sometime yesterday. The diary for 1943 was missing. The proof she mentioned on Miss Lacey's answering machine could have been in it."

He gazed at me, one eyebrow cocked. "Sounds like you and Mabel did a lot of pokin' around in Elva's house."

"We were worried about her. And she'd left the place wide open with all the lights on."

"Hmm. Well." His expression was a combination of anger, sadness, and helplessness. "I'd better secure it, get the boys to go over it, just in case she was killed at home. Poor, silly woman. She deserved better. By the way, Miz Julie's car is at the impound lot. We've got to go over it, too."

I'd forgotten about the Buick. All I cared about was that it had been found and Jay wasn't in it.

"Is there someplace I can drop you?" he asked, starting the engine.

I thanked him for the offer but climbed out and let him go, since I was in walking distance of the hospital. I'd started back toward the traffic circle when I saw Henry, his face as droopy as a hound's, waiting for me on the sidewalk.

"A sad mornin', ain't it?" he asked, when I'd reached him. "Things have come to a pretty pass on Innocence when a body can't die in peace in her own bed. Hear tell she was strangled."

"Looks like it."

"Well, I reckon we were overdue for somethin' to happen, but a murder . . . and Julia still missin' too. But about that beautiful car." He yanked a handkerchief from his back pocket and blew, his eyes glistening. "I been down to the impound lot. Couldn't get in to see it up close, but I can tell you, she's waterlogged to a fare-thee-well." He shuffled his feet, gazed up at me from lowered lids. "What I wanted to put to you . . . when Junior and them have finished with it, I'd like to try to fix her up—for Julia, don't ya know. No charge, of course. I'd be honored to do it."

I was touched. "Thank you. I have a feeling you're one of the few people Aunt Jay would trust with Bernice. Speaking of cars, is there a rental agency on Innocence? I have some running around to do and with the Buick out of action, I'm in a bind."

Henry's expression was as close to mischievous as all those wrinkles could probably arrange themselves. Fifteen minutes later, I understood why. Henry E. Henry and his son, Henry E. Henry, Jr., who looked just like him, owned and operated Innocence Island Auto Rentals. The fleet ran the gamut from a couple of two-block-long limousines to imported subcompacts, with several vintage Fifties' Fords and Cadillacs thrown in for good measure. "Take your pick," he said, grinning under his white moustache. I gave in to a whim and selected a late-model Thunderbird complete with mobile phone, since I'd been drooling over every T-bird I'd seen for the last couple of years. I left the rental agency, stopped at the photo shop, and got a color Xerox copy of Mr. Stokes's snapshot and, remembering finally that Miss Potee might still be waiting to have breakfast with me, called her pager from the car.

She called back immediately. "I saw you out yonder, watched everything from the roof of the hospital. Listen, Troy, things have gotten way too dangerous. Whatever's in

that pan of worms Bits heated up must be singeing somebody's behind for them to kill Elva over it. Since the police
are in it now, let them figure out who did what to who and
why. Are you listenin' to me?"

As much as it bugged me to let it go, what she said made
sense. "I hear you, and you're right. I've got to return that
snapshot I borrowed from Mr. Stokes's cabin and then I'm
through. Thanks for everything you've done, though. I
really appreciate it."

She volunteered to go with me to Safe Harbor but I
managed to decline her offer without hurting her feelings. I was too worried about Jay to be good company.
Besides, I needed some solitude. "I won't be gone that
long, anyhow," I told her. "I want to get back in time to be
here when Mr. Primo and his dog begin tracking Aunt Jay."

"Junior's putting Max on her trail? You can rest easy
now, baby. Bits is as good as found."

Yeah. But alive or dead?

My first stop was the police station two blocks from Safe
Harbor. Being fingerprinted and questioned every way
from Sunday for a couple of hours before putting my signature on a signed statement and swearing it to be true and
accurate was a draining experience. I hadn't really done
anything, but my surroundings and the atmosphere and all
those uniforms sure made me feel as if I had.

At Safe Harbor there was a note on Phil's door saying
he'd be in Cabin Eight. I really didn't want to go in there
again. With luck I could knock on the door, hand over the
photo from the porch, express my sympathy, and it-splay,
as my father was fond of saying.

I did say with luck, right? So of course the door was wide
open. Phil was standing in the middle of the room with

such a hangdog, mournful expression that I couldn't have walked away if I'd had to.

"Hi," he said, his welcoming smile a mere twitch of the lips. "Come on in. I've been in here all morning packing his things and getting rid of fingerprint dust."

The room reeked of pine, lemon, and chlorine bleach, an unfortunate combination of scents that made my nose feel as if the inner linings were being scraped with an emery board. All signs of the late Nathan Stokes had been removed, the whole of his life now crammed into seven cardboard cartons stacked against one wall. The room seemed sterile, arid, considerably smaller than yesterday. And very, very sad.

"I'm really sorry about Mr. Stokes, Phil. Have you had any luck tracking down the visitor? They wouldn't tell me anything at the station."

He perched on the end of the bed, scrubbed his fingers through his hair. "The invisible man? This guy meant not to be seen and it's pure luck he succeeded. Alex is a dynamite counselor but he's also blind as a mole. His eyes are so bad, the person he saw could damn well have been a woman. But we're pretty sure now he knew exactly what he was doing with those damned cheese crackers. The receptionist said a man called around noon yesterday, said he was coming to see Nathan, and wanted to know if it was all right if he brought him a birthday cake. Nathan's birthday would have been next Wednesday. Miss Goins checked with the dietitian, who told her to tell him fine, as long as it wasn't a cheesecake. The man asked why and Miss Goins, being helpful, explained in general terms; she's been here long enough to know about that kind of thing. So the bastard knew exactly what he was doing. They'll keep looking for him, but . . ." He shrugged, as effective a period for the end of his sentence as the usual miniature dot.

So I'd been right. It gave me no pleasure at all. In fact, it made me feel all the more responsible. "I'm really sorry," I said. "I'll get out of your hair so you can finish. Here's the snapshot. I hope you haven't sealed the boxes."

Phil frowned. "This is the one you took? I thought . . ." He seemed puzzled.

"What's the problem?"

"I thought you took the big picture, the one on his dresser. We were going to use it for the program of his memorial service, and for his obituary in his hometown newspaper. What the hell could have happened to it?"

I sat down, trying to juggle this new information without dropping other bits and pieces I'd been tossing about. "The picture was of him? Mr. Stokes, I mean?" For some reason, that had never occurred to me.

"Yeah. He won it, a sitting for a formal portrait, I mean, at a local photo studio, one of those deals where you wind up with sixteen million wallet-size copies for free but you pay through the nose for an eight-by-ten. We couldn't make him understand that he wasn't obligated to buy any of them. After we saw it, we decided to let it drop because it was a dynamite picture. He was a good-looking guy." He laid the photo I'd returned on top of one of the cartons.

I felt bad that my one and only view of Nathan Stokes was such a long way from Phil's description of him. "What happened to the sixteen million wallet-sized pictures? I'd really like to see one."

He grinned, stood up, and retrieved the cleaning rags he'd left on the chifferobe. "Follow me." We left the cabin and went across to his.

I hadn't really noticed the interior yesterday. He'd made the small space very comfortable, the decor slightly reminiscent of a dorm room, with beige, red, and black plaid bedspread and matching curtains, and the kind of cheerful litter that marked him as a carefree house-keeper.

He opened the top drawer of a desk and removed a fat, business-size envelope with a rubber band around it. "Take as many as you like, maybe give them to the people who used to know him. Every couple of weeks, he'd give me one." His voice cracked. "I'd remind him that he'd already given me one, but he'd insist I should have another. I finally just took them. I'm glad now I did."

I slid the rubber band off and opened the flap. There had to be at least a dozen wallet-sized snapshots in it. I removed one slowly, stared at it, unable to move, unable to speak. It was the same face, a little fuller and softer, but otherwise a dead ringer for the man Jay had identified and the teenager in front of Taine's General Store.

12

"Uh . . . maybe you'd better sit down," Phil said, emptying the desk chair of a stack of magazines and a red and white yo-yo. "You just turned the most interesting shade of . . . well, rye-bread brown."

I plopped in the chair and slid the rest of the photos into my hand. They were all copies of the same pose, and the faces of Vinnie Quarles and Mr. Light Eyes, aged by fifty years or so, smiled up at me from every one of them. Phil was right. Nathan Stokes had indeed been a handsome man, every bit as drop-dead gorgeous as his mother's boarder, but with intensely blue eyes.

"How long ago was this taken?" I asked.

"January, I think, right after the new year. Mind telling me what this is all about? Why did you come to see Nathan anyhow?"

"How much time ya got?" I asked, stalling while I tossed a mental coin. Heads I'd tell him everything, tails he'd get an edited version. The damned thing landed on its edge. Nothing was going right today.

"How about a cup of coffee?" He stood up and crossed to a small wooden cabinet under a side window. The only thing it held was a Mr. Coffee, a model I'd never seen before. He went through the brewing ritual, tending to it with an attention to detail that branded him as a devout coffee drinker. No plain old Maxwell House for this kid. He ladled several scoops of dark, glistening beans into the maw of the coffee maker, pressed a button, and a startling combination of rattles and a teeth-gnashing whine filled the air. The thing was grinding the beans! Then the hot water began to trickle through the ground beans, sending an enticing aroma wafting around the small room.

Phil withdrew two exquisite china cups, saucers, and spoons from his cabinet. "How would you like it?"

Normally I preferred my java black, but the inkiness of the liquid filling the coffeepot was all the warning I needed. "Cream and one sugar, if you have it."

He poured, dosed mine with lump sugar and honest-to-God table cream from a miniature refrigerator. I knew what was expected and, thank God, was able to oblige him.

"Thank you. This is terrific stuff." It was also so strong, I'd be awake for the next three days.

From the smile on his face, you'd have thought Ed McMahon had just shown up on his doorstep. "Glad you like it. Now, are you going to tell me why you're here or not?"

After the big deal he'd made of the simple act of brewing two cups of coffee, I figured I owed him. I launched into the basic story line, emphasizing how important finding out precisely what had happened in '43 was to Jay, the part it may have played in the death of Nathan Stokes, and almost certainly the murder of Elva Peterson.

Halfway through the recital, I sensed I'd done the right thing. Phil's expression began to change from that of a listener intrigued by a bizarre tale to that of a person for whom the narrative had begun to have special meaning. His eyes grew thoughtful and turned inward. When I'd finished, he sat absently stirring his coffee, still off somewhere, perhaps drawing conclusions of his own. I clamped my lips together and gnawed on my tongue, determined not to blow whatever was going on.

After an interminable wait, he pushed his cup to one side. "Be right back," he said, and sprinted out. He meant it, returning in less than a minute with one of the cartons from the cabin next door.

"I'm going out on a limb here," he said, ripping off the tape and pulling up the flaps. "But I figure I owe you. What you've told me gives us a clue to one of Nathan's problems. It's a damned shame to find it now that he's dead."

"What was wrong with him?"

He paused, gazing up at me. "Do you know anything about autism?"

Oddly enough, I did. Not a hell of a lot, but at least I wasn't completely ignorant about the condition. "Uh . . . a person who's autistic has difficulty relating to his surroundings and seems to exist in a world where he's the only inhabitant, or acts as if he were. So he may or may not respond to someone speaking to him. Oh, yeah, and he can't handle changes. He wants things to be or to happen just so with absolutely no variation. I know that's simplifying but it's the best I can do."

"Your best isn't bad. Nathan was autistic, but God knows how old he was before he was diagnosed. Thirty, maybe forty. Before then he was labeled schizophrenic. And actually, he wasn't as severe a case as some. Once they realized what they were dealing with, it became a bit easier to help him. He'd never be cured, but he improved to the point where he could relate to others on a limited basis and survive out there with all the people who're allegedly sane when he had to. Took them ten years to get him to that point."

This was all very interesting, but I knew there was more important stuff to come and I didn't have all day. I wanted to be on Innocence when Mr. Primo's German Shepherd found Jay.

"But," Phil went on, "and this will mean something to you, starting around the first of July of every year, he'd regress, turn into a kid, hiding in his closet and chanting 'Natie's been a bad boy,' over and over. By the Fourth, we would have to sedate him. After a couple of days, he'd be fine, or as fine as Nathan was going to get."

I sat riveted, trying to remember what the Misses Lacey and Potee had said about him. Something about being large for his age, but for the life of me, I couldn't remember how old they said he was in 1943.

Phil began rooting in the carton. "Every now and then, he'd get onto a death kick. He had a real flair for art." He paused until he'd found what he'd been looking for, an illustration pad. Easing it from under several things packed on top of it, he pulled it out and flipped back the cover and the first few sheets. "Here, take a look at this."

I took the pad and felt my cheeks go cold. To say that Mr. Stokes had had a flair for drawing was a masterpiece of understatement. He was damned good, his strokes firm and sure, catching movement and mood with an economy of lines. I dropped the pad on the desk and dug into my bag for my glasses. I didn't really need them but I simply wasn't willing to trust my eyes. With them on, the penciled strokes were a bit darker, sharper-edged. The two figures in the drawing seemed to come to life, the shades and shadows behind them giving a three-dimensional quality to the scene, like a black-and-white hologram.

There was no mistaking what he'd depicted. A man lay stretched prone on a brass bed, and above him, straddling his backside, a woman, the folds of her long flowing gown billowing out around them both, her arms extended straight down, fingers splayed as she pressed with all her strength against the pillow covering the man's head.

"It's all wrong," I protested. "Aunt Jay didn't smother the man, she—" I shut up, and let the gears of my brain engage for a change, because the operative word was indeed *wrong*. First, Jay had only bonked the man. Second, the drawing was done from the vantage point of someone near the door or perhaps out in the hall; the window wall against which Jay had found herself trapped on the floor on the far side of the bed was clearly outlined. Nathan could not have seen what had happened between Jay and the boarder; the man had closed and locked the door. Third, the woman appeared to be considerably taller than Jay. The lines of her body in relation to the man's were longer than Jay's would have been, and the hands pressing down on the pillow were much larger. Jay's hands were tiny, the size of a child's. Fourth, the back of her head wasn't right. The woman's face was turned away from the viewer, as if she'd glanced out of the window for a second. The hair in the sketch was short and curly, like a bob. I'd only seen Jay with her hair down once and was astonished at how long it was, practically to her waist. According to her, she had never cut it and never would.

"Phil, I don't know what to make of this," I admitted. "It's definitely not what Aunt Jay said happened. And I don't know who this woman is but I know who she ain't, pardon the grammar. She's not Julia Wingate. How did Mr. Stokes explain the sketch?"

"He didn't." Phil scooted backward on his butt until his back was against the side of the bed. "Nathan drew a lot of those, or variations on the same scene, but he would never talk about them. The director before the one we have now checked with the Innocence police years ago, but they claimed there had never been a homicide in the island's history. But after what you've told me . . ." He left the rest dangling.

I wasn't quite ready to put the drawing down as a figment of Mr. Stokes's imagination. It was close enough to the truth that it would be stupid to ignore it. But it still didn't make sense. If Mr. Stokes had sketched what he'd seen, the boarder had been smothered after Jay had rung his bell and left. But by whom? Nathan's mother? And why? And if that's the way the boarder had died, how could Mrs. Peterson have had proof that he'd left the island alive—unless this attempt on his life had failed?

"Phil," I said, closing the cover, "I know it's asking a lot, but could you loan this to me? Not the whole pad, just this one sheet."

He gnawed on his bottom lip. "I'm not sure I'm in any position to do that. I mean, Nathan's will is pretty explicit. All this stuff—"

This was my morning for the unexpected. "Mr. Stokes left a will?"

"Not a real one," Phil said, returning to the carton. "I mean, it was never signed by witnesses or anything, but we feel an obligation to honor his wishes. We're shipping everything to his brother in—"

"Excuse me? His b-brother?" I was so stunned, my lips were flapping. "Mr. Stokes had a brother?"

"Has," Phil said, gazing at me as if he thought I might be a candidate for residency. "He lives in Hawaii. Every time Nathan got a postcard or letter from him, he'd show it around until it was frayed at the edges. Then he'd frame it."

"Whoa. Just whoa," I said, my hands up in self-defense. At no point had anyone ever mentioned a brother. "Do you know for a fact the guy in Hawaii is his brother or do you assume he is because Mr. Stokes said so?"

"Why would he lie?" My question, however, must have generated second thoughts because he cocked his head to one side, mulling it over. "You know, you may have something there. The first time I remember him mentioning a brother was over the Christmas holidays, a few years back. The other residents usually go home for Christmas or their relatives come here for the big party we throw for everybody. We were feeling sorry for Nathan because he had nowhere to go and no one to visit him. That's when he showed us a postcard and said it was from his brother in Hawaii. The man exists, I know that for sure, but whether he's actually Nathan's brother, that might be open to question. Regardless, if it weren't for him, Nathan wouldn't have been here. He footed all the bills."

"You have to pay to live here?" I asked.

"You betcha booty. Granted, it's not fancy but it ain't cheap either. There's room and board, there's therapy twice a week, more often if it's needed, a medical staff to oversee health and medication for those who need it. This guy in Hawaii may have been Nathan's guardian. The way I hear it, he's supported Nathan for years."

I got up and paced, trying to fit together the pieces of a puzzle without knowing what the finished product was supposed to look like. "Could you give me the man's name?"

Phil backpedaled. "Uh . . . I don't know whether that's privileged information or not. I could ask him when I call him about shipping these things. Nathan wanted him to have them, especially the Purple Heart."

I closed my eyes, took a deep breath. My systems were being overloaded. "What was Mr. Stokes doing with a Purple Heart?"

"He said his brother gave it to him."

The only person in this cast of characters who qualified for a Purple Heart so far was Vinnie Quarles. He and Nathan must have been very close for him to have given away a symbol most veterans cherished. Brothers? Half brothers? What else was in that box?

Either I was eyeing the carton more covetously than I thought or I was living up to my reputation as a rotten poker player. Phil wandered over to the door and gazed out. "Ms. Burdette—"

"Troy."

"Troy, there are things I'm in a position to do," he said, still facing the screen, "and things I'm not. I've already crossed the line showing you that sketch, but I gotta tell you, I think you're right. The things you're trying to find out have something to do with what happened to Nathan to send him into Never-Never Land every Fourth of July. Hell, it may have even sent him to his maker yesterday. And nothing would give me greater pleasure than nailing the son of a bitch who slipped him those cheese crackers. So . . ." He turned to me, a solemn figure in cut-offs and a tank top. "I've got to run over to the infirmary. I'll be back in—say, fifteen minutes. If you'd like another cup of coffee, help yourself."

I blame how slow on the uptake I was on the stresses of the morning. "Oh. Yes. I would like another cup, thanks. Take your time."

"Fifteen minutes," he repeated, and left.

I doubt he'd gotten two steps from his front porch before I'd started rooting in the box. It contained only paper in one form or another—the photographs, postcards, and five-and-dime prints I'd already seen, several sketch pads, and a bunch of large manilla envelopes which turned out to be medical records. I flipped through them hurriedly.

His application for approval to become a resident of Safe Harbor was only ten years old. Otherwise, he'd been in two institutions, the first confinement beginning in 1947 when he was fifteen, the second from 1960. The poor man had been locked up most of his life.

I was shoving the records back into the envelopes when I sensed that I might have missed something. I slid the forms out again, noting nothing worth the precious minutes I was wasting—until I came across the personal information sheet filled out when Nathan was institutionalized in 1947. Date of birth: June 19, 1932. Father: Jacob E. C. Stokes, deceased. Mother: Lucille May Dalton Stokes, deceased. I yanked out my notepad and began scribbling. The only piece of information I needed now was the name of the mysterious benefactor/brother in Hawaii.

I put the medical records back and checked the remaining envelopes. One contained old photographs of Mr. Stokes as an infant, then as a toddler with a mop of dark curls that dangled to his shoulders. There were a few of his mother as a very young woman, one in what appeared to be a maid's uniform, posing self-consciously in front of an impressive white house with an enormous veranda and columns that stretched beyond the limits of the photograph. There was something rather fragile and vulnerable about her. Life must have dealt harshly with her after that; the few pictures of her as an older woman showed clearly the toll alcohol had taken on her.

I paid particular attention to her hairstyles. In most of the photographs it appeared to be shoulder length, but at some point she had worn a bob. Miss Lucy Stokes was looking more and more like a suspect by the moment. But a suspect guilty of what? Even if she'd tried to smother the bum, considering the message Mrs. Peterson had left on the answering machine, the attempt had failed.

The very last envelope made a deep dent in the force field I'd erected around my emotions. I'd found the will of Nathan Dalton Stokes. He'd have never won a Pulitzer, but his intent was clear.

> *My will*
> *I, Nathan, make this will like on Perry Mason.*
> *Give my radio to Pearl since she got a hearing ade and can hear good now.*
> *Give Maxie Gross my wates to help him get some more muscles on his week side.*
> *All the rest for my bruther Bubba in Hawaii, specially the Purple Heart. He give it to me to show he trust me to keep my word. I did. I never tell anybody. He taken care of me and kep me out of the state hospitals where the others wanted to put me when Mama died. Tell him Nathan loved him.*
> *Love, Nathan*

I folded the will and slid it into its envelope, swallowing around the boulder in my throat. My fifteen minutes would be up shortly, if they weren't already. Regardless, the least Nathan Stokes deserved was a moment of grief and respect for a life spent making the best of things. He was so fortunate to have had someone who'd stuck with him. Not like me, who . . .

I screeched to a halt midthought. I'd waltzed around the dance floor with self-pity more often in the past two days than I had in over three years. How dare I equate my problems with the difficulties Nathan Stokes had faced. All right, Wade had deserted me, not in the legal sense, but the bottom line was that he'd opted out. Once he had gone, I was still in control of my life, could still function, make a living. If Bubba in Hawaii had deserted Nathan, heaven only knows what vegetable bin he'd have been in yesterday. I screeched to a halt again, remembering the kind of bin he was in now. What was it he'd never told anyone? What was the secret he'd taken to his grave?

A Bubba. In Hawaii. Vincent Quarles was called Vinnie. So who was Bubba? Who would be notified in case of emergency? I checked his first application again. Josiah S. Allenby, Innocence Island. Reverend Allenby?

That made sense. If there was an emergency and an immediate decision was called for, it would be logical to have the name of someone local to handle the problem. Considering how long the Reverend had been on Innocence, he would certainly have known Nathan and his mother. He might even have been their minister. Damn it, I still needed Bubba's real name.

I replaced all the envelopes and papers, closed the flaps, and whopped myself on the forehead for being an idiot. There on the boxtop was the label with the name and address of the recipient of Mr. Stokes's personal effects: Progressive Movements, Inc., 818 Key Point Road, Honolulu, HI. Terrific. A corporation. Well, it was better than nothing.

Phil's return, preceded by foot-stomping and throat-clearing from the porch, was almost comical. He opened his door with the kind of caution one would use entering someone else's domicile. "I'm back," he said, his glance skittering to the carton and away again.

I finished scribbling the address and put my notepad away. "Thanks for the coffee and everything, Phil." I'd left the sketch pad on the desk. Phil opened it, carefully tore off the drawing he'd shown me, removed a super-large envelope from his desk, and slipped the drawing into it. "Anything else I can do for you?" he asked, handing it to me.

I took the hint. "You've been super. Thanks."

"You'll let me know if you find out something?" He looked like an anxious little boy.

"You'll be among the first. Thanks for caring about him, Phil."

His face fell. "If I'd cared a little more, he might still be alive. I feel responsible somehow."

"That makes two of us," I said, understanding perfectly.

I checked in by car phone with Mr. Haskins before leaving the grounds of Safe Harbor. He said Mr. Primo wasn't back and might be flying in to Savannah, Hilton Head Island, or Charleston. Either way, he'd still be some distance from Innocence.

"You'll probably get here before Jesse does," Mr. Haskins said. "So take your time. Nothing you can do after you get here anyways."

He was right, but it didn't make things any better. I'd been feeling helpless and ineffective for two days and I was getting sick of it. I use that as the excuse for my behavior when, halfway back to Innocence I realized that the big metallic smile on the grill of a car behind me had been a fixture in my rearview mirror for quite a while. It had eased up behind me as I'd waited at a red light right after I'd left Safe Harbor. And again when I'd missed my turn and had had to double back to damned near where I'd started from, since it was the only route I knew. The reason I'd seen it then was because I'd been stuck behind a tractor pulling a load of rolled-up sod at a brisk ten miles an hour. My only consolation was that I was not alone. A convoy of grumpy drivers was strung out behind me; in it, two vehicles back, the big silver car with the black top.

By the time I spotted the gaudy neon sign towering above a tired-looking strip mall up ahead, I'd had enough. I took the first entrance, realizing at the last minute that all I'd probably done was to put myself farther back in the parade, since sooner or later I'd have to hit the main road again. If I could find a map in one of these stores, I could plot an alternate route back to Innocence.

I stopped at a crosswalk and watched a young mother push a stroller in front of her with one hand and drag a toddler along behind her with the other, fussing at him all the way. Once she'd cleared the diagonal lines, I glanced in the rearview mirror before easing ahead and there it was again, poking along a good distance behind me, the big silver-colored car with the black top. I squinted, trying to see who was behind the wheel, but the sun turned its windshield into a sheet of yellow-orange, completely obscuring the driver.

There really wasn't any reason to think it was following me and any other time, it probably wouldn't have crossed my mind at all. Except that, come to think of it, that big gray monster had been behind me before I'd missed my turn. On top of that, it looked just like the car that had been parked in front of Safe Harbor yesterday, the one that had taken off in one hell of a hurry, almost turning me into a hood ornament on the Buick in the process.

I felt my temperature begin to climb and tried to talk it back down. This was dumb. It had to be a coincidence. But there'd been far too many coincidences already. I had to satisfy myself that I wasn't being paranoid or convince myself that I was.

The driveway circled around behind the row of stores so I followed it at the posted speed limit of five miles an hour, one eye glued to my rearview mirror. Sure enough, I was passing the third store when my silver shadow careened around the turn behind me, almost hitting a couple of teenagers who yelled obscenities after it. It slowed to a more decorous pace and trailed me as I circled back around to the front again.

I'd had it. I made a sharp left, pulled into a parking space, got out and ambled toward the nearest store. I faked a bit of window-shopping, watching the Lincoln's reflection in the storefront as it pulled into a row one over from where I'd parked the T-bird. And sat. No one got out.

My forehead had blossomed with perspiration the minute I'd left the car. The sun was flexing its muscles today, the temperature on the digital display in the window of a bank flirting with ninety degrees. If I stayed on this sidewalk much longer, I'd be soaked. It was too damned hot for fun and games.

I ducked into the first shoe store I passed and tossed a "Just looking" at the nearest clerk before she could pounce on me. Considering my passion for shoes, I didn't have to pretend to peruse the sandals in the window. There were several pairs singing a siren song to me and it took every ounce of willpower to ignore them and glance casually outside. The phantom in the Lincoln hadn't moved.

Who the heck could it be and why was he/she following me? It really bugged me that I couldn't see the driver. The longer I stood there, the madder I got. I was tired of this cat-and-mouse business.

There was a door opening onto the rear parking lot. I replaced the sandals I'd been holding, smiled a goodbye to the clerk, and walked straight through the store and out the back door. The heat and humidity slapped me in the face and I hugged what little shade there was under the awnings as I hurried toward the end of the row and rounded the last store. I stopped and peeked around the corner of it. The Lincoln was facing the other direction. Perfect.

The parking places on each end of the strip were reserved for oversized vehicles. Using as a shield a pair of battered yellow school buses parked nose to tail, I darted behind them and kept going until I was too far out in the parking lot for the driver of the Lincoln to see me in his mirrors. Cutting across from one row to the next, I worked my way toward him at an angle, trying to get close enough to see and memorize his tags. Then I could head for the Thunderbird and casually glance over at him as I passed. That's the way I had it planned, anyway. Unfortunately, the driver didn't know that.

I was in the row behind him, three cars to his right, when the door of the Lincoln opened and he got halfway out, leaning over the top of his door as if trying to peer into the shoe store I'd gone into. I began cataloguing data. Male, white, medium height. Dark hair. If he'd only turn around so I could see what he looked like.

Mom drives me nuts saying be careful what you wish for, you just might get it. You'd think after thirty-one years I'd have learned that mothers are almost always right. I kept walking, narrowing the distance between us, when the driver got all the way out of the car and slammed his door closed. He turned to lock it and I got an unobstructed view of his face. I stopped dead in my tracks in shock, which wasn't all that smart since I was smack in the middle of the aisle with a pickup approaching. It halted and waited. I was greatly appreciative, since I couldn't have budged if you'd paid me.

Finally the driver of the pickup lost patience. He rolled down his window and stuck his head out. "Lady, you fixin' to set up housekeepin' on that spot or what?"

That caught the attention of the driver of the Lincoln,

who glanced up, and saw me. He did precisely the same thing I'd done, froze for a good ten seconds. Then, as if someone had zapped him in the fanny, he jumped back into his car, started the engine, and hightailed it out of his parking spot. He sped toward the nearest exit, and, ignoring oncoming traffic, bulldozed his way onto the highway and was gone. I'd have probably been standing there still if the man behind the wheel of the pickup hadn't leaned on his horn and kept leaning. I mouthed a "Sorry" at him and walked wobbly-legged to the Thunderbird, got in, and just sat there trying to make sense of what I'd seen. The driver of the Lincoln had been, at a guess, between forty-five and fifty, his thick, dark hair graying at the temples, his facial features so familiar it was like *Invasion of the Body Snatchers* come to life. He looked just like Aunt Jay's light-eyed assailant. And Vinnie Quarles. And Nathan Stokes. Exactly like them.

13

I headed back to Innocence and the courthouse with the single-mindedness of a homing pigeon, my brain tied up in knots trying to figure out who this clone was, and how he figured into the scheme of things. One thing was certain: he had to be related to one or more of the other two. But how?

Miss Lucy's boarder would be several years older than Jay was now, which would put him in his mid-eighties. Gauging from the Jacques Landing snapshot, Vinnie would be a few years younger, perhaps in his late seventies. Mr. Stokes . . . I did some fast second grade arithmetic . . . had been in his mid-sixties, and the man following me looked to be in his late forties. That was one hell of a spread, more than forty years, so it wasn't likely that they all were half brothers.

Was this Bubba? Uh-uh. Nobody who lived in Hawaii could be as pale as this guy had been. That didn't mean he wasn't related to Mr. Stokes in some way, a cousin or half

brother. So whose son was he? I doubted he was Vinnie's.
Since the look-alike's eyes were either a pale gray or blue—
I wasn't close enough to tell—I'd be nuts not to put my
money on Miss Lucy's boarder as Father of the Year. And if
I was anywhere near the ball park about the age of the
driver of the Lincoln—late forties—that put his date of
birth sometime after 1943. If I was right, his father had survived Jay's whack on the head with the thunder jar and,
assuming the woman in Mr. Stokes's drawing was his
mother, her attempt to smother him. So why all the mayhem now? What was there to hide? And why had Light
Eyes the Second been following me? I was willing to bet
he'd been driving the car that had almost flattened me in
front of Safe Harbor. Whether he'd trailed me there or had
been there when I arrived was open to question.
Whichever, I doubted he'd gotten out of the car.
Considering how much he looked like Mr. Stokes, he'd
have attracted someone's attention.

By the time I'd passed the gatehouse on Innocence,
another thought had occurred to me. The island was small
enough so that everyone was at least a familiar face to
everyone else. I hadn't seen today's paper but the editor,
knowing a dynamite human interest story when he saw one,
had promised Miss Potee to print the enlargement. Except
perhaps for Mrs. Peterson, however, no one had recognized the picture of Miss Lucy's boarder. Since this fourth
look-alike was a dead ringer for the boarder, it wasn't likely
that he lived or worked on Innocence, or someone would
have called Junior Haskins by now, saying, "You know, that
picture puts me in mind of the young feller works in the
bank. Sure does." Evidently the newspaper story had drawn
this last one out of the woodwork.

Four men who looked enough alike to be quads. Was
that the problem? Was the fact that a face from the past

was being circulated all over the island a threat because three others wore that same face? Was a set of dominant genes blowing some family's secret out of the water? Somehow it felt right. That's what this was all about: some family's dirty laundry.

I'd been woolgathering with such intensity that I'd done it again, missed the turn off Main that would have taken me over to the courthouse. I got my bearings, eyed the traffic behind me, and saw no trace of the Lincoln. Relieved, I backtracked toward the police station. The sooner I let Officer Haskins know about this latest development and my theory about the reasons for what Jay had stirred up, the better. Jay. God willing, she was still alive and unharmed. God willing the bomb in her abdomen hadn't exploded yet.

Slowing for a stop sign, I noticed a magnificent brick church at the intersection: New Faith Evangelical Church. The topic for next Sunday's service: "If Thine Eye Offends Thee." Guest Pastor: Reverend Josiah Allenby. If he'd agreed to be the contact on Nathan's application, perhaps he could fill in some gaps about the Stokes family.

At the police station, I bumped into Mr. Haskins, literally, at the door. "Gotta run," he said, and grabbed my arm, walking me back out toward his cruiser. "There's a fire over on Sixth Street. And just so you know, Jesse Primo came in up at Charleston. Henry's gone after him. You take that picture back?"

"Yes, but I have another one to show you," I said, and handed it over. "That's Nathan Stokes."

Mr. Haskins's jaw dropped a full two inches. "How many men have been walkin' around with this face?"

"There's a fourth one," I said, and, talking fast, told him about the game of tag with the driver of the Lincoln.

"You sure he wasn't just the same general type and your imagination plastered these other faces on his?"

I decided not to be insulted. "I was three cars away. It was like looking at Miss Lucy's boarder and her son. They're related, I'm sure of it. And he hadn't meant to be seen, that's for sure."

"Did you get his tag number?"

I shook my head. "I was so shocked. . . . Sorry."

Mr. Haskins gave me a pat. "We couldn't pick him up anyway. Technically, he hasn't done anything."

"One last thing and I'll get out of your way," I said, and passed him the envelope with the sketch.

He opened it hurriedly, almost tearing the paper, snatched it out and stared at it. "Where'd this come from?"

"Mr. Stokes drew it. And—" An unintelligible squawk from the cruiser's radio cut me off.

Mr. Haskins understood it. "I'm sorry, Miz Burdette, I've got to skedaddle. They need somebody for traffic control." He shoved the drawing and envelope into my hands, climbed behind the wheel, and started the engine. "Look, I need you to put down on paper everything that happened this morning, everything you learned. And don't worry. When Jesse gets here, I'll find you." He snatched the gearshift into Drive and sped off.

I stood there for a moment, trying to decide what to do first, find a typewriter or a computer so I could give Mr. Haskins something on paper, or pursue an idea that popped into my head back at New Faith. The latter won hands down. I'd talk to Reverend Allenby.

From the street, the minister's old house looked sad and forlorn, as if it were on its last legs and was embarrassed about it. It seemed to be hiding behind its drawn shades and curtains. In comparison, even with the crime-scene tape strung around it, Mrs. Peterson's house next door still bore the aura of its late resident. The swing on the porch moved, nudged by a midday breeze. The cement frog in the yard and the gnome under the toadstool by the front steps appeared to be waiting patiently for the return of their owner.

Her property was immaculate, grass clipped, flower beds weeded. The only thing that needed tending was a broken branch halfway up the beautiful oak tree in the side yard that towered above both Mrs. Peterson's house and the Reverend's next door; the tree obviously predated both of them. The branch was mortally wounded, hanging from a strip of bark slowly peeling away from the trunk. Perhaps it had been struck by lightning. A cluster of baby branches littered the base of the tree, victims of the larger one's slow descent. Other than that, it was obvious Mrs. Peterson had tended to her house and property with a fine hand. For the second time today I felt guilty that I hadn't liked her more.

I rang Reverend Allenby's doorbell twice before it occurred to me that it probably wasn't working. I knocked firmly and almost jumped out of my skin when the door opened almost instantly.

"Miss Burdette." Reverend Allenby looked as surprised to see me as I was to see him, since I'd about convinced myself that no one was home. "Come in, come in," he said, pushing the screen open for me. "A sad day, isn't it? I think now I was too hard on Elva sometimes; she could be so frivolous. But down deep she had a good heart." He moved around the dark, musty living room, plumping pillows on the sofa and lifting a cloud of dust in the process. This place hadn't been aired out in months. It felt close, confining, and faintly perfumed, as if by spicy air freshener.

"Have a seat," the Reverend said. "Forgive me if I don't open the curtains. The sun's so hot that it tests the poor air conditioning. I try to help it any way I can, closed the vents on the upper floors years ago, keep the windows covered. It makes quite a difference in my electric bill. By the by, I want you to know I've been praying for your poor aunt. I know in my heart that God's watching over her. Now, what can I do for you?"

Suddenly I wasn't sure how to begin. "Uh . . . I was wondering if you're planning a memorial service or something for Mr. Stokes."

He gave me a blank stare that made my heart plummet. "Mr. Stokes?"

"Nathan Stokes. You were notified, weren't you? Mr. Stokes died yesterday. I just assumed . . . I'm sorry, Reverend Allenby. It never occurred to me they hadn't called you."

"Nathan. Lucy's son?" His Lincolnesque features settled in mournful lines. "I hadn't heard. Why would anyone have notified me?" he asked, lowering himself onto a straight-backed chair.

Something was not computing. "You were listed as the person to contact in an emergency." I hoped he wouldn't ask how I knew that.

"After all this time?" He appeared genuinely surprised. "I haven't seen the boy in years. After his mother died, he was sent to—my goodness, where was it now? Spring Grove, that's it. But—" He got up, wandered over to a lamp table, and turned on a light. It was so welcome it felt as if the sun had just come out after days behind clouds. "Now that I think on it, I did agree that they could call me if he needed something. I went up to Spring Grove to see him once, but he didn't say a word, just acted as if I wasn't there. His doctor said that would probably never change and . . . well, the whole experience was so distressing, I didn't see any point in going back."

I swallowed my anger at the system that had left Mr.

Stokes in his personal prison for so long and at Reverend Allenby for not having tried again. "Well, it turns out he'd been misdiagnosed. He was autistic and did improve. Here's his picture."

His eyes widened as I handed it toward him. Reverend Allenby was no poker player; he was stunned. "Why, he looks like—" He stopped, as if speech had momentarily deserted him.

"Like the man I've been trying to identify for Mrs. Wingate," I said, finishing it for him. "Enough like him to have been his brother. So I was wondering, Reverend. You've been on Innocence for so long and since Mr. Stokes and his mother lived nearby, I thought maybe you could tell me something about the family. I know the name of his father, Jacob Stokes. Did he and Miss Lucy have any other children?"

The Reverend was lost in his scrutiny of the photo. Outside, the plaintive wail of a siren rose and fell as it sped fast, the sound pulling him back to the moment. "Sorry. Lucy's husband? All I remember is that she was a widow. She moved in with the boy when he was just a little nipper."

"She wasn't a native of Innocence?"

"Oh, no. I don't remember where she was from originally. She wasn't all that neighborly, probably because of the boy. She took more comfort in the bottle than the Bible, I'm afraid."

I grimaced, slamming head first into a dead end.

"She didn't begin taking in boarders until little Nathan was school age," he said, sitting down again. "Of course, he never actually went to school, not in his condition. Oh, yes, and during the war, she hosted very noisy parties with drinking and card playing and the like. Really shameful behavior. To be honest, the only reason I agreed they could call me if there was a problem was because there was no one else. It was my Christian duty. That's all I can tell you."

I took a deep breath, wrestling with my disappointment, and got up. He walked me to the door. "Well, thank you anyway, Reverend Allenby. Can you think of anyone else on Innocence who might have known the family well?"

He paused, one hand on the doorknob, head lowered in thought. "Not a soul. You're too young to appreciate the mores of the times. Back in those days, good families didn't associate with a hard-drinking woman like Mrs. Stokes. As a result, few of us got to know her. I would never, for instance, countenance my daughter attending the parties Mrs. Stokes used to host for visiting servicemen. Angela was such an innocent," he said, his eyes straying to the portrait of the girl I'd seen in Mrs. Peterson's photo album. It dominated the wall above an old upright piano opposite the door.

"She's beautiful." It seemed the polite thing to say. Besides, she was.

"Thank you. Angela Marie, the image of her mother, who died many, many years ago. Angela was so talented. She wanted to be an interior decorator. The showplace she made of her room . . . People talk because I've never changed a thing in it, but it's the only reminder I have of how talented she was." His thin lips widened in a shy smile. "Would you like to see it? I rarely let anyone up there, but since you didn't know her . . . "

"I'd be delighted," I said, surprised and touched that he'd offered.

"It's upstairs." He started for the steps, but hesitated, distracted by the sound of the second emergency vehicle to go by. His eyes clouded with concern. "That was a pumper."

Having grown up four doors from a firehouse, I

understood what he meant immediately. "There's a fire down-island of here. Sixth Street, Officer Haskins said."

"Oh, dear. I hope it's not the home of one of my people. There are several shut-ins on Sixth, members of New Faith when I was pastor there. Forgive me, Miss Burdette, would it be a great inconvenience for you to give me a lift so I can make sure they're all right? I promise to show you Angela's room before you leave Innocence."

"I'd be glad to drop you anywhere you like." As curious as I was about the shrine he'd made of his daughter's room, I was a little relieved. This place made me claustrophic.

Outside, he locked the door, which surprised me. According to Miss Potee, the only locked doors during the day were in the hotels and that was because the people behind those doors were strangers and didn't realize that on Innocence there was no reason to lock anything, even car doors. As far as I was concerned, the Reverend was doing the smart thing. I'd locked the Buick. A fat lot of good it had done me.

Reverend Allenby seemed to try to mask his anxiety about his former church members by offering a running commentary as we headed south on Central, describing the island in the days before the Renaissance, as he called it. Pricey single-family houses backed up against the strand of shore where fishing and shrimp boats had docked with their day's haul decades before. There were boats docked there now, too, sleek fifty-footers and longer that belonged to the residents of those homes.

We passed a succession of tasteful midrises that had replaced a veritable swamp. "The biggest mosquitoes south of the Mason-Dixon line," Reverend Allenby said, warming to his subject. "They used to eat us alive."

His Cook's tour became more erratic the farther south we went, primarily because of the fire equipment zipping past us, sirens blaring. "They're from the North End station. This must be serious, to pull in a second company. You can drop me anywhere along here. I'll walk the rest of the way."

We wouldn't be able to proceed much farther anyway. A police cruiser, chase lights a-spin, sat dead center of the intersection at Central and Sixth, diverting traffic westward. I pulled over to the curb, parked behind a plumber's van, and got out with the Reverend. People seemed to be coming from all directions, their anxiety obvious.

Keeping up with the Reverend was as much a challenge as matching strides with Miss Potee. We turned left toward the ocean on Sixth, which began to look familiar. I'd been here with Miss Potee. This was the street the Reverend's new house was on. And that's what was burning, fully engaged, flames spiking from every window.

"How horrible," Reverend Allenby said. "I don't know who lived there—there are so many new people now—but I pray to God no one was home."

A veritable mob stood watching from across the street, standing on lawns, in driveways, on front porches, lined up behind the barricades to separate them from the fire equipment and hoses snaking across the tarmac. Firefighters scurried back and forth, but it was obvious the house was beyond salvation. A loud, splintering sound rent the air, followed immediately by the collapse of the roof as it pancaked what little was left of the exterior walls. The crowd moaned and moved back a step, hands to their mouths.

A buzz, barely detectable above the other noises, began as people recognized the minister. One woman saw him and wailed, "Oh, Reverend. Your poor little house!"

"Josiah!" I'd heard the voice often enough to recognize it instantly. Mayor Leland Stokes, who'd been standing on the porch of a bungalow, waved and began weaving his way down to us on the curb.

"Leland." The Reverend, on automatic pilot, extended his hand. "Who lives here? Was anyone home, anyone hurt?"

Hizzoner hesitated, then shrugged, realizing there was no point in keeping anything from him. "There was no one home, Josiah. The house was unoccupied because it was going to be yours come Sunday."

"Beg pardon?"

"Some very grateful people in the business community purchased the house for you, and the good people of Innocence pooled their resources and furnished and decorated it. It was all ready. We were fixing to present it to you on a special ceremony on Sunday after church services."

From the expression on the minister's face, the mayor might have been speaking a foreign language. "But . . . why would they do that? I already have a house."

"Which is about to fall down around your ears. It's in such bad shape, New Faith decided they couldn't afford the upkeep any longer. It's been sold to Hospitality House so they can tear it down and expand. But everyone wanted to see that you were taken care of, Josiah. This was to have been their gift to you. What happens now, I don't know. Hospitality House agreed to delay their plans until we'd moved you here. They're in a bind, contracts and deadlines, you understand. I suspect they'll move you into temporary quarters until another place can be found for you."

"I . . . I . . ." Reverend Allenby was speechless. I suspected I was witnessing a first. He began to sway, as if battered by a stiff, swirling wind.

"Jesus, man, don't you pass out on me!" Mr. Spates grabbed him around the shoulders. "Somebody get a chair off a front porch! For God's sake, make it quick!"

"No need to blaspheme," the minister said weakly. A sturdy white wicker chair was passed above the heads of the crowd and whisked under the Reverend's rear end. He sank into it with obvious relief.

"Put your head between your knees," Hizzoner instructed, then turned and shouted, "Is there a doctor or a nurse out here?"

Down the block a well-muscled bronze arm shot up and David separated himself from the group he'd been with, among them Miss Potee and another Patient Helper whose name I couldn't remember.

"What's the problem?" David asked as he approached. "Hi, Troy."

I nodded my greeting, a little rattled by how happy I was to see him, and not because the good minister needed ministering to. I averted my gaze. This wasn't an appropriate place or moment for drooling, which I was damned close to doing. I made a mental note to give myself a stern talking to. I'd just met the man, for Pete's sake. And after everything had been settled here for better or worse, I'd be heading north again and David would be moving on, too, pursuing his own goals.

It was just as well. I'd just about decided there was little reason to become a Mrs. again. Any man as nice and grounded and gorgeous as David Baskerville, M.D. would make some woman a first-prize husband. Just as important, in my book, anyhow, he'd make a first-prize father for some lucky child or two. Since the latter part of the equation was not in my book, I might as well cool it. Look but don't touch. Ah, well.

Josiah Allenby had begun to rally. "I'm fine, son, just overwhelmed. Leland's just told me what everyone did for me. I can't tell you how grateful I am. I will be sure to include my thanks in my sermon on Sunday. But to move,

Leland? I've been in that house so long, and let's be honest, I don't have many years left."

David's smile began as a twitch before it escalated into full-scale laughter. "You are the healthiest ninety-two year old in the state, Reverend Allenby. They don't make them like you anymore."

The minister had the good grace to look sheepish. "I have been fortunate to have maintained my physical and mental health. But to leave my house . . ." His eyes became tortured. "I can't bear to think of it. There are so many memories, especially of Angela. No. Moving's out of the question. We'll work something out."

"What?" Mr. Haskins, emerging from behind a tanker, held a walkie-talkie against one ear. "Say that again." He moved toward us, frowning, then stopped. "What! Goddammit, what is going on around here?"

The Reverend's heavy brows flew sky-high. "Junior!" the mayor said, and tilted his head in the minister's direction.

Mr. Haskins set off at a trot toward the nearest cruiser. Something about the urgency of his gait made me follow him. I caught up with him just as he reached the car and opened the door.

"What is it?" I asked, my gut telling me that whatever had happened would have an impact on me and mine. "What's wrong?"

Rage contorted his fleshy features. "Grady just got a call from Vera Primo. Some son of a bitch has poisoned Jesse's dog."

14

Mr. Haskins sped away with an angry blast of the horn that scattered people standing in the street. I closed my eyes, the taste of despair on my tongue. Until that moment I hadn't realized how much I'd been depending on the wet, black nose of Officer Primo's German Shepherd. Now he'd been sacrificed, too, along with Mrs. Peterson and Mr. Stokes. Any hope that Jay would be found soon was gone.

I felt a hand on my shoulder. "Hey," David said. "I've never seen Junior Haskins move that fast. Is something wrong?"

"Someone poisoned Mr. Primo's dog. David, what condition do you think Aunt Jay's in about now?"

His silence, spun out for so long I thought he might not answer, was telling. "Not good, Troy. I just wish we'd had a chance to complete all of the angiographic studies. The abdominal pain she experienced is one of the signs of an actively dissecting aneurysm, which means a section of the artery has weakened to the point that it's being stretched to the max. Once that begins in a vessel of this size, we're talking minutes to hours before a full rupture occurs and the patient bleeds to death. All we can hope is that, since she hadn't been symptomatic until very recently, perhaps the dissection isn't too far advanced." His voice was soft, his hand on my arm gentle but supportive. "If I were you, I'd be prepared for the worst. I'm really sorry, Troy."

I'd accepted from that first evening that Jay might not survive. But the thought of her somewhere bleeding to death whittled away at all the defenses I'd constructed to keep functioning. I wished I'd told her how much she meant to me, to Wade, to scores of people.

She'd affected the lives of so many. She had organized a program of support for the children of mothers who were incarcerated. She'd ferried kids to jails to see their mothers, taken them on camping trips and outings, had even over-seen shopping trips for school clothes. It was Julia Wingate who, after my divorce from Wade, had steered me toward the kind of work that would make a difference in the lives of others and bolster my own self-worth. It had been my salvation. Jay deserved better than this.

"Thanks, David," I mumbled and started back toward the Thunderbird. The wind had changed, blowing the smoke and soot from what remained of the fire in our direction.

"Hey." He caught up and stopped me, brushing a bit of ash from my cheek. "Where are you going?"

Until that moment I hadn't really decided. "Back to Hospitality House. The brochure in my room says they have a Business Center with computers guests can use. Would you mind giving me Mr. Fontaine's number? I need to ask him if he knew the name of Vinnie Quarles's father."

"Sure. I'll call you with it as soon as I get back. But why? How would knowing that help you?"

"My gut feeling is that what we're dealing with here is some family's dirty laundry. Thanks, David." Again, I started toward Central.

Once again, he blocked my way. "Hold it, lady. What do you mean?"

It was clear I wouldn't be going anywhere without giving him an explanation first. "Miss Lucy's boarder, Vinnie Quarles, Nathan Stokes, and some joker who tailed me from Bluffton all look—"

"Someone followed you?" David interrupted.

"Right. They look alike, David, all four of them." I whipped out the picture Phil had given me. "This is Nathan Stokes." He looked appropriately shocked. "They've got to be related, David. We know they don't have the same mother, but either they have the same father or their fathers are brothers."

"What if they are? What does that have to do with Mrs. Wingate and the boarder?"

I tried to muffle my irritation. The last thing I needed at the moment was the voice of reason. "I don't know, but it's all I have to work with so I'm going to run with it. Mr. Haskins and his men are up to their armpits. They don't have time to pursue this. I do. Aunt Jay may die, but by God, if she does, I'm going to see to it that everybody knows the reason for it."

David studied me, gauging whether or not I was stoppable, I suppose. "Okay. But if someone's following you, Troy, you may be in danger. I came with the ambulance, so I've got to hang around until it goes back to the hospital. I'll call you with Mr. Fontaine's number as soon as I can. But listen, my shift ends in a couple of hours. Promise me you'll stay put until I'm free. I don't want you running around alone. I'm serious."

That pierced my armor for a second but I welded over

the rent. There was no point in reading too much into his concern. Still, what he'd said made sense. "I'll wait for you, scout's honor. Can I go now?"

He released my arm. "Okay. But don't forget, you promised. I don't want you disappearing, too."

I jogged toward the car, feeling a bit like a teenager wondering if the boy she likes is watching. I thought about that ten pounds I'd been meaning to lose. Lord knows every ounce of it was around my hips. Then I remembered the super-sized Hershey bar from Hospitality House's gift shop. I was ravenous and it was waiting for me, calling my name. To hell with it. I couldn't have David but the Hershey was mine, bought and paid for. Then I remembered that Hersheys were Jay's favorite candy and my appetite vanished. If we found her dead, I'd never eat a Hershey again. Oh, God, where was she?

At Hospitality House I stopped by my room first to check on The Deacon, who greeted me with a yawn so wide I could swear I saw daylight out the other end. He then curled into a ball, one paw over his eyes, and in no time was snoring. So much for feline companionship.

Munching on a breakfast bar, I dialed Miss Potee's pager number. I hadn't noticed whether she was still at the fire when I left. I'd give her fifteen minutes and then go on down to the Business Center. I didn't dare wait any longer than that.

The phone rang six minutes later. "This is Mabel Potee. Who called me?"

"It's Troy. I—"

"Oh, baby, I just heard about Max. He's at my boy's veterinary clinic, and it looks like it's gonna take a while to get that crap out of his system. At least he'll survive. But what are we gonna do now? We've got to find Bits!"

"I'm doing what I can," I said, "which amounts to still

trying to pin down the motive for all this insanity. I have a question for you. Was Nathan Miss Lucy's only child?"

"Far as I know. Why?"

"Because Mr. Stokes claimed to have a brother in Hawaii, a brother old enough to have been in the service. He gave Mr. Stokes his Purple Heart, so he was probably wounded during World War Two." Like Vinnie, I mused. Another one of those damned coincidences?

"Uh-uh." There was no doubt in Miss Potee's voice. "Couldn't have been a child of Miss Lucy's if he was old enough to be in the service. She was too young. Blanche says she remembers her parents thinking Reverend Allenby might hitch up with Miss Lucy, but once she started hitting the bottle, that took care of that."

The upright Reverend Allenby and Miss Lucy? I couldn't imagine him considering her as a stepmother for his beloved Angela.

"I'm really sorry about his house," I said, remembering the interest she'd taken in it.

"So's everybody. We're just praying it wasn't arson."

"Why would someone do that? I thought everybody worships the ground he walks on."

"Most do," Miss Potee said, "but he's made an enemy or two over the years. He's hell on what he calls adulterers-and-fornicators—never one without the other, the same way people say sick-and-tired. He's even accused people and named names from the pulpit, so not everybody loves the man. You want me to pump Blanche about what she remembers about Miss Lucy?"

I allowed as how that might be helpful, rang off, and went down to the Business Center, which was better equipped than I had expected. Their four computers and printers weren't top-of-the-line but they'd do. I settled in front of a PC, turned it on, watched it go through its warmup exercises, and placed my fingers on the keyboard. It was better than therapy. I was at home again, in familiar territory. I clicked open the simple word processing program, took a deep breath and began inputting everything that had happened in the last two days, all the bits and pieces of Jay's mystery. I cut and pasted, deleted this, revised that, printed it out and read it through with a sense of satisfaction, perhaps because it was the only thing I'd accomplished since arriving on Innocence.

I perused it a second time, just to make sure I hadn't left anything out, and finished with an even stronger conviction that in trying to atone for a wrong she thought she had committed, Jay had inadvertently opened a closet door and the skeletons of several generations had fallen out. And for the first time I thought I saw a picture coming together. Granted, it was still unfocused, with key elements missing, but if I could find them . . . I needed the help of someone who could access databases and records that were off-limits to me. Graham. I don't know why I hadn't thought of it sooner.

There were phones beside each computer. I checked to be sure the nearest one was plugged in, arranged for all calls to be charged to my room, and dialed my brother. Graham and a high school friend had left good, steady government jobs to set up shop as an Internet access provider. There was no reason for America Online or Prodigy to worry about his service quite yet, but give him a few years and he'd be a source to reckon with. Most important, thanks to his years in government with a top-secret clearance, Graham had contacts all over the globe. And he owed me.

"Graham?"

"Squeak!" As in Pipsqueak, the name he'd pinned on me as soon as I was old enough to hate it. "Where the hell have you been? I've been trying to get you. The parents called from Nassau and are having a ball. What are you up to?"

"Calling in favors, brother mine."

"For what?" he asked, with just the right amount of outrage.

"For that eight forty-five dash to the mall I made a couple of months ago to buy a gold bracelet for a certain jackass who'd forgotten to get an anniversary present for his wife."

He groaned. I had him and he knew it. "How much do you need?"

"Not money, big brother. I need you on-line in whatever direction it takes to get some information for me. Start writing. The name is Jacob E. C. Stokes, deceased. I need to know whatever you can find out about him, especially how many children he laid claim to. Unless I miss my guess, he had a big problem keeping his zipper zipped. There's one son on record, a Nathan Stokes, born in 1932 in Charleston, South Carolina. Hold it a sec."

I read through the paragraph detailing our conversation with Mr. Fontaine. Uh-huh, Estelle had left Jacques Landing to work in Charleston. And if I remembered correctly, Miss Lucy's boarder had told Jay he would show her how they treated thieves up in Charleston. "Stokes probably lived in Charleston. It may be a family hub, or something."

"You wouldn't, of course, have a Social Security number on him."

"Sorry."

"Sure you are. Is that all?"

"Not by a long shot. Do you still have that contact in the Veterans Administration?" It was a dumb question. Name a place and Graham knew someone who lived, worked, or computed there.

"Shelly? Yeah. Why?"

"I'm also trying to trace a Vincent William Quarles. Born on Jacques—French spelling—Landing, South Carolina. Mother's name: Estelle Quarles. Father's name may be Jacob Stokes."

"Ah, an illicit liaison."

"Without a doubt. Estelle was black. Stokes wasn't. I want to know if Quarles is still alive. He was in the service during World War Two and lost a leg, so he had to have been in a VA hospital at some point. If he's dead, I need the name of whoever filed for a Basic Burial Allowance."

"You couldn't do this yourself? Or write off for this stuff?" Graham sounded much put-upon.

"And miss an opportunity to put the squeeze on you? I'm doing this to help Aunt Jay and time is critical. I'll fill you in later."

"Well, if it's for Aunt Jay," he grumbled. "What else?"

"Find out who owns and or runs a firm called Progressive Movements in Honolulu. And, if you can work it, if there's anyone associated with the business whose nickname is Bubba."

"Bubba? In Hawaii? Please! Next."

"I need all of the above, like, yesterday. You can do it. You love a challenge. Here's number. Now get off the phone, Grammy. The clock's ticking."

I hung up on a series of colorful expletives. I dearly loved getting Graham's goat.

Posted on the wall behind each computer were directions for accessing the Internet. Browse through the Web long enough and you're bound to hit on something interesting. I logged on and headed straight for Genealogy. It wasn't a subject I normally pursued so I wandered around a bit before I discovered that there were a lot of people wandering around out there with me, looking for kinfolk. Each state seemed to have a mail drop, as it were, where you could post the name of the family or relative you were researching. Unfortunately I didn't have time to take that route. What I needed to know I needed to know *now*.

There were scores of home pages that included family trees. "Hi! We're the Higglypoohs. Welcome to our home page. To introduce ourselves, etc, etc." Some family trees were so extensive and detailed I suspected that if I followed them back far enough, I'd run into Noah and his brood.

By pure luck I stumbled across a home page for Jacques Landing, a surprise considering how closemouthed they were supposed to be. Along with the usual commercial extolling the virtues it claimed made the Landing attractive to business, its webmaster had embedded a link to the history of the island that included a couple of hundred years of genealogy, tracing the begats of the founding fathers. I couldn't wait to break the news to David.

The three generations of the Quarles family branch was one of the shortest. Estelle had been an only child and had died before her fortieth birthday. And there it was, the date of birth of Vincent William, May 2, 1922. No name in the place for Vinnie's father, no date of death for Vinnie, but I hadn't expected one, since no one had heard from him after he'd had the mausoleum constructed for Estelle. He'd be seventy-five now, so there was every possibility he was still alive.

I grabbed a Hospitality House notepad and jotted down Vinnie's birthday, then Nathan's. I logged off, and went back upstairs to think and wait for David's call while I scanned my notes.

Vinnie would have been twenty-one in 1943 and Nathan eleven. At what point had their paths intersected? Obviously after 1939, the year the snapshot of Vinnie and Estelle had been taken, but when and on what occasion?

Was the resemblance between them that obvious even then? Since there were four men so far with almost exactly the same features, it was fairly safe to assume that they were part of a family, no matter how distant the relationship, in which the males bore a strong resemblance to one another. Using that line of reasoning, Miss Lucy's boarder and her son were related. If Vinnie had been one of the servicemen ferried over for the Fourth of July celebrations and had run into Miss Lucy's boarder, assuming they hadn't known one another before, how would they have reacted? Perhaps the boarder had taken Vinnie to Miss Lucy's. What then?

A great deal might hinge on whether or not they'd realized that Vinnie was black. If they had, would his existence have exposed the extracurricular activities of a member of the family, activities which if known, might have caused irreparable harm? Was blackmail in the air? It was a cinch the boarder must have done something to push Miss Lucy so far that she'd try to kill him. I could envision her acting in her son's defense, striking out in the heat of the moment to protect him if he were being mistreated. But the little I knew didn't fit that scenario.

Jay had beaned the man and left him lying face down, the same position shown in the sketch. So he was either still out cold or asleep when Miss Lucy decided to take advantage of the opportunity and smother him. Perhaps she was protecting someone's reputation. Her own? I doubted it. Her reputation was already shot, thanks to her love of the grape or corn or whatever kind of hooch she drank, and the weekend parties she hosted for servicemen. Who else might have meant that much to her? Her late husband? Made sense, if he'd been someone allegedly above such things as a roll in the hay with a woman of color. But again, that hinged on their knowing that Vinnie was black. David maintained that the residents of Jacques Landing were very proud of their ancestry and would never think of passing themselves off as anything other than African American. That was now. This was then. Would Vinnie have 'fessed up that readily back in 1943? Had he been a member of a black regiment? I was getting a headache. There were too many unknowns.

The phone rang, waking The Deacon. He jumped down and disappeared under the bed. I made a mental note to check under it before we left for good. It was one of the places The Deacon used as a stash at home. No doubt he'd done the same here.

David was on the line. "Everything okay?" he asked.

"Fine. You have Mr. Fontaine's number?"

"I called already. All he remembers is that Estelle left the Landing as soon as she was of age—I guess that means sixteen or so—and got a job in Charleston working for a family as a domestic. Couple of years later she returns to the Landing great with child." Behind me, The Deacon began a rough-and-tumble with whatever toy he'd dug out from under the bed. "He says he doesn't think Estelle ever told anyone the name of the baby's father, but the family she worked for had a son about her age and Estelle's father suspected he was the culprit. Troy, what is all that noise?"

It took me a second to figure out what he was talking about. "My cat. It's playtime. Now that I think of it, perhaps I should meet you downstairs. The Deacon isn't the friendliest feline in the world."

"Not on your life. I'll come to your room and your cat can like it or lump it. Moore just walked in, early for a change, so I'll be there as soon as we've compared notes on a couple of patients. In the interim, you stay put. That's an order." *Click.*

I wished he hadn't put it quite that way. I didn't respond

well to being bossed around. But I didn't dare leave, either, damn it.

I wandered out onto the balcony to get some air and think. There were so many other things I could have asked Graham to dig into but they would take more time than I could spare. As it was, shadows were long now, daylight taking on that sharp-edged quality it assumes before dusk begins to settle. The rear of Reverend Allenby's house had the same sad, shuttered look as the front, the angle of the evening sun clearly illuminating the screened-in porch. It was empty and undoubtedly had been yesterday morning as well. Next door, the tape had been removed from Mrs. Peterson's property. I could see her garden, its neat rows of tomatoes and beans snaking their way up poles, and other green things I couldn't identify from this distance. Who would tend it now?

A black cat was perched in the tree in the side yard. I sat on the balcony for the next half hour, watching it. It was either stuck up there or sublimely content because it never moved. I envied it its patience, its ability to wait for whatever, something I don't do well under most circumstances. Given the present situation, each minute felt like a calendar year. What must it feel like for Jay?

Inside, the phone chirped again. I caught it in the middle of the second ring.

"Hey, Squeak, you need to check the source of your information about the Quarles character. There's no record he was a veteran. He doesn't show up in VA records of any kind and Shelly's tapped each of the services. She's checking National Records now, but, dead or alive, if he was in WW Two, his name should have popped up by now. Later. Bye."

Typical Graham. He hadn't let me get a word in edgewise. Before I could call him back, there was a knock at the door. I checked to see where The Deacon was, then went to open it.

"You're supposed to ask who's there," David said, scowling. "I could have been anybody." Then he spotted The Deacon, who, true to form, was on Full Alert at the foot of the bed in a half-crouch. "What have you been feeding him? That's the biggest damned cat I've ever seen. So, what's been happening?"

I closed the door, waved him to the chair, and told him of Graham's failure to come up with any record of Vinnie's military service.

"That's weird," he said, and did precisely what I hoped he would. He picked up the phone and called Jacques Landing. I made no pretense of not eavesdropping. It was frustrating as hell getting just one side of the conversation, but I figured that listening in on the extension by the bed would be pushing it.

David "uh-huhed" and "uh-uhed" until he finally hung up. "I don't know what the problem is," he said, with a troubled frown. "Vinnie came home after Basic Training and one other time before he was shipped overseas. Mr. Fontaine says he was definitely in an Army uniform both times."

Then why couldn't Graham's contact find him?

"But," he continued, "and this is interesting, he said everyone was surprised he'd passed the physical, because Vinnie had a heart murmur and had been originally classified 4F. He figures Vinnie must have gotten a doctor to swear that the condition wouldn't affect his performance. He wanted to enlist so his mother would get his allotment and benefits. She needed lots of medical care."

"TB," I said remembering. "But what happened that the money stopped coming?"

"No one knows. He was in a German prison camp, but

that still shouldn't have affected his allotment. And his name should be in their records somewhere." He scowled. "Something's not right here."

Sensing movement, I looked around to see The Deacon, belly low, sneaking up on David, one slow step at a time. It occurred to me that after that first look at him, David had ignored The Deacon altogether. Perhaps he didn't like cats, in which case, I'd have to alter my opinion of him. "You're being stalked," I warned him. "I'll put him out on the balcony."

"Leave him alone. What time is your brother supposed to call back?"

"I gave him two hours," I said. "Why?"

"Because I'm getting sick of hearing your stomach growl. Don't you believe in eating?"

I pressed my hand against my midsection, embarrassed. "I just had a breakfast bar," I protested.

"You don't eat properly. That's why you're so thin. You could stand to put on another few pounds, you know."

My mother would *love* this man. *I* was beginning to love this man. Perhaps it was just as well he didn't like cats.

The only cat I was concerned with had reached his quarry. Slinking around to the left of David's chair, he stood up on his hind legs, sniffing at David's backside.

"Deacon—" I began.

"Stop worrying about him. I'm taking you out to dinner and before you start squawking, we can forward calls from this phone to my cellular. Forwarding is one of the amenities Hospitality House offers since most of its guests are usually across the street at the hospital." He began pushing buttons on the phone while The Deacon, a southpaw, slowly raised his left front and with the finesse of a first-class pickpocket, patted David's rear. David grinned, dialed again, and made a reservation somewhere or other, haggling with the person on the phone about which table he wanted. I watched, fascinated, as The Deacon poked and nudged at the back pocket of David's jeans.

David hung up the phone and twisted around to look down at the cat. "Well, at least his nose is working." He stuck two fingers into his pocket and removed a small flat packet of aluminum foil. "Now, let's get something straight," he said, waving it under The Deacon's nose. He had The Deacon's complete attention. "I'm a human, you're a cat. I happen to like the human who belongs to you, so you might as well get used to me. Behave yourself and there's more where this came from. We'll be leaving," he said to me, "as soon as I make this cat my love slave."

I gnawed the inside of my cheek raw to keep from howling with laughter as he very slowly fed The Deacon a good dozen popcorn shrimp one tiny morsel at a time. The Deacon sat and waited patiently for David to extend each shrimp. I had never been able to get him to eat from my hand. And nobody, but nobody, had ever won over this cat. I was witnessing two firsts. I don't know which pleased me more, that David liked me and had expressed it in no uncertain terms, or that he liked the cat and the cat obviously liked him. I felt guilty being almost happy while Jay was hidden somewhere dying.

"Let's go," I said, "before you seduce my cat away from me altogether. You're sure we won't miss Graham's call?"

"Positive." He folded the empty square of aluminum foil and put it back in his pocket. "I'll use a trash can at the restaurant or your room will smell like a fish market when you get back."

Considerate, too. This was more than I could stand.

"I need to wash my hands," he said, nose wrinkled.

I pointed him toward the bathroom and used his absence

to rake a comb through my hair and apply lipstick for the first time since I'd arrived.

The Deacon, feeding time over, disappeared under the bed. He began backing out from under it, tail first, just as David returned. I moved to the desk to put the notepad into my purse and turned to see my cat with something white clutched between his teeth. He bounced to David and stood on his hind legs like a meerkat with his offering.

"He plays tricks, too?" David asked.

"It's a bribe for more shrimp. That had better not be what I think it is," I said and skirted the bed to see him more clearly.

"Missing one of your credit cards?" David asked. Gingerly, he removed it from The Deacon's mouth and passed it to me.

"Deacon!" I bellowed, in my best I'm-gonna-kill-a-cat tone. He looked at me, confused, pupils dilating, and slithered under the bed.

How could he have gotten the card out of my wallet? I turned it over and felt my stomach lurch. It wasn't mine. The name embossed across its bottom: Elva L. Peterson. Too rattled to say a word, I handed it to David.

"Elva . . . What the hell? How'd he get this?"

I sank down on the end of the bed. "I don't know. She used it yesterday; I saw the receipts. And The Deacon hasn't been out of this room."

David stared at it, eyes narrowed. "I'm going to try something." He stepped out into the hall, closed the door and was back in less than ten seconds. "Talk about a fifty-cent lock," he muttered. "I think it's safe to assume she came in the same way I did."

"I had the feeling someone had been in here yesterday," I said, "because of the way The Deacon was acting, all puffed up and twitchy. He's as close to a guard cat as there is; he'll attack if someone comes in and I'm not around. But it couldn't have been Mrs. Peterson yesterday, David. I met her at Miss Lacey's a few minutes later and there wasn't a scratch on her. Oh, my God." My cheeks went cold.

"What?" He slipped the credit card into his shirt pocket.

"She was all scratched up this morning. Mr. Haskins thought the scratches had been caused by someone dragging her. She must have been here, David. She probably dropped the credit card when The Deacon jumped her. But if I didn't answer her knock, why would she slip the lock and come in anyway?"

"Perhaps she wanted to leave something," he suggested. "Why don't you search the room? I'm going downstairs and ask around. Someone may have seen her come in. I'll be back."

As soon as he left, The Deacon stuck his head out to see if the coast was clear. I leaned down and scratched behind his ears in apology, then began the same kind of search I'd performed the day before, starting with the dresser. That took less than a minute. The items in the closet, what few there were, seemed undisturbed. There was nothing new in my pockets.

I opened my carry-on, checked it thoroughly. Nothing. I removed Jay's little suitcase from the shelf, remembering after I'd done it that I'd forgotten to look to see if the strand of hair I'd positioned between it and the shelf was still there. Oh, well.

I opened Jay's overnight case. Her jewelry was as I'd left it, all those tiny little rings. I closed the case and put it aside, unable to look at them any longer.

The bathroom yielded nothing. Neither did the drawers of the night table and desk. I even looked under the bed. All I saw was a collection of The Deacon's menagerie of toys.

David tapped at the door. "I found the guy in charge of security. He'll ask the staff on the night shift, but there's a possibility Mrs. Peterson came in the side door, in which case no one would have seen her. Did you find anything?"

"Not even dust balls."

"Well, it occurred to me on my way back up here that your phone's forwarded to the one in my car and we're not in it. Let's drop off the credit card at the police station and go on to dinner."

I grabbed my bag, told The Deacon to behave himself, and followed David out, checking to be sure the door locked behind me, as if that made a hell of a lot of difference. I left with little expectation of ever sitting down in that restaurant. So far something had always happened to prevent my eating a square meal. It just wasn't in the cards. All I could do was hope that whatever the snag was this time, I'd manage to survive it.

15

The police station was lit up but vacant, which David greeted with an equanimity I found hard to fathom. What happened if there was an emergency? What were you supposed to do, let the phone ring until someone finally showed up to answer it? He found an envelope, wrote a note explaining where the credit card had come from, and left it in a prominent place on the desk. "I let them know where we'll be in case they want to talk to us immediately," he said, buckling up, "and left the cellular phone number, too." As if summoned, the thing sounded off. David answered and after a second, handed it to me. "I think this is for you," he said, grinning.

"And who the hell was that?" Graham demanded.

"None of your business." That was guaranteed to drive him nuts. Ever since the divorce, Graham took being a big brother far too seriously for my own good. He hated Wade. "What have you found out?" I asked.

"Shelly says it's definite. Vincent Quarles was never in

the service. So I went poking elsewhere. Southerners are deep into the genealogical bag. I got a hit on the dude you thought might be his father, in fact, two of them."

"Two fathers or two hits?"

"Two Jacob Stokes, dummy, Junior and Senior. Turns out to be an old Charleston family. There are Stokeses all over the place. The family tree is like a maze. I've got a buddy who works on a newspaper in Charleston poking around for me. It might take longer than a couple of hours, though."

"Well, it would help to know which one married Lucille Dalton, Nathan's mom, and how many other sons each of the Jacobs had. God knows I've seen one face on too many men for them to be unrelated. Anything else?"

"Progressive Movements. Found the phone number and an answering machine saying they're closed because of a death in the family. They manufacture electronic components. I've got another friend looking into who owns it."

At least Nathan had mattered enough for Bubba to shut down the assembly line for a while. It made me feel better. "Okay, Grammy. You're almost off the hook."

"Brat. Did that guy say 'doctor' when he answered the phone?"

"Yes, he did."

"Are you sick?"

"Healthy as the proverbial horse, thanks."

"You're dating a doctor? Mom will freak! What's his—"

I hit the End button with the greatest pleasure. I'd gotten Graham's goat twice in one day, a record.

"So what'd he say?" David asked, waiting at a red light.

"One, if we're to believe VA records, Vinnie was definitely not a veteran. Two, there's a Jacob Stokes Senior and a Junior. Which one was Nathan's dad, we don't know yet. The light's green."

He jerked to attention, waved at the driver behind who had honked, and proceeded through the intersection. "It would make more sense for Jacob Senior to be Nathan's dad and Junior his half brother."

"So there's a good chance he was Miss Lucy's boarder. And her stepson. Which doesn't feel right. According to Miss Potee, Miss Lucy probably wasn't that much older than I figure the boarder was."

"Perhaps a May-December romance," David suggested.

I was so engrossed with trying to work out the potential relationships among the Stokeses that I admit to paying little or no attention to my surroundings as we entered the restaurant and were led to a prime piece of real estate by the window. The view overlooked a park-like square complete with a fountain spurting geysers two stories high, walkways radiating from it to the outer perimeter, and benches under massive shade trees. Fake gaslights ringed the area, unlit at the moment. All of the surrounding businesses had fronts that were much alike, Doric columns along a deep veranda.

"Ground rules," David said, holding my chair for me. "We forget everything for the next hour and concentrate on the food, the ambiance, and one another. Agreed?"

The "one another" had been added in such an offhand manner that I almost missed it. "Agreed." It would be easy. The restaurant featured the kind of atmosphere that, located anywhere else, could have claimed responsibility for the births of a heck of a lot of children. Lights were low, the music soft, heavy with strings, and downright mushy, while candles threw shadows across the linen-covered tables.

"Except," I said, remembering, "one last thing. It turns out that Jacques Landing has a home page on the Internet complete with history and the genealogy of all the families on the island."

David groaned. "Are you telling me that all this time all I had to do was turn on the damned computer and browse the Web to find out if my grandmother's granddad founded that blasted island?" I nodded, the disgust on his face launching me into a fit of giggles. "I feel like a first-class idiot," he said, scowling. "And if you don't quit laughing, this meal will be Dutch." He went to ground behind a menu large enough to cover his face and two or three more, but I could see his abs contracting spasmodically as he laughed at himself.

We placed our orders—guinea fowl for David, London broil for me (and The Deacon)—and lapsed into companionable silence over a tangy shrimp cocktail. He was smooth, was David Baskerville. He waited until the appetizer and a marvelous wine had lulled me into a mellow mood before saying, "Tell me about your ex-husband. Wade, right?"

I looked him dead in the eye and called him a bastard.

"I beg to differ," he responded with almost comical hauteur. "My parents had been married nine years by the time I was born and had had a kid a year. I was the last."

"You've got eight brothers and sisters?" And would probably expect to have a big family himself, I mused dolefully.

"Four of each. It was hell sometimes. We were't dirt poor, just dust poor. But there was always food on the table and everybody worked and all nine of us went to college. And once we were all out of the house, my parents filled it up with foster kids. Don't think you've detoured me off the subject. Come on, tell me about Wade. Considering the lengths you've gone to to help his great-aunt and to keep the situation from him because of his recent fatherhood, I figure he must be a dynamite guy."

I took my time answering because I needed to hear it

myself. "I thought he was. Our relationship was a vital com-
ponent of my very foundation, only the relationship turned
out to be a lie. I may never forgive him for that."

David broke a roll in two, buttered both sides, and
placed one half on my bread plate. "You're being evasive.
What did he do, Troy?"

I couldn't figure out what there was about this man that
made me feel obligated to spill my guts. But spill them I
did, gave him the whole story, from the time Wade moved
into the neighborhod when I was eight until the night he
packed a bag and said goodbye almost four years ago.

David made no comment during it all, simply listened.
His eyes were like a kaleidoscope. I'd never seen irises
change color the way his did, from a mesmerizing green to
a deep hazel to an intense brown and gold. The hues
shifted with his moods. Since I didn't know him well
enough, I wasn't sure what the soft greenish gray they'd
become revealed about his present state of mind. And even
if he'd been inclined to tell me, he never got the opportunity.

The sun had eased below the horizon but a flaming
pink sky, along with the gaslights which had flared to life
sometime during my recitation, combined to supply
more than enough illumination to see the features of
people outside quite clearly. While I'd been laying out
my life's history, I had focused on the activity down in
the square to avoid seeing any pity in his eyes. The
strollers—human, not the four-wheeled kind—were out
in force, crisscrossing the park at a leisurely pace.
Directly opposite us, a limousine was pulling to a stop in
front of one of the white-columned business establish-
ments. The driver hopped out, hurried around to the
rear door, and opened it, leaning in to give his charge a
helping hand. An elderly gentleman emerged, his age

betrayed by his posture and an uncertain gait, his thick, dark hair throwing off glints of yellow as he stood under one of the gaslights. He straightened up and glanced around the square. Then, shaking off the driver's assistance, he walked slowly to the door of the building and disappeared inside.

"Hey, what's wrong?" David reached across the table and pinched the back of my hand gently. "You look as if you're about to keel over."

"I just saw one of the clones! Honestly! He got out of the limo and went into that building."

"Are you sure?" David peered at me with outright suspicion.

"I admit that face has been burned into my brain, but I did not imagine it. I'm farsighted, there's plenty of light, and I saw him clearly. He's one of them, David. I don't know which one, but I'm damned sure going to find out." Plucking the napkin from my lap, I dropped it on the table and got up, almost colliding with our waiter, who managed to lift the enormous tray he was carrying just in time to avoid dumping its contents over my head. "Sorry. Put those in a warmer," I said to him. "We'll be back. You coming, David?"

He grimaced and got up. "Keep this table for us, Cody, and I'll double your tip."

"You got it, Doc," the waiter said, and made a U-turn back toward the kitchen.

Outside, David grabbed my hand to slow me down. "Cool it, Troy. Just what do you plan to do?"

I hadn't a notion. "Play it by ear, I guess. Improvise. I just want to see him up close."

"Has it occurred to you that you don't know who you're dealing with? One of the clones has been trailing you, remember? And one of them is probably a murderer, maybe the same clone, maybe not. You don't even know how many of them there are."

That gave me pause but only for about half a second. "I don't care. The least we can do is try to get his name, find out something about him."

"And then what?"

"I'll work that out when the time comes." We had cut directly across the square and were now approaching the limo. The driver lounged against the front fender, arms folded, ankles crossed. I skirted the vehicle and came abreast of him, David lagging slightly behind. "Hi," I said. "I could swear I just saw a former boss of mine get out of this limo. Was that James Burdette?" What the heck, Dad would never know.

The driver shook his head. "No, ma'am. Name's Crandall."

Crandall. I glanced at David, whose response was an eloquent shrug. I tried again. "Then he's got to be related. Is Mr. Crandall from Charleston?"

"Ya got me. I picked him up from the airport. Doesn't talk much, but don't sound like anybody from around here."

I was stuck, but only temporarily. I stared meaningfully at the door of Tyler and Sons.

"Oh, all right." David chuckled. "We'll go on in. I can have a word with a buddy while we're here. Take it easy, man," he said to the driver and ferried me toward the entrance. "Are you always this stubborn?"

"Yeah. What kind of business is this? Why are they open so late?"

"Funeral homes tend to have rather fluid hours," he said dryly. I balked, unprepared for this turn of events, and he nudged me inside with far more enthusiasm than I felt was warranted. If one of the clones was in here, however, the only logical reason was to arrange for the final rites of another of his clan, Nathan Stokes. Considering what the limo driver had said about his passenger's accent, there was a distinct possibility that Bubba had arrived. I'd only been in the Hawaiian Islands once, but I'd been struck by their distinctive intonation. So Bubba's name was Crandall. I wondered which branch of the Stokes family the Crandalls had sprouted from.

Inside, we were immediately surrounded by hush and plush. There were viewings going on in two of the four reception rooms opening on either side of the foyer.

"David, I'm not dressed for this kind of thing." Somehow my denim skirt and vest and cotton shell seemed even more casual than usual. The visitors in the viewing rooms were gussied to a fare-thee-well.

"Chicken," he whispered and stepped inside the door of Parlor One, nodding to this one and that, but for the most part simply looking around. "Not in there," he said, when he came out a minute later, and crossed the hall to Parlor Four. That took a little longer but the result was the same. "Come on," he said, taking my arm. "If I can find Charlie, he may be able to help us."

He proceeded through a door at the end of the hall and led me past a series of offices, sticking his head in each one. All were empty.

"Wait a minute." I pulled up short before the territory he was about to invade. The sign beside this door said: All guests must be accompanied by Tyler and Son personnel. "I draw the line at barging into the room where they prepare the bodies."

"It's nice to know you draw it somewhere," David said, and opened the door. "Ah, there's Charlie." I stuck my head in, not quite ready to trust him yet, and found I could relax but only by a degree or two. It was the display room for the coffins. They lined the walls and were back-to-back down the center of the long, softly lit room, bronze-colored, platinum, woods of various hues, velvet-flocked models, lids opened to expose satin-lined interiors.

David's friend, Charlie, who looked as if he belonged in a body builders' competition, stood just opposite us entering notes on a hand-sized computer. Seeing David, he placed a finger to his lips. There were chairs between every second or third coffin but I decided that just inside the door was fine with me. I didn't understand the need for silence until I became aware of a second person moving slowly along the aisle formed by the coffins farthest from us. I couldn't see who it was until he passed a niche where a seat had been placed between the coffins in the center aisle. I stiffened and David squeezed my hand, hard.

It was definitely one of Them. I could only see him in profile for the moment but there was no mistaking the width of the brow, the angle of the jaw. "This one, Mr. Tyler," he said, and I could almost smell the sweet bouquet of the islands. "Write it up, please. I'll be paying with traveler's checks."

Charlie cleared his throat. "For the coffin or—"

"For everything."

Charlie appeared to eye him with renewed respect. "It should only take a moment. If you would care to wait—"

"Here's fine. Leave space for an additional entry. Might as well pick out one for myself while I'm at it."

"Yes, sir!" Charlie looked as if he'd just hit the jackpot, then evidently remembered a solemn demeanor would be far more appropriate. "Yes, sir," he said again, his tone somber. "Dr. Baskerville, you wanted to see me? Why don't you accompany me to my office?"

David turned to me, a question in his eyes. "You go on," I urged him. "I'll be fine right here."

"Troy—"

"Please, David," I whispered. "He's Bubba, I'm sure of it. I have to talk to him. Look at him. Does he look as if he could harm anybody?"

David hesitated, assessing the situation. "All right, but I'll be right beyond that door if you need me."

"My hero," I said, and fluttered my lashes.

With a smile playing around his lips, he followed his friend from the room.

Now that I was alone with the man, I wasn't sure what to say or do, so I opted for what came naturally, given the circumstances. I began a slow visual examination of the coffins, stopping before each. They really were quite beautiful, but I felt like a ghoul, pretending to be interested in them.

Bubba had stopped at a bronze model toward the end of the row. I made my way slowly toward him, my heart pounding, watching him from the corners of my eyes. He was taller than I'd thought, despite being slightly stooped with age. In fact, he was a gorgeous old man. The intense Hawaiian sun had burnished his skin a deep tan, yet there was an unhealthy pallor to it. Forgetting all pretense, I stared at him with a growing certainty that his decision to select a coffin for himself had not been made on a whim. This man was not well.

I assume he felt my gaze. He turned toward me, brows raised. I saw him straight on for the first time and lost every bit of cool I claimed to have. "My God, it's Vinnie Quarles!"

He was probably a good poker player. His only reaction was to tilt his head to one side, his expression guarded. "Pardon?"

"You're Vincent William Quarles. I don't believe it."

"That's just as well, young lady, since I'm afraid you've mistaken me for someone else. The name is Crandall, Edward Crandall." He smiled and I almost wished I were a couple of decades older or he a couple of decades younger.

I wasn't going for it. "If that's the name you prefer now, that's the name I'll use. But Mr. Fontaine said you had jet-black eyes. Your name may have changed but your eyes haven't."

"Which Fontaine?" he demanded, astonished. "Kenneth or Hoover?"

I shrugged. "Whichever owns the store."

"Hoover? He's still alive?" There was no masking his incredulity. "Cousin Hoovy's still alive?"

"And well." I went rooting in my bag and held up the snapshot of Vincent and his mother.

His face hardened. "Where did you get that?"

"It's a copy. The original was hanging on the wall of Nathan Stokes's cabin. It's being shipped to you with the rest of his things."

He heaved a sigh that seemed to come from deep within his soul. "I'm afraid you have the advantage of me, young lady. You are . . . ?"

"I'm Troy Burdette. I was the one who found Mr. Stokes yesterday. I can't tell you how sorry I am that we couldn't save him." Since I'd already blown it, I figured I might as well be up front with him, because I was not letting him off the hook. "Look, Mr. . . . Crandall, under normal circumstances I wouldn't dare invade your privacy at a time like this, but the circumstances aren't normal by a long shot. On July fourth, 1943, this man—" I went into my bag again and extracted the enlargement— "roughed up a young woman named Julia Brownlee, my great-aunt, in an upstairs bedroom of Miss Lucy Stokes's boarding house. In defending herself, she bashed him over the head with a chamber pot and killed him."

"What!"

"Well, she thought she had. It's haunted her ever since. She came back to Innocence three years ago to confess, and later that evening someone shot her, I assume to shut her up. She came back again on Monday to confess, and no one knew what she was talking about. No one had been reported dead. No body was ever found. Now she has delayed surgery that will save her life in order to find out once and for all whether she'd really killed this man. The daily paper printed the story yesterday and all hell broke loose. Since then Mr. Stokes has been killed and also a local woman who claimed she could get the proof that this man left the island alive. On top of everything else, someone has abducted my aunt from the hospital. We don't know why. But she's critically ill, with an aneurysm that may explode any minute. We've got to find her. I figure if we can get at the truth of what happened that night in 1943, it'll lead us to whoever's holding her. Can you help us?"

His eyes had been fixed on the enlargement. He rubbed his forehead. "And I thought I had problems. I can tell you what I know, but I'm not sure it'll solve anything. Your aunt didn't kill Jake Junior. No indeed. My brother Nathan did."

16

I couldn't figure it out. Half an hour ago when David and I had sat in that restaurant, its ambiance had seemed romantic in the extreme. Now, back at the same table overlooking the same square, the atmosphere seemed completely different, with a surreal quality, perhaps because the subject matter we were discussing was so at odds with our environment.

I'd burst in on David's conversation with his friend and had dragged him back to the display room to introduce him to Vinnie Quarles and to repeat the bombshell Mr. Quarles/Crandall had dropped. A fifteen-minute delay ensued while the bill with the funeral home was settled, after which Mr. Crandall paid off the limo driver and came back to the restaurant with us. He'd made us an offer I wasn't about to let David refuse: he'd fill us in on the whole sordid story (that's a quote) if we'd join him for "lunch."

"I'm still on Hawaii time, so it's lunchtime for me, but that's when I normally have my heaviest meal."

If what he finally ordered, soup and a small salad, was his heaviest meal of the day, I shuddered to think what he ate for breakfast and dinner. Once this feast arrived, he popped several pills into his mouth and downed them with a glass of water, David eyeing him with an intensity I'd learned meant he'd gone into a diagnostic mode.

"Forgive me," Mr. Crandall said, "but I have to ask you to let me explain what happened in my own way. That means starting at the beginning, in this case with my father, Jacob Edward Crandall Stokes Senior."

David and I exchanged a look, since that last statement had answered a couple of questions right off the bat.

"My father was an utterly amoral man. He preyed on women as if it was his profession. He had three wives that I know about, a string of mistresses, and hundreds of one-night stands."

"How many children?" I asked.

"None by his first wife; allegedly he drove her to suicide. One son by his second wife, who already had one child when he married her, another son by his third. How many illegitimately? Your guess is as good as mine."

That explained to a certain extent the nut case who'd followed me. Whether he was a son or grandson of Jacob Senior we'd probably never know.

"My mother had the misfortune of working as a maid in his house during his marriage to his second wife," Mr. Crandall continued, lines of anger around his mouth. "It took him two years to do it, but he finally got her into his bed."

"There's no way to put this delicately," I said. "Did he know she was black?"

His smile had a bitter quality. "Knew and didn't care. He considered her a novelty, a white black girl. He never saw me after I was born, never acknowledged me. She was a single mother back in the days when that was a mark of shame, yet she made sure I never felt I had anything to be ashamed of. She did her best for me, but when it was my turn to do for her, I wasn't able to."

"You mean when she contracted tuberculosis," David said.

He lowered his head, as if still feeling the sting of his shortcoming. "I was eighteen. There were no jobs except on fishing and shrimp boats. Her case was advanced and they were short of beds in the colored sanitarium. I was desperate. I tried enlisting, figuring at least if I sent most of my allotment, she might be able to go into a private hospital. But I had a heart murmur. They declared me 4F, unfit for service."

"Yet you had a Purple Heart," I said.

"Yes." His lips tightened and he poked at his salad.

"So you were in the service. You were wounded during the war."

He rapped on his left knee, which emitted a hard metallic sound. "I'm fitted with a prosthesis using electronic components I designed and patented. My son and I ship them all over the world. As for how I wound up in the Army in spite of my heart murmur, I went looking for my father to ask for help for my mother. At that point I knew nothing about him, only his name. I was too late. He'd died of syphilis a month before. That's when I met Jake Junior, the one in the photo, for the first time. He was in the catbird's seat. He'd inherited everything, the magnificent old house on prime acreage. He had a maid, butler, chauffeur, gardener. When I told him what I wanted, he literally fell off his chair laughing, said if he offered a dollar to each of his father's 'doxies,' he called them, and the children he'd spawned with them, he'd be in the poorhouse the next day. He most certainly had no intention of sharing his inheritance with one of his father's black bastards. That meant he'd known about me, because race hadn't come up until that moment."

"Sounds like a real winner," David said.

"He'd come by it honestly. He was about to kick me out when a maid came in and dropped the tea tray she was carrying in shock. She said something about not knowing Jake Junior had a twin brother. I don't think Jake had realized how alike we were until that moment. Or perhaps he just preferred not to acknowledge it until it occurred to him that it could be of benefit to him. You see, he'd just received his greetings from Uncle Sam and was not happy about it."

"Ah," David said. "It couldn't have come at a worse time for him. He'd just inherited quite an estate, from the sound of it, and he stood a good chance of going overseas and getting his head blown off."

"Precisely. He offered me a deal. If I went in his place, he would see that Mama was taken care of. He would have his family doctor find a private sanitarium for her and would pay for everything for the duration of her confinement. I went for it, even though I didn't trust him. But a little cash under the table to his doctor got me through the physical, don't ask me how. They acknowledged that I had a heart murmur but certified that it posed no danger. I was fit for service. And before I reported for duty, Mama was in a really nice sanitarium in the Pennsylvania mountains."

"Segregated?" I asked.

"Black patients in one wing, white in another. She was in; that's all I cared about. I went into the Army as Private Jacob Edward Crandall Stokes Junior and no one ever questioned it. Jake Junior got such a kick out of the wool he was pulling over the eyes of his Uncle Sam. As for me, I was sent overseas, got caught in an ambush, and spent seven long months as a guest in a German prison camp."

"You were wounded in the ambush?" David asked.

"No, during an escape. There were three of us. They carried me for six days until we ran into one of our units. By that time the leg was past saving. They took it off and shipped me to a VA hospital stateside. That's when I discovered I'd been listed as Missing in Action for months. I called the sanitarium as soon as I could and they said Mama was no longer a patient. I couldn't call home; there were no phones on the Landing then."

"And Jake Junior?" I asked.

"No answer there either. By the time I finally got home to the Landing . . ." He looked away, pupils contracting with pain.

"We heard the rest from Mr. Fontaine," David said.

"As soon as Jake found out I was MIA, he'd pulled the plug on the payments to the sanitarium. My allotment wasn't enough to keep her there and the colored sanitarium near here was so small and packed, they had patients in beds out in the halls. Mama said she'd just as soon go home and die there, and that's what she did. And I went looking for Jake and got lucky; he'd sold the homeplace in Charleston and the buyers were moving in when I arrived. They told me where to find Jake. I planned to kill him, I admit it. I was too late. By the time I traced him to Lucy's, Nathan had already done it for me. Now that he's dead there's no reason to protect him any longer."

"It couldn't have been Nathan," I protested. "He was only a kid."

Mr. Crandall nodded. "Eleven, but tall for his age and very strong."

"I'm sorry," I said, "I don't understand."

"Did your great-aunt do laundry?"

"Her mother did. She helped."

"Then I can assure you, all she did was knock Jake silly. When I arrived and asked Mrs. Stokes if he was there, she said he was upstairs nursing a granddaddy of a headache. According to her, he'd made the mistake of manhandling the laundry girl and she'd knocked his block off."

"Mrs. Stokes actually saw Jake, talked to him after Aunt Jay had left?" I asked.

"Yes indeed. She said he was sitting up there with a huge knot on the side of his head, raising hell about the kind of people she let into the house. She said he'd been trouble since he'd first shown up, throwing his money and his weight around, and taking advantage of island girls. She'd already given him his eviction notice. He was supposed to be out by midnight and she was worried he'd use the incident with the laundry girl to stay longer. I told her I'd be more than willing to get him off her property and then I planned to kill him. She asked me why and I told her."

"Had she known about you before?" I asked.

"No, and I didn't realize she'd been married to my father until that moment. She'd inherited a lot of property he wanted, and he'd married her to get it. Then Nathan was born. As soon as my father realized he wasn't normal, he divorced her, saying that Nathan was not his child. In those days there was no way to prove it. But as I was saying, Jake had shown up at her house out of the blue, said his father had treated her shamelessly, and he'd come to see how he could help her with Nathan. I found out later he knew I was back in the country and figured I'd come looking for him, so he'd skipped, thinking I'd never be able to find him." He picked at his salad, probably because it was there. "Anyway, he'd settled in at Mrs. Stokes's and had caused an uproar ever since. She also suspected he might have been knocking Nathan around. That was enough for me. She took me upstairs and there he was, lying on his stomach, as dead as the proverbial doornail."

"But what makes you think Nathan killed him?" I asked.

"He as much as said he had. He was hiding in the hall closet across from Jake's room, clutching one of those old-fashioned cast iron doorstops his mother said had been holding Jake's door open. The poor kid had been beaten pretty badly; his nose was bleeding, he had a split lip and the beginning of a shiner. He kept slapping his own face, saying, 'Bad boy, Natie's a bad boy.' From what little we could make out, he had wandered into Jake's room, attracted by the diamond cuff links on the dresser. His mother said he liked shiny things. Jake turned over, figured the boy was about to steal them, and jumped him. Nathan must have defended himself by striking out at Jake with the doorstop. A blow to the head, from somebody as strong as Nathan was, killed him."

I sat back, imagining the scene and wondering why I still wasn't satisfied with the way things were turning out.

"Why was Jake's body never found?" David asked.

Mr. Crandall hesitated, then shrugged. "I guess there's no point in keeping that a secret any longer either. And if it will help your great-aunt in any way, Miss Burdette . . . "

I decided to think positively. Julia Wingate had to survive to hear all this.

"We stuffed him in his own steamer trunk, threw in every book in the house for ballast, rented a fishing boat, and dumped him as far out in the ocean as we dared go, considering all the patrol boats on the prowl for enemy submarines. It might not have been the most ethical thing to do but, damn it all, Nathan was my little brother, a child with a mental disorder that made him a victim twice over. Mrs. Stokes said the people on the island were already afraid of him. If they'd found out what he'd done, they'd have insisted he be put away. He'd have wound up in an asylum for the rest of his life when all he'd done was defend himself. I was not about to see him subjected to any further trauma."

Despite all the wrong things he'd done—assuming his brother's identity in the service and passing for white in the process, and feeding Jake's body to the sharks and sea anemones, I couldn't help but like this man because he'd done all those things for the right reasons. He'd gone out on a limb to protect a younger brother he'd just met.

"Poor Nathan," David murmured.

"It took some doing to make him understand that he must never tell anyone what he'd done," Mr. Crandall was saying, "but he promised he wouldn't and I promised him and his mother that as long as I was alive, I'd see that he was taken care of. It was time someone in the family did some good. And since Jake had stashed in his valise almost fifty thousand dollars from the sale of the house, we had a pretty good start on Nathan's security."

"That much money in 1943?" David said. "I should imagine you did."

"Mrs. Stokes insisted on splitting it with me—sharing the guilt, I guess. I'm ashamed to say I took it with no hesitation and left before sunup the next morning."

"Where'd you go?" David asked.

"I headed west. There was nothing left for me on Jacques Landing. I arranged for a decent mausoleum for my mother, and went on doing what I'd been doing for the last few years, being Jacob Edward Crandall Stokes Junior. From California, I worked my way to the Hawaiian Islands, dropped the front and back part of the name, and built a new life as a black man among a population of brown-skinned people. This is the first time I've been back. I had to see that Nathan had a proper burial."

"And you'd be willing to explain what happened that night to the Innocence police?" David asked.

"Why not? Getting rid of Jake's body was a crime but I doubt I'll live to spend any time in jail."

"The problem?" David asked, probing gently.

"Prostate cancer." The tone of his voice seemed grounded in acceptance and resignation. "Your dinners are cold."

I had long since lost what appetite I had, and still had questions that needed answers. "And you never met your father."

"No. It's just as well. Nathan's mother filled me in on the kind of man he was. He must have hated women to treat them the way he did. He had no shame. He even seduced his stepson's wife and made her pregnant."

"Good Lord," David said.

"That almost got him killed, especially after the poor woman died giving birth."

I'd had trouble following the snarls in his family tree. "So in your generation there were actually four of you, since Jake's mother already had a son when she married your father."

"Yes, my stepbrother. He was living on Innocence at the time, too. In fact, he was the one who encouraged Lucy and Nathan to move here after our father walked out on them. He sort of took them under his wing. I suspect he's dead now. I wanted to meet him, but after what happened that night, I thought it wise to put as much distance as possible between me and this island. Lucy said he'd become a minister, so evidently he was old enough when my father married his mother not to be influenced by him. Jake, though—he was his father's son. Mrs. Stokes said he was cutting a swath through half the girls on Innocence."

For once I kept my mouth shut, determined not to make

a mistake and raise his hopes. I whipped out my Hospitality House notepad and began adding and subtracting years and estimating ages. Satisfied with the answers, I said, "Mr. Crandall, what was your stepbrother's name?"

"Josiah Allenby."

David, sipping water, almost choked on it. "You're kidding."

Mr. Crandall patted his back. "You knew him?"

"Present tense," David amended. "Know him well. He's still here, a proverbial pillar of the community."

"I'll be damned." His gaze strayed toward the window and lingered. "I'm not sure whether to get in touch with him or not, since he might not want to acknowledge that he has a stepbrother who's black. He's the last link with this side of my family, though. I'd like to thank him for taking Nathan and his mother under his wing."

He had lied to me! It hit me like a damp towel across the face. The upright Reverend Josiah Allenby had lied to me! He'd claimed to know little or nothing about Lucy Stokes and her family. Granted, in age, he probably hadn't been more than five to ten years older than she'd been, but the way things had stacked up, Lucille Stokes had actually been his stepmother. Nathan had been his stepbrother! *And Jacob Stokes Junior had been his half brother!* He'd known the identity of Miss Lucy's boarder from the very beginning! Why hadn't he come forward with Jake's name? Why had he lied?

He had brought out a mean streak in me that didn't surface that often. Nothing would please me more than watching the Reverend's face as his oldest stepbrother expressed his appreciation for the alleged help and support he'd offered his younger stepbrother and his mother. I wanted to witness that meeting, to look him in the eye as a reminder of the snow job he'd pulled on me and Jay from the very first.

David's features were undergoing a series of changes of expressions as the truth began to dawn on him as well. His eyes locked with mine, startled and troubled. "Reverend Allenby was at the hospital all day yesterday," he said, with a trace of defiance. "Tuesdays and Thursdays are his days as chaplain."

David, I realized, was one step ahead of me, supplying an alibi for the man of God to account for his whereabouts during the time Nathan was receiving his last visitor. I was getting hotter under the collar by the moment, angry at myself for not having thought of it first, angry at David for defending the man and, despite the two precious days he'd caused us to waste trying to find out Jacob Stokes's name, angry for still not being able to think of Josiah Allenby as a potential murderer, especially the murderer of his own stepbrother.

He'd also been on site when Jay had disappeared. Could he have been responsible for that? Probably not. He'd volunteered to take me upstairs to show me his daughter's room, so obviously he had nothing to hide.

"He still has a lot to answer for," I said. "He lied to me, David, a flat-out, in-your-face lie."

Mr. Crandall's head swiveled from side to side, watching us. "Am I missing something?"

"Why not help these two get together?" I suggested. "The Reverend's had a hard day, considering he lost a brand-new house he didn't even know he had. Maybe meeting a brother he didn't know he had will make up for it."

David fixed me with an assessing gaze, a finger raised to signal the waiter. "I'm willing, but I've known this man for several years, Troy. If he held out on us, he must have had a good reason."

"Fine. I want to hear it. Are you ready to go, Mr. Crandall?"

"You'd take me?" His lips curled in a sheepish smile. "It's

ridiculous, a man my age nervous about how he'll be received, but I really would appreciate the moral support. Let me settle the bill." He whipped out a platinum credit card, the first I'd ever seen. "Add a tip of forty percent, young man, for keeping my friends' dinners hot. Just bring it, I'll sign it."

"Yes, sir!" Cody scrambled off with the card and was back in record time with the receipt.

"How far away does Josiah live?" Mr. Crandall asked, scribbling his life away.

David, who had fished his tiny cellular phone from his pocket, was busy pushing its buttons. "Nothing's all that far on Innocence. I'm just checking to see if anyone's at the police station. We can wait until you've talked to Reverend Allenby, but Junior Haskins needs to hear what we have to tell him. It answers a lot of questions."

But not all, I thought. Not by a long shot.

There was a hush over the neighborhood as we arrived at the Reverend's sad house, which was dark, as usual. Next door at Mrs. Peterson's, the porch light and the security floodlights mounted at the corners of the house had been left on, spilling amber orbs onto the lawn. Otherwise, the area was clothed in night colors.

"This is where Josiah lives?" Mr. Crandall said, climbing from the front seat of the Honda. "My God, I remember this. Mrs. Stokes and Nathan lived over there near that corner. I remember this particular house because it looked so out of place, more like New England Gothic than Low Country Beach Cottage. There was a church on the other side, wasn't there?"

"There used to be. It was Reverend Allenby's old church," David said. "This house was the manse."

Mr. Crandall gazed around. "Yes, I do remember it. There were children playing stickball in the middle of the street and a bunch of servicemen watching and cheering. And a couple of girls sitting in a tree, chatting away. That one, I think. I kept hoping Jake wasn't there. It was too friendly a neighborhood to be the site of a murder. That's about when I decided I'd have to get him off the island first. That's what I did, just later than I'd counted on."

I led the way up the walk and knocked on Reverend Allenby's door, once, twice. No response. David squeezed behind a rust-spotted lawn chair and peered in the window to the left of the front door. "There could be a mob in there and we wouldn't be able to tell. How can he live with the house all closed up like this?"

I peered in the window on the other side, hoping to detect a glimmer of light through the drawn shades and heavy damask draperies. It was hopeless. I wasn't ready to throw in the towel quite yet, though. I was too angry. The good Reverend had some explaining to do.

"David, let's check around back, in case he's in the kitchen."

"Hold on a minute." He strode to the Honda, opened the trunk, and removed a utility lantern. A wide yellow beam scythed across the darkness. "Wait here, Mr. Crandall. If he's not home, our next stop's the hospital."

We stepped onto the grass, circling the house counterclockwise. The windows on the up-island side were almost invisible in the darkness, so David swept the area in front of us with the flashlight as we walked. We rounded the rear of the house where it wasn't quite as inky; the flames in the Japanese stone lanterns along the walkways behind Hospitality House warmed the night with a soft golden haze. I wondered if The Deacon was on the balcony watching, but there was no way to tell. I wasn't even sure which room was mine.

"Has it occurred to you," David said dryly, "that someone has probably called the police by now to report prowlers skulking around Reverend Allenby's house?"

"Has it occurred to you that it probably did them no good at all? There's no one to report to."

"Thank God," he muttered. "Watch your step."

The back of Reverend Allenby's home was no more welcoming and even more desolate than the front. The screened porch was a black hole, deeper than it had appeared from my vantage point on the sixth floor. I moved as far back as I could and peered at the second and third floor windows as David fanned the lantern's beam across the wooden slats that covered them. They were in dire need of scraping and painting but were otherwise intact. And like the ground floor, completely dark. As were the windows on the far side, although it looked as if a few of the slats over the windows on the top floor weren't as secure as they could be. Still, up that high, it probably didn't matter.

Mr. Crandall, leaning against the fender of the Honda, waited patiently. "Anything?" he called.

"Not yet," David responded. "You okay?"

"Just fine. Admiring that tree."

We approached said tree and I stopped, looking up at it. It was indeed a grand tree, the kind parents hang tires from, the kind kids remember long after they're adults, the kind neighborhoods fight to protect. The uppermost branches soared a good fifty or sixty feet in the air. Considering how tall it was, it probably contributed a great deal to their property values. There was quite a distance between the two houses, yet its branches spanned the gap, some brushing against the eaves and roofs of both.

I was about to head for the Honda when I remembered

the cat I'd spotted this morning. He'd obviously gotten down or he'd have been raising hell for us to come rescue him. I took the lantern from David and played its beam upward, searching past the dangling broken branch, and suddenly there he was. I couldn't be certain whether he was higher or lower than when I'd seen him earlier, but I felt a blip of alarm because, like this morning, he was completely, utterly still. "Oh, Lord."

"What's the matter?" David stepped closer.

"There's a cat up there. I saw him this morning from my balcony. He's still there. See?"

He took the lantern and narrowed its beam, capturing the dark shape in its glow. Edging a few steps nearer the trunk, he squinted at it. "He's awfully still. He may be dead." The sound that escaped from my throat was completely involuntary. "Oh, for pete's sake," David grumbled. "Lord protect me from cat lovers. Let me see if there's a ladder in one of these utility sheds." He angled off toward the rear of Mrs. Peterson's yard.

By the time David returned with a six-foot ladder, I was waiting for him with a stake I'd yanked from Mrs. Peterson's garden. It might take a poke or two to get the pussycat to release his hold on his perch.

David settled the ladder against the tree. "You know, you are the weirdest date I've ever had. I must like you one hell of a lot."

I decided not to push my luck by confessing that I hadn't realized we were on a date, because on the whole, the more important part of that little speech was that he liked me. It was the second time he'd said it.

"Hold the ladder steady, please. If I fall and bust my butt, my reputation will be shot." He chucked me under the chin, began to climb, then reached down for the garden stake.

Mr. Crandall stepped over the plastic fencing and came to stand beside me. "Why's he doing that?"

"There's a cat up there. He's been there all day."

"Then that's where he wants to be." He moved to my side and held the other side of the ladder. "When he gets hungry enough, he'll come down."

"This one won't," David said, stepping off the ladder onto the lowest branch. "Whatever that is, it's not a cat. Here, catch it." He poked the dark blotch and it bounced its way down through the leaves.

Mr. Crandall snared it easily, chuckled, and handed it to me. "There's your cat."

It was a hat. A black, plastic, floppy-brimmed rain hat. I stared at it, astonished, as an absolutely preposterous notion began to form. Too preposterous, I decided, and held my peace.

David climbed down and brushed bark grit from his hands. "What exactly did I rescue?"

I held it up for him. "Sorry."

"You're telling me I risked life and limb and umpteen years of medical training for a hat? You owe me one. I'll put the ladder back and then we'd better get over to the hospital. Why not leave him a note, Mr. Crandall, in case he's not there either. You can bunk with me tonight and since I go on duty at six, Miss Cat Fancier here can bring you back in the morning."

"My, how surly we've become," I said, with a grin. "I have a pad and pen, Mr. Crandall." Flipping back the cover, I tore off the top sheet on which I'd been calculating assorted ages, then saw that the handwriting on the loose one under it wasn't mine. It wasn't even the same kind of paper. "Shine the light on this, please," I asked David. He obliged and Mrs. Peterson's round, tiny letters jumped into focus.

"What is it?" David moved behind me to read over my shoulder. Mr. Crandall, uncertain whether to snoop, took a step backward. "Read it aloud," David suggested.

"*. . . warned her Jake was too old for her and just inter-ested in you-know-what. He sweet-talked his way into Betty Lou's and Sylvie's and Mary Ann's pants and those are just the ones I found out about. Angel's just another notch on his bedpost, but she won't listen. She really thinks he'll take her with him when he leaves tomorrow night. She's going to slip out the usual way and meet him at the boat dock at eleven. I'll believe it when I see it. I'll go ahead and leave her suitcase under our tree after the picnic dance is over, but I don't like it. Ronnie U. keeps saying some-body should tell the Reverend about Jake and Angel but I can't betray my best friend like that. I'm afraid what Ronnie might do, though. He hates Jake for being so fresh with me. Besides, I think Ronnie's got a crush on her. And Angel's so . . .*"

The rest was gone. I really didn't need it anyway. "This is why she broke into my room, to leave this. Angela Allenby was planning to run away with Jake the night of the Fourth." Jake, of course, hadn't shown up. It would have been difficult, given his condition. So Angel had run away alone, probably rebelling against the tight rein her father had kept her on. But Mrs. Peterson wouldn't have known that. She was still under the impression that Angel had left with Jake.

"Why the hell didn't she leave it where you'd find it sooner?" David demanded.

When I thought about it, she had. "I saw this stuck cross-wise in the pad and assumed it was just another one of my lists. I tucked it in and put the pad in my purse. I've been walking around with the evidence tucked under my arm all day!"

"I'm not sure I understand this," Mr. Crandall said slowly. "Exactly who was this Angel that Jake was going away with?"

I was too distracted to respond. I'd missed something. Needing my usual aid to help me think, I opened the maw of my bag to find my glasses, and my fingers passed along the edge of the ten-by-thirteen envelope containing Mr. Stokes's drawing. The light, as they say, dawned hot and bright, searing the back of my eyeballs.

"Ohmigod, I was wrong," I said, pulling it out and opening the envelope in such a hurry that I almost tore it.

"Hey, slow down." David took it from me and slid it out. "Wrong about what?"

The mistake I'd made had been a natural one, but I kicked myself anyway. "I thought this was a nightgown or a peignoir. It's a robe, a pastoral robe. Damn it, this isn't a woman."

"Oh, God," David said softly.

"Ever since Phil showed it to me, I've had the feeling that this wasn't artistic license or some bizarre flight of fancy. Nathan drew what he saw."

"He must have found out." David's voice was heavy with dread. "Somebody told him about Jake and his daughter."

"Wait a minute," Mr. Crandall said. "How many children does he have?"

"Only one natural child," I responded. "Angela. She ran away from home and never came back. He adored her. I saw that for myself."

"Perhaps, but she wasn't his child. I told you my father had seduced his stepson's wife, remember? Josiah's wife. The child she had was my father's. She was my half sister, and Nathan's."

"And Jake's," David finished for him. "The rotten bastard."

"He might not have known," I said, and marveled that I could make excuses for Jake Junior.

"He knew." Mr. Crandall's eyes glowed dark and hot. "Mrs. Stokes said everyone knew. That's why Josiah left Charleston with the baby after his wife died giving birth. Jake Junior seduced his own half sister!"

The question had to be asked, if only to help David accept the truth about the man he held in such high esteem. "You know the Reverend, David. Miss Potee said he's hell on quote, adulterers and fornicators, unquote. Do you think he could have killed Jake if he found out what he'd done?"

His response was a shrug of helplessness. He leaned back against the ladder. "You've heard the expression, the wrath of God? One of my patients was dying last year and her granddaughter had been given permission to bring her new baby to see her great-grandmother. Reverend Allenby stopped in. When he realized the granddaughter wasn't married and had no plans to be, he flipped, began raving about fallen women and the wages of sin and protecting the innocent. Freaked out the grandmother, sent the granddaughter into hysterics. When you consider that the young woman he had raised as a daughter had been taken advantage of by her—and his—own half brother . . ." He sighed, unable to finish. The voice of his pager sounded and he snatched it from his belt. "Be right back," he said, returning to his car. "Gotta call in."

Mr. Crandall leaned back against the ladder. "I'm not sure about all this. If Josiah killed Jake, why would Nathan say he'd done it?"

"He didn't actually say he had, did he? All he said was 'Natie's a bad boy.' He had the doorstop in his hand with blood on it, probably his own. Jake was dead so the logical assumption was that Nathan had done it. Was there blood on Jake's head?"

He hesitated. "I remember . . . a knot—"

"Where Aunt Jay had beaned him. Was there blood anywhere at all?"

"The knuckles of one hand, his shirtsleeve, and a little light stuff around his lips."

"Seems to me I read somewhere that sometimes there's bloody froth around the mouth when someone suffocates. Or maybe when they're strangled. David would know."

"I've got to go," David called from the car. "Problem with a patient. I may be gone a while, so, Troy, can you see Mr. Crandall gets to a hotel?"

"We'll check Hospitality House first." I wanted to keep him nearby. "And if you have a chance, look to see if Reverend Allenby's at the hospital."

He nodded, clearly disturbed at the latest turn of events. "Don't do anything dumb, okay? Promise me you'll stay out of trouble."

"How can I get in trouble between here and Hospitality House? You'd better get going."

"I'll be in touch," he said, and sped away toward the corner.

"Where's this Hospitality House?" Mr. Crandall asked.

I turned and pointed. "That's the back. It's not fancy but it's close. You could check into someplace else or stay with David tomorrow night. Let's . . ." I stopped, my train of thought having veered in another direction. "He certainly would have had the opportunity to kidnap Jay."

"Josiah?" Mr. Crandall peered at me in the darkness. "What reason would he have? The only eyewitness to the murder is dead—"

"A victim of murder himself," I reminded him. "Reverend Allenby lied to me this very afternoon, Mr. Crandall, claimed to know nothing about Miss Lucy's background and family. If he lied about that, he probably lied about not knowing where Mr. Stokes was living now."

He could also have been the caller who'd wanted permission to bring a birthday cake and had been given a list of items that were a danger to Mr. Stokes. But even as I thought it, I ran headlong into a wall of ambivalence, finding it difficult to believe the man capable of cold-blooded murder. In the heat of passion, yes, but with malice aforethought? I hated myself but I'd begun to waffle.

"Well, to be honest, Miss Burdette, I doubt this sketch would be accepted as proof of anything," Mr. Crandall was saying, "because of Nathan's emotional problem."

"In other words, all we have is a big, fat zero," I said, seething. "Thanks to Mrs. Peterson, we could guess the motive for Jake's murder. But we can't prove this Ronnie U. in the diary actually spilled the beans about Jake and Angela to the Reverend, so our guess isn't worth squat."

"Even if Mrs. Peterson were still alive," Mr. Crandall pointed out, "her testimony would be inadmissible because it was hearsay."

So it looked as if the Reverend was untouchable. All threats to his freedom had been removed, even Jay, which still didn't make sense. She'd have made a perfect scapegoat, a willing confessor to a murder he committed. I was convinced, justifiably or not, that it all came down to Elva Peterson's presence in Jay's room last night. The only reason I could see for her visit was to show what she considered proof that Jake had left Innocence with Angela. What if the Reverend had overheard that conversation? He might prefer that no one knew his beloved daughter had planned to run away with Jake umpty years ago. But what difference could it make now—unless he thought Jay might insist on confirmation from Angela, assuming she was still alive and could be found after all this time.

I juggled that thought for a few moments. I'd gotten the distinct impression no one had heard from her since she'd run away, not even Mrs. Peterson. Why wouldn't Angela get in touch with her very best friend to let her know she was all right, even if she'd had to wait a while to do it? My brain began to sizzle as a brand-new horror slithered in from under a rock. Had Angela died that night, too? Was that the sin Reverend Allenby wanted hidden at all costs? Had that possibility finally occurred to Mrs. Peterson as well? I shuddered, my fists clenching tight, and the vinyl rain hat squeaked a protest at the abuse it was suffering. I'd forgotten I had it.

"What are you thinking, Miss Burdette?" Mr. Crandall asked. "I can practically see the wheels turning in there."

I looked up through the leaves. "I think this is the tree Mrs. Peterson referred to in her diary, where she was supposed to leave Angela's suitcase. I bet that's how Angela was slipping out to see Jake, too. And I think Mrs. Peterson climbed this tree last night."

"What?"

"Sure, she was seventy-plus, but she mentioned going to aerobics and she certainly moved as if she had no physical problems. I think she was trying to get into Reverend Allenby's house through the third floor windows."

"What in the world for?"

"I'm not sure," I stalled. "Perhaps some sort of communication from Angela to her father after she ran away." I focused the beam of the utility lamp on the third floor window again. "The slats over that one aren't secure. They're the only ones that aren't."

Mr. Crandall stepped back and gazed up. "I'll take your word for it. Your eyes are better than mine. I do see that this place is falling apart everywhere else; the termites have probably had a field day. If there's a slat loose, that's probably why."

"One other thing," I interrupted, remembering. "One of the policemen said it looked as if Mrs. Peterson had a broken ankle. That branch up there might account for it. It may have given under her weight and she came down. She was not exactly a petite woman. I'm going up to take a closer look."

"I must say, hanging out with you young folks is certainly adventurous," Mr. Crandall said. "I don't think it's a good idea, but if you insist on doing it, the least I can do is brace the ladder."

It was nuts, I admit it, but the longer I thought about it, the more certain I became that the answer to everything was under the roof of this house somewhere. I would examine the slats and if it looked as if they'd been pulled off forcibly, and especially if someone had gotten in, I'd . . . I'd what? Tell Junior Haskins? He might feel called upon to verify that there's been a break-in, but if the Reverend maintained that nothing had been stolen, that would be the end of that. I was sure Mr. Haskins wouldn't consider our suspicions justification for a search warrant of the Reverend's premises. Why was I so certain that it was important to get into this house? What it came down to was another of what my mom called "a feeling," similar to the one I'd experienced the day before standing outside the door of Mr. Stokes's cabin, a feeling that something wasn't right and I shouldn't leave. It was even stronger tonight.

Wishing I'd worn slacks or jeans, I started up the ladder, the utility lamp hanging from my wrist. At the top rung, I stepped onto a heavy branch and tested it gingerly. Satisfied that it was stout enough to hold me, I reached up and tugged on the next branch, pulling on it with all my strength. Suddenly a pale, translucent strip, shaken loose by my tugging, I guess, dropped toward me, snagging on twigs before continuing its fall. Yes! One of Mrs. Peterson's ribbons, I was willing to bet, proof she'd been up here. Reaching out, I caught it as it bounced off a slender branch. To my surprise, it wasn't fabric at all. It was a soft, rubbery plastic.

I could swear my heart stopped. I felt a chill deep into my bones. I slipped the utility lamp off my wrist and aimed it at the thing in my hand. Jay's hospital identification bracelet. Its edges were jagged, as if it had been cut from her wrist with something that needed sharpening.

"She's in there," I croaked, starting up again. "She's in this awful house. Damn him, if she's dead . . ."

It was time to shut up and save my breath for the exertions ahead. I'd been an incorrigible tree-climber in my tomboy days and was in pretty fair shape now, but getting to the edge of that roof was a lot harder than I'd have thought. I couldn't imagine how Mrs. Peterson had managed it. I hoisted myself onto the next branch, then the next, and gingerly stepped onto the roof. Some of the tiles were loose. The slope of the roof was gentle, but a single misstep and I'd find myself on the way to the ground the hard way.

"Everything all right up there?" Mr. Crandall called softly.

"So far, so good. Just looking around."

The third floor was considerably smaller than the lower ones, consisting of, at a guess, either one medium-sized room or two small ones, the kind of space that would be used as servants' quarters or a place to store junk. There was a pair of windows looking out on each of the side yards, one overlooking the back and one facing the street.

I inched toward the windows. Now that I was level with

them, I could see a faint gleam behind the slats, which were angled so that it was impossible to detect the light from the ground. Lying snug up against the house, directly under the window where it couldn't be seen from below, nor from inside if anyone looked out, was a crowbar. There was no rust on it so it couldn't have been there long. Mrs. Peterson must have brought it with her.

I examined the windows closely. On the rearmost one, the whole frame in which the slats were anchored had been separated from the siding, leaving a gap of several inches. Within the frame itself, several of the slats were held in place by nails on the right side, but they'd been pried loose on the left. Had we been standing in any other spot when David had directed the lantern's beam up here, I wouldn't have seen it. They had been loosened, then pushed back so they wouldn't be noticed.

I picked up the crowbar, inserted it under the loosened side, and pulled back on it. The frame came away easily and, to my surprise, quietly, opening like a book to expose the double-hung window. Its panes were frosted, admitting light but making it impossible to see in or out.

I said a mental prayer, crossed my fingers for luck, then tugged at the lower sash. It resisted at first, then slowly and again, quietly, inched upward.

I pushed harder and the bottom pane slid all the way up. A pungent odor wafted from the room beyond, a combination of eau de toilette and unwashed bodies. Breathing shallowly, I stared in astonishment at the decor inside. People were right; the Reverend hadn't changed a thing of Angela's. It was her playroom, a faded pink and white, the wall directly opposite me lined with shelves of varying heights, dolls of all sorts, none of recent vintage, sitting primly on the upper ones. The middle section contained dollhouse furniture, exquisite miniature chairs and tables, beds, dressers, cradles, kitchen accessories. Books filled the lower shelves, slender volumes that appeared to be the sort of picture books a small child would read.

The furnishings were spare, a white spindle bed, a white rocking chair decorated with tiny pink roses, a wardrobe, a writing desk, and padded stool. A toy chest sat at the end of the bed, a three-story dollhouse near the corner. Next to the only door was an antique high-sided bathtub on stubby legs. A bathbrush hung from a hook on the wall, a thick pink towel next to it.

Four stout posts, roof supports I supposed, dominated the room. Wrapped once around the far left post was a sturdy chain secured by a formidable lock. The other end of the chain, which was perhaps twelve feet in length, circled the slender waist of a reed of a woman, so frail she reminded me of dandelion fluff. The comparison was further enhanced by a head full of long, platinum tresses as fine as angel hair. She stood on the far side of the bed, staring at me with wide, pale blue, startled eyes. Her skin was colorless, unhealthily so, the veins underneath were visible. Regardless, it took little imagination to see the resemblance between this wan, fey old woman and the wisp of a girl she'd once been. Angela Allenby.

17

"What's today?" she asked, breathlessly, her fingers splayed across her chest. "Which day of the week?"

It was not quite the question I'd have expected. "Wednesday."

"I was right!" Her face blazed with triumph. "Wednesday. I still have all my faculties. Did Sugar Babe send you?"

"Who?"

"Elva."

Uh-oh. "Well, I guess you could say that."

"Praise be! I knew she wouldn't fail us. I'd have opened the window for you but as you can see, the chain won't allow that. What's your name?"

I climbed over the sill into the room. "I'm Troy Burdette. Miss Allenby, you've been up here all this time?"

"Call me Angela. Didn't Sugar Babe tell you?" She moved from behind the bed, the chain clanking as she walked. Shades of Marley's ghost. "I've been locked up in this playroom since July fourth, 1943. Sugar Babe climbed the tree, the way we used to years ago, and found me. She climbed our tree! At her age!" She laughed, the sound a girlish tinkle. "She was going to go downstairs to see if she could find any letters I'd written my father after I was supposed to have eloped. As if I wouldn't have written to my best friend in all these years."

Somehow I found it difficult to believe that Elva Peterson would go to such lengths simply to help Julia Wingate identify the man she thought she'd killed. Since Mrs. Peterson had heard nothing from Angela after that night, I suspected she'd begun to wonder whether her best friend had ever gotten off Innocence alive.

"I can't tell you how grateful I am you came," she was saying. She began removing items of clothing from the bed one piece at a time, folding each carefully. "Until yesterday evening, the only face I've seen was my father's. He made certain I never saw the other one."

"What other one?" I asked, intrigued at how gracefully she moved in spite of the chain.

"The one who pushes books and my meals through the flap in that door, and hot water for my washups. Where's your bag?"

My bag. "Outside on the ground. I needed both hands to climb the tree. And I'm not alone. Don't worry, we'll find something to cut that chain." David had said Mrs. Peterson's utility shed was full of tools. Perhaps she had something I could use. If she didn't, the police would, and I'd find somebody in uniform, no matter what it took.

"My prayers have been answered," Angela said, as if she couldn't quite believe it. "But what took Sugar Babe so long to reach you?"

"Circumstances beyond her control." She had to be told, but it would have to wait.

"Please don't think I'm complaining. I was just so worried." She picked up a long skirt and looked at me expectantly. "Aren't you going to get your bag?"

What was this thing she had about my purse? I crossed to the window. "I'll ask my friend outside to toss it up, but there's nothing in it that will help. I've got a Swiss Army knife but that won't even make a scratch on a chain that heavy."

"Swiss Army knife?" She halted her folding, confusion clouding her blue eyes. "You don't use scalpels anymore?"

"Excuse me?" I felt as if I was fighting my way out of a maze. "Scalpels?"

"For surgery." She dropped the skirt. "Aren't you a doctor?"

"Me? Lord, no. What made you think I was?"

"Oh dear, oh dear." She began to wring her hands. It was the first time I'd ever seen anyone actually do it. "Sugar Babe left to find a doctor. I told her I'd waited fifty years for freedom, I could wait a little while longer, but Julia couldn't."

I almost fell out of the window and barked a shin getting back in. "Julia Wingate? Where is she?"

The few remaining pieces of clothing on the bed began to move. "Troy?" The voice, barely audible, was one I'd begun to think I'd never hear again.

"Aunt Jay!" I flew to the bed and began tossing frilly garments off of it.

"It may be the ague," Angela said, helping me to uncover her. "She's hot one minute, freezing the next. Elva changed clothes with her, since she was wearing long sleeves and her trousers would cover Julia's legs. Everything I have is light in weight because it's always so hot up here."

Jay's face had finally emerged, gleaming with perspiration, her eyes barely focused. Despite the mountain of clothes she'd been under, she was shivering. "'Bout damned time," she whispered hoarsely.

Hurling the remaining dresses onto the floor, I gathered her in my arms, reveling in the feel of her. "Lord, Aunt Jay, I've been so scared."

"Me, too. Get help, baby." I could barely hear her. "Quickly."

"Hang on, Aunt Jay," I said, releasing her. "Please."

"Go, daughter."

"I'll cover her back up." Angela began retrieving clothes from the floor and piling them on the bed again.

I nodded, terrified of leaving Jay, even for a minute, and climbed out the window. "Mr. Crandall." Inching my way to the edge of the roof, I peered down.

"Here." He stepped to the far side of the tree so I could see him.

"Bang on the door of one of these houses. Ask them to call for an ambulance first, the police second. Aunt Jay's up here and she doesn't look good. Angela Allenby's up here, too. Has been since '43. She's chained to a post."

"My God! Josiah must be insane! Wait, Troy. What's the address?"

"Just tell them Reverend Allenby's house. Everybody knows where it is. Hurry! And be sure they understand that they'll have to break in downstairs and then up here on the third floor."

"My God." He wasted no more words and started toward Mrs. Peterson's.

"Not there!" I called. "That house is empty."

He turned and hurried toward the houses across the street. I worked my way back up to the window and this time took the crowbar with me.

Back inside, Jay was no longer visible. Miss Allenby saw

the crowbar and shook her head. "We tried that last night. The chain's too strong."

"What about the door, then?" But it took only a glance to see that it was hopeless. The door was metal and opened outward, the hinges on the other side. The lock was a double cylinder deadbolt.

I knelt and examined the pet door, enraged that she'd been treated with even less consideration than a dog or cat. At least a pet could go in and out. I was encouraged, however, at its size. It looked as if it might accommodate a fairly large dog. The height of the chamber pot in the corner supplied the reason. I'd never seen one that tall, an antiques collector's dream.

"I used to hate that little hole," Miss Allenby said. "But sometimes when I can't stand the sight of anything in this room any longer, I lie down and use the handle of the dust mop to push the flap open just to see real sunlight."

"They don't lock the flap?" I asked, my throat closing at the thought of the desperation she must have felt.

"They used to. Then I reckon they realized there was no need since I can't reach the door."

I dropped onto my stomach and pushed the flap up to expose the worn oak flooring of the third floor landing. A dim bulb glowed from somewhere above the door, illuminating the window positioned directly opposite.

I stuck my head through the opening, then my shoulders, and immediately dismissed any notion that I could go any farther. There was no way my fanny would squeeze through this hole. It was one hell of a graphic illustration of the difference ten pounds could make.

Retreating a little, I turned onto my back and pushed myself out again to see if there was any chance that the good Reverend might have left the key in the lock. I wasn't sure what I'd do if he had. Heaven knows I couldn't reach it. But it wasn't there, so I didn't have to worry about it. All I could see was the underside of the doorknob, the housing of the lock, a small wooden shelf beside the door, and what I could swear was a fifteen-watt bulb in the ceiling. Leaning against the wall was what looked like a large cutting board with at least a four-foot handle on it.

I backed in again and asked Angela what it was.

Her lips formed a hard, straight line. "That's how my meals are served. The other one places the plates and silverware on it and slides it in to me."

Flames of anger seared through me. There was nothing I could say. But I did have a question. "How often does your father open the door?"

"Every Sunday night." She sat down on the bed next to Jay and began dabbing her forehead with the end of a lacy scarf. "He sets that time aside to come up and preach at me about the sins of the flesh and the purification of my soul. He says if Mary Magdalene could be saved, so can I. He's keeping me from temptations of the flesh, you see, protecting my innocence. I may burn in hell for it, but I hate him!"

I sympathized completely, but I had other matters to pursue. "Do you know whether he keeps the key on his person or on that shelf outside? Think. When he leaves and locks the door, do you hear him place the key on the shelf?"

She shook her head. "I can't hear anything outside this room. Years and years ago he brought up some squares and put them on the walls and ceilings. After that I couldn't hear birds or cars or anything. When I was a little girl, though, the key was kept in a box on the shelf. If I was naughty, he'd lock the playroom as punishment, with me on the outside. I look back on those days with longing."

If the box was still there, I couldn't see it. My only hope

was that her father was a creature of habit and had taken the path of least resistance.

I got up, and checked on Aunt Jay. She opened her eyes but I had the distinct impression that she didn't see me or if she did, didn't recognize me. In panic, I opened the closet beside the bed. It was jammed with clothes, neatly hung. I grabbed an armful. "Help me. I need hangers, at least four of them, straightened out."

"All right." Angela asked no questions. Yanking dresses off onto the floor, she managed to straighten two of the hangers. With the two I'd straightened, I twisted the ends together and stood on them to close the loops, leaving the hook on the one on the end. Outside, a throaty scream, a pure animal sound, interspersed with several male voices, drifted through the open window from some distance away. Perhaps someone had been hit on the traffic circle. The thought was more than I could deal with at the moment.

"What are you going to do?" Angela asked.

"If it's still there, knock the box off and get the key. We've got to get this door open."

"Oh. I see."

It was obvious she didn't, but I didn't have time to elaborate. I stuck the hangers through the pet door, then wedged myself as far out of it as I could. The next few minutes were the most frustrating of my life. A bit of probing on the shelf with the hook of the coat hanger alerted me that there was indeed something there. Pulling it to the edge of the shelf, however, was as close to hard labor as I'd ever experienced, because all I could see was the underside of the shelf. By the time I'd maneuvered the thing to the edge and nudged it off, I was drenched. And lucky. The box was cardboard, so it didn't make much noise when it hit the floor. The two keys in it, however, went skidding across the wooden planking. The contortions required to flip onto my stomach and wield the hangers to keep the keys from flying off the landing sent spasms of pain across my shoulders and back. But I did it. Trembling from the strain, I raked them within reach and grabbed them.

At some point, Angela had joined me on the floor, a good two feet from the door, as close as the chain allowed her. "You got them?" She held out her hands, palms up. "You really got them?"

Scooting over to her, I placed the keys in her hand and closed her fingers around them. "Here. Squeeze them. Enjoy the feel of them, but for just a minute because I need them back to see which one unlocks the door. Aunt Jay's in critical condition and I've got to get her out of here."

She closed her eyes, shaking her head as if in disbelief. "I'm free. Free!" Then, with a smile, she opened her hand. "You can take them now. Thank you."

The smaller of the two keys unlocked the deadbolt easily. I went out on the landing and listened, but heard nothing from below. So far our luck was holding. If we could just get out of the house before Reverend Allenby showed up.

I gave the second key back to Angela. "You've earned the right to open your own lock. I'll get Aunt Jay ready."

Leaving Angela to free herself, I knelt beside the bed and pushed all the clothes to the foot. I'd have to carry her and pray I didn't drop her on the way down the steps. I wished now I'd listened to my brother Jimmy when he'd suggested that I add weight training to my exercise routine. "Aunt Jay, it's time to go."

She didn't respond, didn't even open her eyes this time. Grabbing her wrist, I checked her pulse. I couldn't find it. Panic gripped me in a half nelson. "Please, God," I whis-

pered and glued my ear to her chest. If I had to begin
CPR, I wouldn't be able to stop until the medics arrived
and Lord knew how long that would take. I was about to
ask Angela if she'd go down and unlock the front door so
there'd be no further delay when help finally arrived,
when it came vaulting in through the window instead.
David.

"You promised you'd stay out of trouble." He glowered
at me, then nodded at Angela as he came around the bed.
"Miss Allenby, I'm Dr. Baskerville. Your nightmare is over.
Oh, God," he said, getting a good look at Jay for the first
time. Kneeling, he probed for a pulse at the base of her
neck, then pulled back her lids. "We've got to get her out of
here *now*." Yanking the sheet up from the foot of the bed,
he wrapped it around her, picked her up, and strode out.
"I'll need somebody to open the front door for me," he
tossed over his shoulder.

"Right behind you." I had followed him out, when
Angela's plaintive cry stopped me cold.

"Please, please don't leave me! I can't get it open!"

I looked back to see her struggling to get the key into the
lock at her waist.

"My hands are shaking so. Help me, please." Her wide
blue eyes were a scream of pure panic and despair.

Darting back in, I took the key from her and jammed
it into the lock that secured the chain around her waist.
It resisted for a second before I felt the mechanism
inside yield and finally open. She began to cry as I
removed the thing and the chain fell to the floor with a
clatter.

"We must hurry," I said, envisioning David standing at
the front door waiting impatiently for me. That, under the
circumstances, would have been the best of all possible
worlds. Instead, when I reached him, he stood at an open

door deep in the shadows at the top of the stairs from the first floor.

"Shhh," he said and jerked his head toward the lower floor. I stopped, gesturing for Angela, behind me, to be quiet. "Listen," he mouthed at me.

Squeezing past him, I knelt at the door. That's when I heard it, a low baritone mumble above the sound of something being moved across the floor. After a second, I could make out occasional phrases.

". . . adulterers and adulteresses, know ye not that the friendship of the world is enmity with God? Whosoever therefore . . . friend of the world is the enemy of God. . . . Resist the devil, and he will flee from you. . . . Cleanse your hands . . . purify your hearts, ye double minded."

Reverend Allenby.

I looked at David in horror. What were we going to do? There was no way we could get out without being seen. And as much faith as I had in David, I could not envision him climbing down the tree with Jay slung over his shoulder like a sack of potatoes.

Angela tapped me on the shoulder. "I brought this along," she whispered and lifted the crowbar so I could see it. "I'll use it if I have to." Hatred blazed from her eyes.

I shook my head and removed it from her hand. I wouldn't have the least hesitation about using it either, but better me than her. If she managed to get in a lick that killed him, she'd have exchanged one kind of prison for another.

Still shielded by the shadows on the second floor landing, I moved down a step and froze as the Reverend shoved the old upright piano past the opening at the bottom of the stairs and out of sight. He'd picked one hell of a time to rearrange the living room.

"I will not, I will not be moved," he sang in a full, rich

baritone. "Like a tree planted by the water, I will not be moved." The song having ended, he began talking to himself. "This is my temple, sacred ground, a place of purification. I will not allow it to be taken from me. They have no right! Yea, verily, I will hold sway against the agents of Satan. I will not be moved." Breathing heavily, he crossed in front of the stairwell again and disappeared toward the rear of the house. After a second, we heard a door close.

"I think he's gone," David whispered. He glanced down at Jay, her ashen face barely visible. If we didn't leave soon, the sheet in which he'd wrapped her would become a white percale shroud. "Let's go," he said and moved quietly down the steps, but stopped at the bottom, his gasp of surprise audible. I came down and, stooping, peeked around him. The living room was in shambles, the settee standing on end against the front windows on the left, a pair of heavy upholstered chairs stacked one on top of the other in front of the window on the right. The upright piano was positioned with its back against the front door. The man was barricading himself—and us—in.

"He's lost it," David said softly. "We'd better get out of here while he's in the back." Carefully, he sat Jay on a straight-backed chair at the foot of the steps. "Hold her shoulders. She's drifting in and out of consciousness."

"Am not," Jay responded as I came down and stood behind her. She was with us again!

David strode to the piano and with one great heave, shoved it aside. Under any other circumstances, I'd have been impressed, especially as he was pushing it across carpeting. He unlocked the door and threw it open. That's when our luck ran out. Standing in the doorway, key in his left hand, was a man with the most perfectly coiffed blond hair I'd ever seen and, oddly enough, a dark, bushy beard. He had the unmistakable forehead, pale eyes, and long nose that marked him as one of the begats, perhaps once or twice removed, of Jacob Stokes Senior. I, however, immediately lost interest in his face, because in his right hand he held an ugly, snub-nosed revolver.

18

It was odd. The only thing threatening about him was the object in his hand. His stance held no trace of menace. "Who are you?" he asked. "Where are you taking Mrs. Wingate?"

"Damn it!" David spat in frustration. He'd been so close to escape.

Aunt Jay stiffened under my hands, her head emerging from the sheet like a turtle sniffing a potential meal on the breeze. "Ah, shit," she croaked softly. "He's the one I told you about from the police station. He brought me here last night. You gotta watch him, children. He's as loop-de-loop as a roller coaster."

Despite the danger we were in, I felt immensely better about her. When Julia Wingate resorted to profanity, she was extremely aggravated. That took energy. It was gratifying to know she had any left.

The newcomer looked around the room. "What's been happening in here? Where's Father Josiah?" He started to push past David. "Mrs. Wingate shouldn't be down here. She's very sick. Father Josiah said I should put her out of her misery, but I knew if I brought her here, he could heal her when he goes to the upper room on Sunday. If he finds out she's here before then, he'll be angry with me. I've got to take her back upstairs!"

"Put her out of her misery?" I erupted, enraged. "We're talking about a human being here, not some dog lying out on the road. How *dare* he!"

"Simmer down, Troy," David said, tight-lipped. Whirling around, he came back, maneuvered Jay into his arms again and started for the door. The newcomer still blocked the way. David lowered his head until he was nose-to-nose with the man. "Now you listen to me, Mr. whoever you are. I'm a doctor and this woman is my patient. She is critically ill and needs to be in surgery within the hour, so I'm taking her out of here and the only way you're going to stop me is to shoot me. Either do it or *get the hell out of my way!*"

Stokes Number Four frowned. "An operation will make her better?"

"Yes!"

"But Father Josiah said there was no hope for her and that—"

"He lied to you," I cut him off.

"He would *never!*" He seemed scandalized at the thought.

"He lied to me earlier today. Go, David," I said, sotto voce. If I could keep Stokes Number Four distracted long enough for David to get Jay out the door and to the car before the idiot remembered he was supposed to shoot him, Jay might stand a chance of surviving this night. I was a hell of a lot less sure about myself. I wondered where Angela was but didn't dare risk looking back. I had to keep talking. David edged around him.

"I asked Reverend Allenby if he knew anything about Nathan Stokes's mother and father. He said he didn't. He flat-out lied, because it turns out that Nathan Stokes was his own stepbrother."

"Stepbrother. I don't . . . what's a stepbrother?" He looked at me as if he truly didn't understand. David kept inching toward the door. Where was the damned ambulance?

"After Reverend Allenby's father died," I said, my brain skimming along on two tracks, one watching David, the other sizing up this man, "his mother married again. The man she married became Reverend Allenby's stepfather."

"Stepfather," Stokes the Fourth repeated. It was clearly an alien term for him. His eyes, a familiar pale gray, were wide, his expression ingenuous. Jay was right. This man didn't have both oars in the water, in fact might have no oars at all. And that meant he was even more dangerous.

"Jacob Stokes Senior and Reverend Allenby's mother had a son, Jacob Stokes Junior. Jacob Junior was Reverend Allenby's half brother, because they shared the same mother." David slipped out of the door and disappeared into the darkness beyond. Keep yakking, I told myself. They weren't safe yet. "Years later," I continued doggedly, "Reverend Allenby's stepfather married again and had another son named Nathan by a woman named Lucy. So his stepfather's son, Nathan, was Reverend Allenby's stepbrother."

From somewhere behind me, I heard a strangled sound and realized I'd said far more than I'd meant to. I spun around. Apparently Angela had remained in the shadows of the landing all this time. Now she came slowly down the steps, her cheeks talcum-powder white. "Jake was my father's half brother? Jake was my *uncle?*"

I could have kicked myself. The horror in her eyes made

me want to dissolve in a puddle of goo like the Wicked Witch in *The Wizard of Oz*.

Stokes the Fourth gaped at Angela. "Mrs. Allenby! Father Josiah will be furious. I'll have to take you back upstairs, too. Then I'll bring you your supper. You'll like it. It's chicken salad with raisins and apples."

"You're the other one! You aren't taking me anywhere! And Jake was my uncle? He had to have known it. He courted me anyhow, sweet-talked me into his bed. Sugar Babe was right about him! All he wanted was to have his way with me. And I let him. I *let* him! I loved him! I was going to run away with him!"

"Angela," I said, wondering how on earth to cram the evils back into Pandora's box. At least not all of them were out. She didn't know that Jake had actually been her half brother, and the man she called Father, her stepbrother. In this instance, ignorance was truly bliss.

She sank down on the bottom step, tears streaming down her face. "Damn him! And damn Father for not telling me. God in heaven, what kind of monster would our baby have been if it had lived?"

"Huh?" I said.

"It died right after it was born. I always thought it was my punishment for sinning, for lying with a man before we were married. And I've always hated my father for taking it away without even letting me see the child. He wouldn't even tell me if it was a boy or a girl, wouldn't let me go to the funeral, wouldn't even talk about it."

As far as I was concerned, the question of where in the chain of begats Number Four was linked had just been cleared up. His reaction, however, was not quite what I'd anticipated. He looked crushed. "You knew another man and had his baby before you married Father Josiah?"

Angela's eyes blazed. "What are you talking about? Your

blessed Father Josiah is *my* father, not my husband, you silly fool!"

"But—but he told me you were his dearly beloved and he kept you locked upstairs because a man had forced himself on you and it drove you out of your mind and he didn't want to put you in an institution. That's why I agreed to help him. I know about institutions. I'm an orphan. I grew up in one."

All the pieces of the puzzle were slowly falling into place. The question became whether I'd live to tell anyone else. He still held the gun.

"His daughter," he was saying. "Maybe I just got it wrong. I must have. Father Josiah's a man of God. He said if I do his bidding and help him tend his flock, I could be his disciple. I'd be a reverend, too. Reverend Joshua Allenby. I took his last name because he was so good to me while I was growing up."

Click. Yet another piece of the puzzle. There was a child-like quality about Joshua Allenby, and I wondered if he fully understood how badly he'd been used. He reached up and scratched his head in confusion and suddenly his whole head was askew. I gaped at him and decided there was some question as to who was the bigger idiot, Joshua or me. That beautiful blond hair wasn't his. Without thinking, which was super-dumb since he still had the gun in his hand, I reached up and snatched the wig off. Under it was a full, thick head of almost black hair going gray around the edges.

"Why are you wearing this?" I demanded, handing it to him.

"Father Josiah asked me to. My face seems to bother him when I don't."

I didn't doubt it. At that point another bit of the puzzle became clearer. "You were at Safe Harbor yesterday, weren't you?" I grabbed the beard and yanked. It came away, leaving blotches of adhesive along his cheeks. Behind me, Angela inhaled, a long whistling sucking in of air. "You were standing by the administration building while the ambulance was there," I said, giving her time to recover from the shock of seeing him completely unmasked.

I doubted that Joshua had had much in the way of defenses before tonight. Now he seemed to have none at all. He was in effect a middle-aged child. "I wanted to know how Mr. Stokes was but I was afraid to ask because . . . well, I took something of his and I thought they might put me in jail for stealing."

"The picture from his dresser?" I asked.

He nodded. "Mr. Stokes looked just like me. I asked him if he was my father but that's when he started acting funny and went into the bathroom. He stayed so long that I figured he didn't want to talk to me about being my father and I . . . well, I got mad at him, so I took the picture. At least I would have that. Then you came so I stayed, thinking maybe I could talk to you. Did Mr. Stokes have a heart attack?"

"No." I said, choosing my words carefully. "He ate some crackers that made him sick."

"The ones I had? I ate some. They didn't bother me."

"Where did you get them?" I asked.

"Father Josiah packed a little picnic basket, like he does for the shut-ins he visits. Only there was nothing but cheese crackers in it. He said they were Mr. Stokes's favorites, but that I should bring back whatever was left over. I didn't know crackers could make you so sick. You went back today. Is he better?"

I wasn't sure what to say at first. But he'd been lied to enough already. "He died, Joshua. It wasn't the crackers that made him so sick, it was the cheese. He was taking medicine that makes some types of food turn to poison if you eat them. Cheese was one of those foods."

He looked sick himself. "But Father Josiah called first to make sure what Mr. Stokes could eat. Maybe they didn't tell him about cheese."

Yeah. Right. Perhaps the only way to bring him onto our side was to be brutally honest. "They told him about the cheese, Joshua. He sent it anyway."

"But why?" Angela asked. "Why would he do that?"

"Because he was afraid that sooner or later someone would show Mr. Stokes the picture of a man who was a boarder in his mother's house the night of July fourth, 1943, and ask the man's name. Your father wanted to prevent the man from being identified because . . ." I hesitated, but there was no turning back. "Your father smothered him after someone told him of your relationship with Jacob Stokes."

"No." Eyes widening with horror, Miss Allenby lowered herself onto a step. "Father *killed* Jake?"

Joshua looked from one to the other of us, blinking like some nocturnal animal seeing the sun for the first time. "Father Josiah killed someone? He broke a Commandment?"

"I'm afraid so, a couple of times. He—"

Mr. Crandall strode through the front door, wearing a grin as wide as a city block. I rushed to him, my stomach in my mouth. "She's okay, Troy. David got her to the hospital, but you should have seen the procession following him. The police had bloodhounds out looking for your auntie. They were headed in this direction when David drove past and they took off after his car and dragged their handlers right into the hospital. When I got there, they were running around the Emergency Room, baying their heads off. You should have—" He broke off, frowning, his focus over my right shoulder. "What the hell? What's the gun for?"

I turned around. Angela and Joshua were on their feet and looked as if they were vying for the gaping title in the *Guinness Book of Records*. "Uh, Angela, Joshua, this is . . ." Suddenly my mind went blank. I couldn't remember his assumed name.

"Vincent Quarles," he said quietly. "Pleased to meet you—I think. My God, the Stokes genes are alive and well. Joshua, whose son are you?"

Joshua swallowed. "I don't know. You look like me, too. Are you my father?"

"Me? Good God, no. I have one son, one daughter, and they're back on Oahu. I guess Jake was right. Our father was fruitful and multiplied—all over the state, from the looks of it."

"You're Jake's brother?" Angela said, her gaze scanning his features centimeter by centimeter. "He told me he was all alone in the world. I reckon lying must run in the family."

"Well, I'm in no position to refute that," Mr. Crandall/Quarles said. "I'm sorry, Joshua. I can give you the name of your grandfather, but you'll have to take it from there."

Joshua backed up and sat heavily in his chair. "I wouldn't know what to do. That's why I was following you, Miz Burdette. All my life I wondered who my father was, who my mother was, and all of a sudden, there's this picture in the newspaper on the kitchen table in there and the picture's me, only it's not me. And I thought about it and I figured that for me to look just like that man, I had to be his son. So I wanted to know his name. I figured if I kept close to you, when you found out, I'd know, too."

"What's he talking about?" Angela asked. "Whose picture was in the newspaper?"

Every time I turned around, I seemed to be backing into a wall. "Jake's," I said. "The night you planned to go away with him, he attacked Aunt Jay—Julia—in Miss Lucy's house because he thought she'd stolen something from his luggage. She was defending herself and hit him over the head and knocked him out. She thought she'd killed him and ran away. It's bothered her ever since and she came back to confess, only no one knew anything about it. So she asked me to find out who the man was and what happened to him. We found a picture of him and the newspaper printed it."

She shook her head. "I've always wondered how long he waited at the dock for me. And all the time he was dead, killed by my own father."

Mr. Quarles and I locked gazes and I ducked my head. Damned if I'd be the one to enlighten her. I'd done enough damage for one night. Thank God I'd also done some good. Jay and David were safe. Now if I could just pull my own fanny out of the fire.

"Joshua, why don't you put the gun away?" I asked. To be honest, I'd never gotten the impression he would use it, but it was there and he could if he wanted to. "What are you doing with it anyway?"

He looked at it helplessly. "Father Josiah called me and asked me to bring it to him. I was doing his bidding, like always."

"Well, do us a favor and keep it pointed at the floor," Mr. Crandall said. "Miss Allenby, I sure wish you'd stop staring at me. I'm beginning to feel like a banana split at a dieters' convention."

"It's a lot to take in," she said apologetically. "The only face I've seen in over fifty years was my father's. I'd just about forgotten what Jake looked like and a half hour after I'm free I see it twice. You have his face, older, of course, and your eyes aren't his. Joshua, now, Joshua has his eyes, the very same . . . "

I watched it happen, the dawn of enlightenment breaking slowly across her face. I couldn't understand why it had taken her so long, but then I hadn't been locked up in a playroom for half a century.

"Do you know your birthday, Joshua?" she asked, her voice a whisper.

"January sixteenth, 1944. Whoever left me at the orphanage told them that. I was always proud that I knew my birthday. Most of the other children didn't."

Miss Allenby closed her eyes, swayed, and grabbed the railing to remain upright. She turned, her eyes opening slowly. "And my father, how long ago did you meet him?"

"I don't remember. It seems like I've always known him. He came to the orphanage and brought me and Bobby Lee Silvers here every weekend. Bobby Lee, he got killed in Vietnam."

She averted her face but the raging hatred in her eyes was a dead giveaway. She knew what Josiah Allenby had done.

Suddenly a door banged open at the rear of the house and footsteps pounded down the hall. The good Reverend Allenby strode into the room carrying a hammer and nails and stopped short, stiffening with horror at the spectacle of Angela and Joshua standing side by side. Whether he noticed the gun was difficult to tell.

"Good evening, Father," Miss Allenby said, the ice in her voice cooling the room by a good twenty degrees. "We've been waiting for you, my son and I. And our other guests—"

"My God, boy, what have you done?" he interrupted her. "Take her back up—" He broke off. "Your son? Who told you? He didn't know. Nobody knew."

"Your son?" Joshua whirled to face her. "You're my mother? I don't understand."

"You shouldn't have told him, Angela! It's too complicated for him to understand. Now—" At that point my presence registered.

"You," he snarled, "and that resilient old woman. I just saw them wheeling her to surgery. She's like a cat. Shoot her and she gets up and walks away. Dump her in the bay and she floats to the top."

Ever the obedient servant, Joshua spoke up. "I didn't actually dump—"

"Hush, child," Angela said. Joshua shut up.

I wondered why the Reverend hadn't acknowledged Mr. Crandall. I glanced back to see that he'd positioned himself between the front door and the easy chairs stacked in front of the window. As a result he was in shadow and as far as I could tell, Reverend Allenby didn't realize he was there.

"Josiah," he said, stepping into the light.

Reverend Allenby spun around, saw the speaker, and an inhuman sound exploded from his throat. "You!" he roared. "So you've come back for her, have you?"

"No, Josiah," Mr. Crandall began, but got no further. Reverend Allenby was off and running.

"Just like your demon father. The Book says: Ye shall not afflict any widow, or fatherless child—Exodus, twenty-second chapter, twenty-second verse. Yet he defiled my dear mother, he defiled my beloved Martha, he defiled Lucille and countless others. And the fruit of his loins? You, a satyr, preying on any woman who crosses your path. Nathan, mind eroded by lunacy. Joshua, brain condemned to idiocy." Flecks of foam formed in the corners of his mouth. I glanced at Angela, wondering if there was any way to shut him up before he did any further damage, and saw that it was too late. She'd heard and understood, her face a mask of horror.

I heard a car door slam and laughter building slowly, growing louder. Two men, perhaps more. I wondered how close they were. I appeared to be the only one aware of them. Mr. Crandall stood riveted, listening to his step-brother as if mesmerized.

"The only one of his issue born pure and perfect was Martha's child," Reverend Allenby ranted on, "because in giving birth to her, my beloved Martha gave up her life and in so doing made a gift to the child of her soul. She was pure and perfect, an innocent, and then you, spawn of Satan, appeared." I detected a hellfire and brimstone sermon brewing. "Like the serpent tempting Eve, you lured her into your bed and left your seed—in your own half sister!"

"God help me." Angela moaned and covered her face.

"I've kept her away from the world ever since, praying your evil from her soul and body. I've shredded the Sixth Commandment, sent poor bedeviled Nathan to his maker. I've also dispatched Ronald Unthank—no one's missed him yet—and that whore of Babylon next door."

Belatedly I remembered that Ronnie had been one of the names Mrs. Peterson had volunteered to show the enlargement to, evidently the same Ronnie she'd mentioned in her diary, the one who'd threatened to tell the Reverend about Jake and Angela.

"You killed Sugar Babe just for finding me?" Angela had lowered her hands. She stared at her father as if seeing a monster. "And Ronnie and little Nathan? In God's name, why?"

"I did what I had to do to keep Jake's name and memory out of your life. Now here he is again. Not this time, little brother! Not this time!"

Darting to his left, he snatched the revolver from Joshua's hand and came back toward Mr. Crandall, the weapon extended. As he crossed in front of the open door, Mr. Haskins's voice penetrated from somewhere on the porch. "Reverend! Police! Drop it!"

If Reverend Allenby heard him, he gave no sign. He lifted his arm until the pistol was level with Mr. Crandall's forehead, his intent clear. The retort that followed was deafening. Time slowed to a crawl. The Reverend stiffened, then like a rapidly deflating balloon, slumped to the floor, the area above his heart blossoming with an ever-widening stain. Joshua gave a shriek and Angela pulled him close, one arm around his shoulder.

Mr. Haskins stepped into the room, weapon still aimed, and kicked the Reverend's revolver out of reach. Kneeling, he felt for a pulse at the minister's throat, then ripped his shirt open to expose the gaping wound in his left side. "Aww, damn it." He shook his head.

"Leon," he bellowed out the door, "radio for the ambulance! Don't think it's gonna do any good, but tell them to make it fast! Everybody all right?" He looked around, saw the furniture stacked against the windows. "What the hell's been going on in here?" His chin shot forward as he squinted at Joshua, then at Mr. Crandall. "What is this, a look-alike convention?"

"Sit down, Joshua," Miss Allenby said firmly. Joshua collapsed in the chair.

Mr. Haskins sighed. "Jesus, I feel bad I had to shoot him. Folks are gonna run me outta town for this."

"Not if we can help it," Mr. Crandall said, shaking his hand. "I'm grateful you're such a marksman. You could just as easily have hit Troy or me. We were right in your line of fire."

The policeman snorted. "Not for a minute. I can blow

the stinger off a hornet at a hundred paces on a moonless night and never touch the rest of it. I didn't know who the Reverend was aiming at, but I wasn't about to let him shoot nobody."

"Father Josiah wouldn't shoot anybody," Joshua said, tears streaming down his cheeks. "He couldn't, anyway. The gun isn't loaded."

"What?" That was a chorus made up of Mr. Haskins, Mr. Crandall, and me.

"He asked me to bring him the gun," he wailed, "but he never said anything about bringing the bullets, so I didn't."

Poor, obedient Joshua. He had done the minister's bidding, no less, no more.

Epilogue

"So, what now?" David pulled up the emergency brake and released his seatback so that he was very nearly reclining. He'd parked in the shadow of the same little lighthouse he'd brought me to nine or ten days before. It seemed more like a decade ago.

"I'll take another couple of weeks off and help Aunt Jay wind up her affairs in North Carolina and move to Innocence." The Deacon and I had been staying with Miss Potee since Jay's surgery. I'd been dubious about the arrangement at first, since she and The Deacon hadn't begun their relationship our first day on Innocence on a very positive note. He, however, had settled in and taken over. Her home was now just another castle in his kingdom, and Miss Potee as foolish about him as I had ever been. Jay was now encamped in her guest room as well, and would be staying there until she could find a house or condominium she liked.

"That wasn't what I meant," David said. "You've been

through a lot since you've been here. Are you going home the same person you were when you arrived?"

I wasn't but also wasn't sure I could articulate it. I'd always taken my family and the love we shared for granted. On Innocence I'd seen firsthand the carnage an unhealthy brand of love could leave in its wake, between man and woman, parent and child. But I'd also seen love in its embryonic state. Once Jay was convinced that Bernice would survive the bath Joshua had subjected her to and, given time, would be as good as new, Jay had refused to press charges against him for the abduction. Make no mistake: the health of the Buick had been the deciding factor. With the prospect of going to jail out of the picture, Angela and Joshua had begun to forge a relationship as mother and son, Joshua introducing her to the marvels of late-twentieth-century technology. They were slowly becoming a family.

And I had come to accept that Wade and I were not a family anymore and that it didn't matter because I no longer needed him. Not that I had any illusions about David filling the gap. He was definitely a family man, the one thing I couldn't give him, so I saw no point in daydreams to the contrary.

"I've grown a little," I said, to close the subject. "So I go back to D.C. a slighter wiser person. Is that good enough for you?"

"Depends. Why didn't you tell me your other brother's a doctor at a free clinic adjunct of your adult ed center? And that's he's been looking for help for months?"

The abrupt change of subject caught me off guard. "How'd you find out?"

"Your phone at Hospitality House was forwarded to mine, remember? Graham called last Thursday to tell you that he'd found a military record for a Jacob Stokes Junior.

Your brother's quite a guy, grilled me as if I'd asked him for your hand, as the saying goes."

I could feel my face flame red. "Sorry. Graham's worse than any father." I wanted to find out if he'd tried any obvious matchmaking but was too embarrassed to ask and too terrified of the answer.

"We talked for quite a while," David said. "He's decided I'm perfect for you, by the way."

"Oh, God." I slid lower in my seat.

"The longer I talked to him, the more I was inclined to agree with him. Mrs. Wingate does, too, of course."

That was no surprise. Jay had been kibitzing and matchmaking from the moment the anesthesia had worn off.

"But when it comes right down to it, the only person's opinion I'm interested in is yours." He swiveled around, his back against the door. "I've watched you with Mrs. Potee's grandchildren. I bet you'd make a dynamite mom."

The compliment pierced me to the core. I assumed he'd spoken without thinking. I should have known better.

"There's no reason you couldn't adopt a child, Troy. Just because Wade refused to consider it doesn't mean you can't."

"A single mom?" The idea had never occurred to me, probably because five days a week at the Center I saw how difficult an existence it could be. But I had parents and two brothers and a job and a roof over my head that belonged to me, support most mothers at the Center didn't have. "I don't know. I'll think about it."

"Will you really? My impression of you is that you're prone to be pigheaded—"

"Excuse me?"

"—and rarely change your mind about something. For instance, the fact that everyone thinks we'd be good for one another probably kills any chance I might have."

I couldn't decide whether to be annoyed, amused, or what. "It just may, since everybody swore they knew Wade and I were bound to wind up together, too."

"You did, didn't you? I expect under ordinary circumstances, you'd still be married to him. But you aren't anymore. And you've been down on yourself for so long because you can't have kids, that you may even prefer to avoid any sort of relationship that may lead to something permanent."

"I beg your pardon." One of the things that bugged me most about David was his tendency to be right ninety percent of the time.

"So. I've turned in my notice at Innocence General and have put the medical group in New Orleans that's been after me to join them on hold until I've had a chance to see what the operation at your brother's free clinic looks like. As important as you've managed to become to me in the space of ten days—"

"I have?"

"—I'm going where I feel I'm most needed and can contribute and make a difference. From Graham's description, your clinic sounds like the kind of place I'm looking for, but I'll reserve judgment until I've seen it. What I'm saying is that you won't be the deciding factor, just one of them, so don't let all this go to your head. I'm curious, though: if I happened to wind up in your neighborhood one day soon and phoned to ask if you'd like to go out for a cup of coffee, what kind of reception would I get?"

It was time to get the ball rolling in whichever direction it was going to go. "A cup of coffee, my Aunt Fanny. You owe me a dinner, buster. And don't show up without a pocket full of popcorn shrimp. If The Deacon doesn't take to you again, you can forget the whole thing."

"Piece of cake. Made a real deal with a wholesaler and

have a ten-pound carton of the little boogers in the freezer just waiting to be thawed." David flashed me a wicked grin, his eyes gleaming like polished jade. For the first time I realized that, especially when he was relaxed, his eyes were the same color as The Deacon's. The Deacon's green eyes were the main reason I'd fallen in love with the damned cat to begin with. The deck was stacked against me coming and going. I threw in the cards.

In addition to having written twenty books, **CHASSIE WEST** has acted in professional and community theaters, films, and commercials. She lives in Columbia, Maryland, and is currently at work on her next book for HarperPaperbacks.

HAPPY NEVER AFTER
Kathy Hogan Trocheck

The sixties and the nineties collide when Callahan Garrity sets out to prove the innocence of a rock idol of her youth.

Also available,
EVERY CROOKED NANNY
HOMEMADE SIN
TO LIVE & DIE IN DIXIE

PARROT BLUES
Judith Van Gieson

When a millionaire's wife and rare macaw are kidnapped together, Neil Hamel enters a dangerous game of bird smuggling and one-upmanship. The only eyewitnesses are parrots, and they're not talking.

Also available,
THE LIES THAT BIND
THE WOLF PATH

A PLAGUE OF KINFOLKS
Celestine Sibley

A pair of distant relatives appeal to Kate Mulcay's Southern hospitality... until Kate realizes their extended visit coincides with an elaborate con game and the grisly murder of a neighbor.

Also available,
DIRE HAPPENINGS AT SCRATCH ANKLE

CRACK DOWN
Val McDermid
A Gold Dagger
Winning Writer

"One of my favorite authors."
—Sara Paretsky

"Kate Brannigan is a cheeky addition to the growing sisterhood of crime."
—THE WASHINGTON POST

Manchester PI Kate Brannigan asks her rock-journalist boyfriend to help her on a case and he ends up behind bars.

Look for CLEAN BREAK coming November 1996

HarperPaperbacks *Mysteries by Mail*